Praise for Jill McGown's
Inspector Lloyd and Judy Hill mysteries

MURDER AT THE OLD VICARAGE

"A first-rate mystery . . . A spider's-web of a tale . . . Fiendishly clever."

—*The Washington Post*

THE MURDERS OF MRS. AUSTIN AND MRS. BEALE

"Sophisticated and satisfying."

—*The Philadelphia Inquirer*

VERDICT UNSAFE

"A cleverly constructed, realistic courtroom drama that keeps you totally involved."

—ANNE PERRY

PICTURE OF INNOCENCE

"A masterpiece of controlled complexity."

—*Publisher's Weekly* (starred review)

PLOTS AND ERRORS

"A dazzlingly devious tangle of clues and coincidences."

—*Chicago Tribune*

By the same author

Record of Sin
An Evil Hour
The Stalking Horse
Murder Movie

The Lloyd and Hill Mysteries

A Perfect Match
Murder at the Old Vicarage
Gone to Her Death
The Murders of Mrs. Austin and Mrs. Beale
The Other Woman
Murder . . . Now and Then
A Shred of Evidence
Verdict Unsafe
Picture of Innocence
Plots and Errors

Jill McGown

SCENE OF CRIME

Ballantine Books
New York

A Ballantine Book
Published by The Ballantine Publishing Group

ISBN 0-345-44313-6

Manufactured in the United States of America

SCENE OF CRIME

Chapter One

"I felt like a prat," said Lloyd as he and Judy made their way downstairs from the room in the Christmas-decorated Riverside Family Center in which the so-called relaxation classes were held. It had been his first visit to such a thing. And, if he could possibly work out how to get out of it, his last, because the one thing it had not been was relaxing.

Judy snorted. "And I didn't?"

"Well, at least you're pregnant. Why do I have to do the breathing?"

"They explained why. Anyway, you're supposed to be relaxing too."

"As far as I'm concerned, relaxing is a malt whiskey and a crossword. Or maybe a video. Or both. Not squatting on the floor making stupid noises."

"I don't think the malt whiskey and crossword method of childbirth has proved all that successful," said Judy.

"I'll bet no one's tried it." Lloyd looked at the people going down ahead of them and lowered his voice. "Apart from anything else, all the others look about sixteen," he said. "And there am I, fifty and bald."

Judy arrived on a landing and turned to face him. "I'm forty-one," she said. "How do you suppose that makes me feel?"

He smiled and took her hands in his, looking at her dark, shining hair, and today's choice of color coordinated pregnancy outfit. She had scoured the county to find clothes she regarded as fit to be seen in when you felt like a whale. Even in her eighth month, she didn't *look* like a whale, pleasant though these creatures were, in Lloyd's opinion. She looked wonderful. There really was a glow. He'd told her that once, and she thought he was kidding, but he wasn't.

"I don't know how you feel," he said. "But you look great."

"Rubbish."

"It *isn't* rubbish," he protested. "You do look great. I think I'll be a little sorry when you're not pregnant anymore."

"Well, I won't." She frowned. "Didn't you go to classes when Barbara was pregnant?"

Lloyd shrugged. "I don't think they'd invented them in those days," he said. He didn't have the faintest idea whether they were fashionable then, but he was fairly safe in assuming that neither did Judy.

Life had been easier back then, he reflected. His marriage had been uncomplicated, basically, until Judy's arrival in his life made it complicated. By and large, Barbara had done the female stuff and he'd done the male stuff. He wasn't the archetypal Welshman; he enjoyed cooking, and he didn't mind housework. He had never expected women to be at his beck and call. But having babies had always seemed to him to be beyond his remit, as the Assistant Chief Constable would say, and he really didn't know if Barbara had done all this relaxation business. He became aware that he was being subjected to dark brown scrutiny, and felt uncomfortable. "It was different then!" he said.

"Different how?"

"I was in uniform. I worked shifts."

It was different because Barbara hadn't been a police officer. Judy was, and she knew what was what; he couldn't plead a heavy caseload or the sudden necessity to work overtime; she would want chapter and verse. And it had been almost twenty years since he'd had anything to do with a pregnant woman; times had changed. Men weren't just encouraged to be involved, they were expected to be.

"Were you present when the children were born?" she demanded.

"Well . . ."

"Lloyd!"

"It wasn't—"

"Don't try telling me they didn't do that in those days, because they most certainly did. Where were you? Pacing up and down outside? Waiting to hand out cigars?"

"No."

"You mean you weren't there at all?"

"I meant to be there, but it wasn't possible. Things came up at work. . . ."

"Both times? Oh, sure they did."

"Look, if Barbara didn't give me a hard time about it, why are you?"

She didn't answer.

"Good evening, Chief Inspector Lloyd," said a voice. "What are you doing here?"

Lloyd turned to see the long, thin frame of Freddie, their friendly neighborhood pathologist, loping down the steps from the rooftop car park. Lloyd had parked in the street—he wasn't a fan of rooftop lots, or rooftop anything elses, come to that.

"I'm here because I'm going to be a father," he replied. "Apparently I have to learn how to bear down. What's your excuse?"

"When it comes to being a father, I think you'd be better off learning how to bear up, but I expect you know that better than I do. I'm here to play squash." Freddie beamed at Judy. "Hello, Judy—positively blooming, I see. And I believe it's Detective *Chief* Inspector Hill now, isn't it? You've caught up to this one." He jerked his head in Lloyd's direction. "And not before time. How's the new job?"

"It's fine, I suppose. I can't honestly say I know what I'm doing yet, but Joe Miller does."

"Ah, yes. He's the computer buff, isn't he? My only regret about your promotion is that I won't see you anymore."

Judy smiled. "Don't take this personally, Freddie, but as far as I'm concerned, the absence of mortuary visits is a major plus about this job."

"Dead bodies are more interesting than most live ones—present company excepted. Besides, you should be used to them by now."

"I'll never get used to them."

"Still—there's always the housewarming. I presume you'll invite me, if I promise not to bring any dead bodies. Have you found somewhere to live yet?"

"No," said Lloyd.

"You mean you're *still* living in separate flats?"

Not exactly, Lloyd thought. He wasn't sure if Judy had noticed yet, but he'd more or less moved in with her.

"We keep looking at houses, but we can't agree on what we want," said Judy. "It's all going to have to wait until after Christmas now."

"Well, there's one for the books," said Freddie, glancing at his watch. "You two failing to agree. Sorry—must dash. I'm on court at quarter past. If I don't see you before, have a happy Christmas."

"Same to you," said Judy. She caught Lloyd's wrist and looked at his watch as Freddie disappeared down the next flight of steps two at a time. "Is that the time? I'm ten minutes late for the rehearsal. She wanted us all there at eight prompt."

Lloyd followed as she made her way down. "I thought you just did their books for them," he said. "How does that involve rehearsals?"

"I'm doing the sound effects tonight because someone's away sick."

Lloyd grinned. "Do you have to moo and things like that?"

"There isn't any mooing in *Cinderella*."

It had been the mildest of jokes. When she was in this sort of mood, he thought, she was hard work. "Can I come?" he asked. "Or would you rather I went home and came back for you?"

"Suit yourself. But if you come, make yourself useful."

Lloyd walked with her through a maze of corridors that would apparently take them under cover to the Riverside Theatre, rather than having to go back out into the rain. The complex had been built with help from the lottery, and as far as he could see, it was still being built. "Watch your step," he said as Judy briskly walked past wooden panels and pots of mysterious smelly stuff.

She didn't slow down.

"What should I do to make myself useful?"

She didn't answer.

Lloyd sighed. "I can make tea," he said. "And you said you would need to eat—I can nip down to the snack bar for sandwiches or something. Will that be useful?"

"Fine. Just don't get in the way."

The theater, which they entered by a rear door that took them along another corridor into the wings, was just about finished. Not too much builders' debris to catch the unwary mother-to-be. They walked out onto the stage, where a spare, tall woman of uncertain years and flaming hair, dressed in what seemed to Lloyd to be a remarkable number of scarves and very little else, was dramatically glad to see Judy.

"Thank *God* you're here, darling!" she said. "I was beginning to think no one was going to turn up."

"Sorry, Marianne, we got held up. This is Lloyd, my partner. Lloyd—Marianne."

"How lovely to see you here, Lloyd." She extended her hand, palm down, and Lloyd felt certain he was supposed to bow and kiss it, but he settled for giving it a necessarily ineffectual shake. "It was my fault that we were late," he said. "I ran into an old friend."

Marianne tilted her head to one side and regarded Lloyd. "I don't suppose you could possibly read Buttons for us, could you, darling?"

Lloyd blinked. "Yes," he said. "If you're serious."

"Oh, I'm *desperately* serious." She turned to Judy. "Dexter rang and said he's come down with something. So I haven't got Buttons *or*

Cinderella now. And I don't know *where* Carl Bignall is. He's supposed to be bringing the chimes, apart from anything else."

"Chimes?" said Lloyd.

"Midnight," said Judy. "The clock has to strike midnight. Carl does the sound effects, and understudies Buttons, amongst other things."

Lloyd frowned. "I thought you said you did the sound effects."

Judy didn't see fit to explain; instead she very obviously ignored his puzzlement. Lloyd blew out his cheeks, shrugged, and threw an it's-her-hormones look at Marianne, which Judy fortunately didn't notice.

"I specifically said I needed everyone here tonight on time, and what happens? Half of them come down with the flu and the other half are late—well, if no one knows where they're supposed to be on the stage, it won't be my fault." Marianne turned to Lloyd. "You might have to double up if Carl's got the flu as well, darling. And if the principals and the understudies all get it, we'll just have to cancel."

"I don't suppose it'll come to that." Lloyd smiled. "When do you open?"

"Not until the end of January, thank God. We were going to open on New Year's Day, but fortunately the Health and Safety people vetoed that because the decorating work isn't finished. There's scaffolding and things blocking the exits. We've got a month, but what with Christmas and the flu, it's beginning to look desperate." She turned as a small group of people arrived. "Oh, darlings, you've made it!" She frowned. "Well, some of you have."

"The traffic's impossible," said one. "The lights have all failed in the town center. We managed to escape down Baxendale Avenue, but I expect some of the others are stuck. Ray's here—he's gone to the café to get sandwiches for everyone. I said you'd settle up with him later—is that all right?"

"Good, good," said Marianne. "Can't leave the house for five minutes without eating," she muttered to Lloyd.

No need for him to go after all. Which was a shame; it might have helped get him back into favor with Judy. He wasn't at all sure how he'd fallen out of favor, but he clearly had.

"Jenny said to tell you that she'll be here," someone said. "She's just going to be a bit late."

"But that means I don't even have Cinderella's *understudy*!" Marianne threw her arms up in the air. "We might as well go home."

"She has to pick her parents up from the station, that's all. She'll be here as soon as she's dropped them off."

"Amateurs," muttered Marianne. "What am I supposed to do in the meantime?"

Lloyd looked at the stage, which was bisected by a backdrop of Cinderella's kitchen. From where he stood, he could see the almost-finished coach and horses behind it; just flat pieces of hardboard cut to shape and painted. And behind them was the exterior of the baron's house, and up in the flies, the prince's palace. With lighting and dry ice or whatever they used these days, he could see that the transforming of the mice and pumpkin into Cinderella's coach and horses would be quite effective, even if it was all done on a shoestring. Providing they managed to fit in enough rehearsal with the actual actors before the curtain went up.

"Judy, darling . . ."

"Oh, no," said Judy, literally backing away as she spoke. "No, Marianne, I can't—"

"Just until Jenny gets here?" Marianne's hands were clasped together in prayer. "Just read the words and stand in the right places, darling, that's all. It's only to give the others their cues."

"But I can't . . ."

"Please, darling. Otherwise we can't even *begin* until Jenny gets here. She's in every scene. And I can't do Cinderella, not with everything else—I'll have to sort out the songs with the pianist when he gets here, and a million other things. Be an angel."

Very reluctantly, Judy agreed, on condition that she would not have to sing, and Lloyd smiled quietly to himself, until he caught Judy watching him and thought it politic to change the subject. "I've never even been to a pantomime," he said, and suddenly everyone was staring at him. It had been an innocent enough remark. "What?" he said. "What's wrong?"

"You've never been to a *pantomime*?" Judy repeated.

"No. Well, they didn't go in much for pantomime where I come from, much less singing, dancing, and clowning."

Marianne's eyes widened. "Where do you come from, darling? Mars?"

"Wales."

"Ah," she said, nodding sympathetically as the awful truth about his heritage was revealed to her. "Wales."

"They have panto in Wales," said Judy.

"Well, maybe they do, but not in my village, they didn't."

"But you had two children," said Judy. "And you lived in London. Didn't you ever take them to a pantomime?"

No, indeed he had not. Amateurs throwing a few songs and dances into *Cinderella* was one thing; showbiz panto was quite another. The very idea of sitting through two and a half hours of B-list celebrities and over-the-hill sportsmen assassinating a perfectly good fairy tale with bad jokes, pop songs, and innuendo, in the company of hundreds of screaming children, was enough to make Lloyd go pale.

"No—Barbara did all that sort of—" He was being scrutinized again. "—thing," he finished.

"Did she?" Judy said, picking up a script and moving away.

Lloyd sighed. He wasn't a new man. Far from it. Tonight, he had felt like an old man. A very old man indeed. But he was going to get to play Buttons, despite his advancing years. Well, read Buttons at any rate. It might be fun.

❦

Ryan Chester, nineteen years old and a useful welterweight at school, was even better at stealing cars than he had been at boxing. He hadn't wanted to box professionally; as a way of making a living, stealing cars was less painful. The one he was driving had been parked outside on the street, a front garden's length from the house it probably belonged to, and inside that house there would almost certainly be kids, a television, people talking; he had taken the chance that no one would hear it start up, and within seconds he was out of sight of anyone in the house who may have heard it.

Now he was on the short stretch of divided highway that would take him toward the Malworth town center, but that wasn't what he had been intending to do at all; this evening was not working out as planned. Still, he thought philosophically, there was no one following him, nothing else on the road, so he could relax a little. He reached into his back pocket, drawing out his cellular phone, and awkwardly pressed the handset buttons with his thumb. Today had been a bitch so far, and the only good that could come of it would be if that stuff was worth something. He swung the car violently around a cyclist he hadn't seen, mainly because the bike had no lights, and slowed down; he didn't want to draw attention to himself like that, for God's sake. He approached the roundabout, signaling as he went into the outside lane for the right turn, frowning as he saw the traffic on the road into the town.

He held the phone to his ear, to hear Baz saying hello over and over again. At least he was answering now.

"Where the hell were you?" Ryan demanded. "I called ten minutes ago."

"Sorry, Ry. I was desperate for a pee."

"Why didn't you take the phone with you? That's the whole bloody point of mobile phones!"

"Sorry, Ry."

Ryan sighed, using both hands on the steering wheel as he negotiated the roundabout and joined the queue of traffic into Malworth, which was moving at half a mile an hour. Why did he feel responsible for Baz? Because blood was thicker than water, he supposed, though no blood had ever been as thick as Baz. He was in court on Wednesday morning because he had been too stupid to get rid of the cannabis he'd just bought when the police had raided the Starland. Ryan had lost count of the number of times Baz had been nabbed for possession. He might even go down for it this time.

He put the phone to his ear again. "It's all right, Baz," he said. "Forget it."

"Where are you?" asked Baz. "Do you want me to meet you?"

"No. Just go home, Baz. I'll see you at the Starland later on."

Ryan terminated the call, and crawled toward the edge of town. One or two of the houses set back from the main road had Christmas lights strung through the trees in their front gardens; it looked nice, he thought. Festive. The town's Christmas lights, lining the main shopping streets, were okay too, he supposed, but he hadn't really expected to have this much time to admire them.

Once he was approaching the one-way system, traffic ground to a stop. It was three days before Christmas, and Malworth was pretty busy, with the shops staying open for the late Christmas buyers and all manner of people entertaining the shoppers in the glistening streets, but this was a complete standstill. He frowned. Maybe there had been an accident or something. He sat motionless behind a bus and tapped his fingers on the steering wheel.

What was the holdup, for God's sake? He wound down the window, admitting flecks of rain and the sounds of a children's choir singing Christmas carols, craning his neck to see beyond the bus, to the traffic lights. But there *were* no traffic lights, and he swore to himself. The lights had failed, and the traffic on the crossroads had no idea who had right of way. The intersection was a snarl of vehicles. Rain spattered the steering wheel, and he wound up the window again.

He'd heard that in-car entertainment was a huge industry in Japan, because the city streets had virtually reached gridlock, and he could see that it would be, if they had to do this every day. The owner of the vehicle he was sitting in was not, unfortunately, big on in-car entertainment, and he had only the children's choir, closer to him now and audible through the closed window, to entertain him. They had gotten through three carols by the time the people in silly costumes who were collecting for some charity, and were turning the traffic jam to advantage by soliciting the drivers for a contribution, got around to him. A large Pink Panther approached him and tapped on the window.

"What's it for?" he asked as he rolled down the window once more.

"Jordan."

For some reason he'd expected a man, but it was a woman's voice, muffled, coming from the pink furry throat.

"Jordan?" He couldn't remember seeing anything about Jordan. "Has something happened there, then?"

Her paw went to her lower jaw and pulled it down a little. "No!" she laughed, her voice clearer. "Little Jordan Taylor. The baby that needs the operation in America?"

"Oh, yeah."

"It's Ryan, isn't it?" she said, as he dug in his pocket and pulled out some change, throwing it into her bucket. "Hello. I haven't seen you for a while."

He stared at the large pink face as she looked down the line of cars, sizing up her next victim. "Hi," he said, as casually as he could in the circumstances. Who was it, for God's sake? He didn't think he really wanted to know. He just wanted out of here. Now.

"Thanks a lot," she said. "Have a nice Christmas."

"Same to you," said Ryan, his brain racing. The lights came back on, to an involuntary cheer from Ryan—and everyone else caught up in the jam, no doubt—and he moved forward on the clutch, his heart beating faster. He was held up on red now, but at least could see the intersection beginning to clear.

He watched the bright pink, slightly bedraggled creature in his mirror as she made her way back to the safety of the pavement. He had no idea who she was; a friend of a friend maybe. Someone's mother. He replayed her voice in his head, and knew that it was familiar. The way she'd said his name had been familiar too. Someone who spoke his name—that ought to be a clue, because people didn't, usually, not in conversation. So who had occasion to use your name a lot? People who told you what to do, he thought. Teachers. Was she a teacher? Could be. But whatever way you looked at it, he had been clocked driving a stolen car by someone who probably wouldn't approve, and he didn't like that. He hadn't been driving the car for ten minutes, for God's sake, and he'd been stationary for most of them.

Carl Bignall ducked down to check himself in the rearview mirror, and persuaded a lock of dark hair over his brow so that it seemed to have fallen there of its own accord. He was thirty-five minutes late; Marianne would not be pleased. The car blinked as he locked it, and he ran down the three flights of stairs from the rooftop car park, his step light for the well-built man that he was, sidestepping hoses and planks and tarpaulins as he made his way through the corridors, arriving in the wings to find some man he'd never seen in his life before reading Buttons. He frowned. It wasn't like Dexter to miss rehearsal. But whoever his stand-in was, he was reading well, which was a refreshing change.

Maybe Marianne was trying him out, but if so, Carl thought, he was a late starter. He couldn't be much younger than Denis Leeward. Maybe he'd just moved here—he might have been the star of whatever amateur dramatic society he'd belonged to before. That could create problems, of course, but Marianne would try anyone out and worry about the politics later. The pool of talent wasn't exactly deep.

And Judy Hill was reading Cinderella, for some reason. The idea of a middle-aged, pregnant Cinderella appealed to him; it could be the story in reverse. A last-chance Cinderella deserting the faithful Buttons for a one-night stand with a flashy prince. Searching for him when she finds she's pregnant, only to find that he doesn't want to know.

"Carl! You've come, you darling man! I'd given you up entirely!"

"I am so sorry, Marianne," he said, his hands held up in a gesture of truce.

"Did you get caught in that frightful traffic jam the others were talking about?"

"No," Carl admitted. "I heard about it on Radio Barton, though. It would have been a good excuse, but I cannot tell a lie—I was nowhere near the town center. I got held up at home. Estelle—you know. She wasn't feeling too good."

"Isn't this her writer's circle night?" said Marianne.

"Yes," said Carl, and smiled. "Of course, maybe she's just playing hookey."

"Dexter's got the flu or something, darling. This lovely man's stepped into the breach."

"Good for him," said Carl.

"The thing is," said Buttons, joining him in the wings, "did you bring the chimes?"

Carl smiled. "I did," he said, pulling the tape from his pocket. "And the ballroom sounds, and the horses' hooves, and all the rest of it."

Buttons shook his head. "On tape?" he said. "Whatever happened to two half coconuts?"

"It's all state-of-the-art stuff now," said Carl, and held out his hand. "Carl Bignall," he said with a smile. "I cheat and copy what I need from CDs."

"Lloyd. I came in with the ersatz Cinders and was commandeered."

"Lloyd, of course! I've heard a lot about you. It's nice to put a face to the name at last. Are you thinking of joining us?"

"No," Lloyd said, shaking his head vehemently. "I'm just helping out."

Carl held up the tape. "Judy? Can you read Cinderella and work the sound effects at the same time?"

"I expect so," she said doubtfully. "If Marianne doesn't need me on stage."

"But I do, darling," said Marianne, with a flick of the scarves with which she draped herself. "Oh, I suppose you can read her lines from the wings, but you'll have to speak up, darling, if anyone's going to hear their cues. God *knows* how we're going to get this production ready on time."

Carl stayed in the troupe because he enjoyed acting and writing the script, but he found Marianne very tiresome. With her, the amateur dramatics were not confined to the stage.

"Has poor Estelle got this awful flu too, darling?"

"Oh, no, she's fine, really. Just a touch of the sniffles." His answer to Marianne's belated concern for Estelle's welfare was far from truthful; Estelle hadn't ever been fine, and this year she'd been seeing Denis Leeward for depression and God knew what else, making his life hell while she'd been at it. The lies were automatic: he had been telling them for years, and could switch off his domestic circumstances as easily as he could switch off a light. "She's having an early night," he said.

"Good, good!"

Marianne went into a huddle with Prince Charming, a bit long in the tooth for the principal boy's part, in Carl's judgment, but her legs were as good as any he had seen, and that was the important bit when it came to fishnet tights and thigh-slapping.

"What do you do when you're not understudying Buttons?" asked Lloyd.

"I'm an Ugly Sister," said Carl.

"He's a wonderful dame," said Judy, taking the tape from him. "Really sexy. What do I do with this?"

"Do you ever wonder about all this cross-dressing in pantomime?" asked Lloyd. "Does it mean anything?"

Carl shrugged. "I think originally it just allowed a bit of gender-bending in safety," he said. "Most people have a little bit of the opposite sex in them, don't you think?" He turned to Judy. "I've put all the effects on there," he said. "All you have to do is play them on cue, then stop the tape. They're all in order."

"Oh, right. So I should mark up a script with the cues."

"Yes—I expect madam will want to hear them all, so you'd better put the tape in, and I'll make sure we're rigged up to the sound system."

"Am I surplus to requirements now?" asked Lloyd. "Or will you want to concentrate on being ugly?"

Carl opened his mouth, but was forestalled by the voice that floated through from the stage. "Where's my wonderful substitute Buttons? Are you there, darling?"

"There's your answer."

Eric Watson's jeans-clad legs descended from the loft and he pressed the button that folded the ladder neatly back up, closing the hatch, then pulled over the hinged ceiling molding so the hatch disappeared altogether. There was no mistaking that knock; he had given his guests instructions to remain absolutely silent. He smoothed his remaining wisps of hair down, and glanced at the clock as he went downstairs and along the hallway to the front door. Ten to nine—it had taken them long enough to get here, he thought as they banged at the door again. He opened the door to a uniformed constable who looked to be about twelve and a half.

"Yes?"

"Constable Sims, Malworth," said the young man. "We've had a report of a suspected break-in at your next-door neighbor's house."

"So?"

"We can't get an answer, sir, and we can't get round the back because the rear gates are locked. We wondered if we could get through from your garden."

He was joined as he spoke by another, older constable.

"Can't you climb over the back gates?" said Eric. "They're not that high. You're young and fit." He looked at the older one and amended that. "Well, he is, anyway," he said with a nod of his head at Constable Sims.

"We think that might be how the intruder entered," said the overweight one. "We don't want to disturb any evidence."

"You're actually going to look for some, are you?" But there was no harm in letting them go over the back wall, Eric supposed. He stood aside, motioning down the hallway toward the kitchen. He let Sims pass, but held up a hand when the other one tried to come in. "I don't think I caught your name," he said.

"Warren."

"You're supposed to give your name and station when you approach members of the public."

He apologized; Eric allowed him entry.

"Did you see or hear anything, sir?" asked Sims as they walked through.

"I heard glass breaking. I thought it was these kids again."

"Again?"

"They come here from the London Road estate. Throwing bottles at the wall and stuff like that. I heard them this teatime. But it sounded a lot closer this time, so I went out and had a look in case it was my greenhouse."

"But you didn't see anyone?"

"No."

In the kitchen, Eric unlocked the back door and took them outside. As they walked out, the security light came on, turning the dark night into near daylight. "There you are," he said, indicating the low ornamental wall that divided the gardens. "Make the most of it before they wall me in."

Sims stepped over the low wall and made his way toward the house. "Window's broken," he called over. "I'll have a look inside."

Warren acknowledged that with a wave of his hand but didn't join him.

"Aren't you supposed to go in with him?" said Eric.

Warren raised his eyebrows. "Know a bit about the job, do you, sir?"

"You could say that. I did it for eighteen years."

"I understand the intruder was seen running away," the constable said. "I think my colleague can handle it on his own. You were saying something about the neighbors walling you in? What's all that about, then?"

"That pile of bricks is for the new, higher wall that my friendly neighbors intend building."

"Are you not on the best of terms, then?"

"Let's just say we're not bosom buddies."

"And you definitely didn't hear anything suspicious tonight?"

"I told you. I heard breaking glass—presumably it was their window. I came out to see if it was my greenhouse, but it wasn't, so I went back in."

"We've had a report of a row going on a few minutes before that. Would you know anything about that?"

Oh, so that's what he wanted to know. "Are you asking if I had a barney with my neighbors? Do you think I heaved a brick through their window or something?"

"No," said Warren. "We've had a report of a disturbance, that's all. I wondered if you heard it too."

"No," said Eric.

"And you definitely didn't see anyone when you came out?" The policeman wandered down the driveway, toward the greenhouse. Eric followed him down.

"No," he said. "No one."

"And you saw no one hanging around before that?"

"No."

"As I said, we've had a report of someone seen running away. You didn't see anyone on the road at the back here?"

"No," said Eric, beginning to lose count of how many times he had said that now.

Constable Sims appeared again. "Kev," he said. "You'd better come in here."

Eric didn't say I told you so.

Tom Finch was working late, catching up on the paperwork that he could no longer ignore. Judy Hill had tried to make him do it on a methodical, regular basis like she did—she said that she had made herself do that right from the start, because she hated it too. But while Tom could see the logic of doing something you didn't like for a half an hour or so in the working day rather than waiting until you would be in real trouble if it wasn't done, and then going at it for three and a half hours for which you would not be paid, he had never had the self-discipline necessary to carry it out. Besides, you got it done quicker in the evening—the bad guys might do their work under cover of darkness, but it was in the daylight that it was discovered, as a rule.

He wrote his signature with a flourish on the very last sheet in his tray, yawned, stretched, and scratched his head, startled, as he still was, to discover the strange bristly sensation.

He'd had his golden curls cut off the last time he went for a haircut; sitting in the chair, looking at himself in the mirror, he realized they had to go if he ever wanted to be taken seriously, and had issued the command to the hairdresser. He had expected an argument during which he could let himself be talked out of it, but she just asked him how short he wanted it, and went at it with the scissors when he had told her to remove as much of it as she liked. He had watched it fall to the ground with a mixture of dismay and satisfaction.

Now, he looked at the phone when it rang with much the same feeling. If he had left at half past five, he wouldn't have been here to answer it. He was tired. It was almost nine o'clock, and he'd worked a twelve-hour day. He wanted to go home. But you never knew—it might be some informant with a juicy piece of news for him. He picked it up. "CID, Finch speaking," he said.

"Sarge," said the girl manning the dispatch room, "Malworth attended a suspected break-in at 4 Windermere Terrace, Malworth, and they've reported finding the body of a woman in the house. She'd been bound and gagged—it looks as though she suffocated. Their inspector wants Stansfield CID to attend."

Tom tried to suppress the little thrill he always got when a really serious crime presented itself. Windermere Terrace was at the moneyed end of Malworth; large town houses that were still owned by people who lived in them, rather than turned into flats. It was his job to investigate crime, of course, and the more serious the crime, the more interesting it was, but he felt that it wasn't a particularly attractive trait. You shouldn't be pleased, however professionally, that someone had died.

Still—it beat paperwork any day. He dialed Bob Sandwell's home number. Bob was the acting Detective Inspector now that Judy had been transferred, and this would be his first real test. He was okay. Tom liked him. But Bob didn't have Judy Hill's flair. If you asked him, they'd have been better off sending Bob Sandwell to HQ to head up this LINKS project, and left Judy here.

"Hi, Kathy. Is Bob there?"

"Oh, Tom—I was going to call tomorrow morning. I'm afraid he's in bed with a temperature. He's got the flu."

Oh. "Right," Tom said. "Look—tell him to get well soon, and . . . we'll soldier on without him. 'Bye."

For the first time in his life, Tom wished that he was an inspector and could take charge of this himself. Maybe he would take the exam again. Judy Hill was always telling him to do it. And maybe he'd pass it now that he didn't look like an angel. But it would need someone more senior than him to deal with this, and Tom felt certain that DCI Lloyd would rather be called before someone he didn't know was drafted from another division, so he'd have to try to get hold of him.

Lloyd's cell phone was switched off, and he wasn't at home, or at Judy Hill's place. Tom left messages on all three phones, and went to assess the situation for himself.

Denis Leeward was sitting in his car in a rest area, one hidden from the road by trees, trying to get his head around everything that had happened. He'd driven toward home instinctively, but then had realized he couldn't *go* home, and pulled up here just before the exit to the village. Meg wasn't expecting him back for another hour and would expect some sort of explanation if he went home now. His ribs ached and he was still shaking; he couldn't go home in this state.

But he couldn't stay here. The pub, he thought, relieved that something approaching an idea had managed to penetrate the fog of fear and worry. He'd go to the pub.

He drove off, turned down the road into the bypassed village and parked, half on the pavement, half off, opposite The Horse and Halfpenny. No one knew how it had come by that name, and people assumed it was one of the new wave of pubs with silly names, but The Horse and Halfpenny, once a coaching inn, had been given its name a hundred years ago. Denis couldn't believe that of all the things he might be thinking about now, when he needed to think clearly, all he could do was wonder how The Horse and Halfpenny got its name.

He moved the rearview mirror and looked at himself, running his fingers through his longish gray hair to neaten it up a bit, straightening his tie. His face looked pale, but that might just be the streetlights. He got out of the car, sucking in his breath as his bruised ribs complained. He'd have to be careful not to do that. He didn't want anyone asking him what was wrong; he had to take a deep breath, calm down, and act halfway normal. He'd had to do what he did, he told himself, justifying his actions to himself, fervently hoping he would never have to justify them to anyone else.

He locked the car, and waited for a motorbike to shoot past him before crossing over the village road to the pub. It was his local spot, but it was far enough away from home for him to be fairly certain that Meg wouldn't see the car. He couldn't think straight. He was going to go and get a stiff drink. He could walk home, leave the car there. And when Meg demanded answers, he might have some ready, or be too drunk to care. He had done something that he would never have believed he'd ever do, and already it seemed like a distant memory, like a dream fragment. A moment of indecision, that was all he'd had, before he quite definitely decided, and committed himself to a course of action from which there was no return.

He ducked under the low beam that had been the painful introduction to the Horse of many a visitor despite its notice warning those over five feet six inches. The pub regulars were playing their weekly quiz game, and above their laughter at the question master's inability to pronounce any word of more than one syllable correctly, Denis ordered a whiskey.

"On the hard stuff tonight, Doc?" the innkeeper asked.

He smiled. A weak, unconvincing smile, but he smiled. "Long day."

"Well, there you are," said the innkeeper. "Get that down you. You look as though you might be coming down with this flu—a bit green about the gills."

"How do you pronounce the name of this pub?" Denis asked, when he had downed the tiny pub measure in one gulp and ordered a beer chaser, and just as the pub erupted into laughter once more. The quiz master took it all in good part.

The innkeeper leaned over the bar, cocking his ear toward Denis. "Say again?"

"How do you pronounce the name of the pub? I've always just called it the Horse—is the rest of it pronounced Halfpenny or Ha'penny?"

The innkeeper looked puzzled at this sudden and rather belated interest in his pub's name. "I say Ha'penny. But the youngsters say Halfpenny. They only know the new money, of course. Don't talk about ha'pence anymore, do we?" He paused. "Come to that, we don't even have the new halfpennies anymore. They soon won't be able to pronounce it at all."

"What does it mean, anyway?" asked Denis. He didn't care what it meant. He had never cared. But he couldn't stop himself fixating on it. He was in denial, he supposed. No, he didn't suppose it. He *was* in denial. Even worrying about the trouble he might be in was part of that denial; he couldn't, wouldn't, think about the rest of it. He found himself wondering then if you could be in denial if you knew you were in denial.

"Don't ask me. The brewery might know, I suppose." The innkeeper frowned. "Are you doing some sort of research?"

"Not really."

"Or are you one of those people who collect pub names?"

"No. Nothing like that. Just wondered."

Denis sipped his beer and looked around at the little room, at the people crowded around small tables, their heads together, or sitting back smugly, having written down their answers to the last question in the ongoing quiz. The ones closest to him were earnestly discussing whether the screen rabbit referred to in the question was Bugs Bunny or Roger Rabbit.

Denis knew they were both wrong; unlike the team, he was old enough to know the answer. He bent down and whispered to the group, "It's Harvey."

"Who?"

"Harvey. He was a six-foot invisible rabbit."

"You don't want to join us, do you? We need all the help we can get."

So do I, thought Denis, straightening up. Oh, God, so do I. He smiled. "Sure," he said. "Why not?"

"Can we have a sandwich break now?"

Judy had played all of Carl's sound effects while Lloyd made good his promise to make the tea, and the chimes, the horses' hooves, and all the rest had passed muster. Now Marianne was sorting out the songs with the pianist, and Judy felt more than a little apprehensive in case she was talked into singing. She had spent two hours learning how to breathe and an hour reading Cinderella's lines and playing the sound effects; she felt as though she had done her bit for the day without a crash course on singing. She was glad someone else had gotten hungry; she wouldn't mind a sandwich.

Marianne reluctantly agreed to a twenty minute break, and Lloyd was at Judy's elbow. "Is there a green room?" he asked.

"Yes," she said. "Why?"

"Do you want to show me it?"

"If you like." She got up with some difficulty, and wished that February had come and gone and that this baby was existing under its own steam instead of making her feel clumsy and awkward and a number of other things she didn't even want to think about. "It's this way," she said, walking through the wings and out into the corridors.

"It's good fun," said Lloyd. "Isn't it?"

"Mm." She couldn't really agree; she preferred a much more backstage role than the one she'd had tonight, but she had known Lloyd would be enjoying himself. "Why have you never joined an amateur dramatic society?" she asked. It had never occurred to her before, but Lloyd, natural actor that he was, had never shown any interest, not even when she told him she did some work for the amateur dramatic society.

He smiled. "Because I'm a professional," he said.

She opened the door and switched on the light. "There you are," she said. "Chairs, a sofa, a table, and some magazines that are probably older than the building." She turned to him as he closed the door. "Why did you want to see it?"

He put his arms around her with some difficulty, and kissed her. "So I could give you a cuddle," he said.

She frowned. "Did I look as though I needed a cuddle?" she asked. "To be perfectly honest, I really need a sandwich a bit more than a cuddle."

"You should eat lunch. Especially now that you're eating for two." He smiled. "I thought you needed reassurance. I want you to know that I will be present at the birth. And I will take Junioress to pantomimes. And I will carry on with the relaxation classes." He kissed her again. "Things really are different," he said. "The world's different. And I'm different. And . . . well, you're different from Barbara. She never expected very much of me, and so she never got very much of me."

Judy knew that Lloyd had no desire to do any of these things. "Is this some sort of bargain? You'll do all that providing I settle on a house and move in with you?"

He shook his head. "You take as much time as you need," he said. "I'm in no hurry."

She felt a little guilty. But then, that was how he meant her to feel. "When do we get to the bit where you tell me I'm selfish?" she asked.

"You are selfish." He smiled again. "But you're frightened. I know you are. And there's no need to be."

"But I thought you'd know all about babies and children, and now—" She sighed. "Have you ever changed a nappy?" she asked. "Because I haven't."

"Oh, yes. I can do nappies. And feeding, once they're past the breast stage. And rocking to sleep." He gave her a little hug. "For the first sixteen years all you can do is keep them dry, warm, fed, loved, and safe," he said. "And after that, it's up to them."

Other couples would have had this conversation months before now, she thought. Other couples would live together, not in separate flats. And Lloyd really, really wanted to be like other couples. She knew she should try harder not to expect things all her own way, but she had never entirely understood how not to be selfish. And she was horribly aware that she had given herself away; now that he knew exactly what was bothering her, he was saying all the right things to reassure her, and she had absolutely no idea whether they were true. She was almost certain that by telling her that she needn't do anything she didn't want to do, and that he would do everything that she wanted him to do, Lloyd was, in his own gentle, charming way, bullying her. Almost certain. But not quite. Because she did feel reassured.

She kissed him this time, and Carl Bignall walked in on them, carrying a plate of sandwiches.

"Whoops, sorry," he said. "I was looking for a Marianne-free zone in which to have a snack. Have you had a row or are you so sickeningly in love that you feel obliged to sneak off and snog in corners?"

"Neither," said Judy, feeling her face grow pink. "He just likes embarrassing me."

"You mustn't be embarrassed on my account," said Carl, making for the sofa. "In fact, you two have given me an idea for a play." He was about to sit down, then straightened up again. "Oh—were you thinking of using the sofa? I can make myself scarce."

Lloyd laughed. "Fat chance," he said.

Carl beamed. "I might use that as the title. It would be perfect."

"Are you a playwright?"

"Not really—I scribble a bit in my spare time. I'm a GP—my practice is just down the road at the Health Center."

"Where the dreaded prenatal clinic is," said Judy, glancing at Lloyd. "Don't forget we've got an appointment tomorrow." She had been told that the father should attend checkups and scans and everything else having to do with the baby, and she'd dragged a very reluctant Lloyd with her whenever she could. It was like taking a very old, very obstinate dog to the vet, and he got out of it every time he could.

"I'm not forgetting," said Lloyd. "And I don't dread it, I just . . ." He shrugged. "I just think you feel more at home in these places if you're actually pregnant."

"You don't," said Judy. "Take my word for it."

"Tell yourself you're a doctor," Carl said, with a grin. "You'll feel much less out of place. Actually, I'm in partnership with Denis Leeward—I think you might know him, Lloyd. He was the FME for Stansfield before he moved to Malworth. It would be a while ago—I think he moved here about seven or eight years ago."

"Oh, yes, I know him," said Lloyd. "How's he doing? I haven't seen him since he left."

"Oh, he's fine."

"Give him my regards."

"Have you had any plays produced, Carl?" asked Judy.

"Marianne produced one once, but two men and a dog came to it. The men fell asleep and the dog thought it was pretentious sub-Chekovian psychobabble."

Lloyd smiled. "Did you ever think of going into the theater professionally?"

Carl shrugged. "At Cambridge, yes. I even did a bit in the Footlights. But I wasn't destined to be plucked from the obscurity of medicine like so many before me, so I write the odd nativity play for five-year-olds to perform and scripts for Marianne's pantomimes. My biggest challenge of recent years has been working 'Walking in the Air' into every script. I'll be glad when Dexter's voice breaks."

"I trust I'm not going to have to sing it," said Lloyd.

Carl smiled. "I thought Welshmen jumped at the chance to give their tonsils a workout."

"Not this Welshman." He grinned. "Well, not singing, anyway." Lloyd was checking his mobile phone, which he'd had to turn off during the relaxation class, and listened to a message; he excused himself and left Judy with Carl.

"Do you have to sing it?" asked Judy.

"I will have to, if Dex isn't back on form by the time we open," he said. "It sounds a bit strange in a not-very-tuneful baritone. I think I would play it for laughs. I'd have to—I'd probably still have the Ugly Sister's makeup on. Doubling up is no fun, believe me."

"You and Dex don't seem exactly interchangeable," said Judy. "Do you have to have Buttons's costume in two different sizes?"

"No. If I had to do it, I'd use a costume from a previous production where I played a footman. It doesn't have as many buttons on it, but it would do, in a pinch. We can't afford luxuries like doubling up on costumes." He smiled. "We don't usually have to use the understudies, but we've never been hit with the flu like we have this year.

You and Lloyd might find yourselves starring in this production on opening night." He pushed the sandwiches over to her. "Have some," he said.

Judy gratefully took a sandwich as Lloyd came back in, his face serious and troubled. "Dr. Bignall—" he began.

"Oh, Carl, please."

"Dr. Bignall, I'm sorry, but I have some very bad news for you."

Chapter Two

Ryan gunned the car down the side street and drove to the storage garages, pulled the bag out of the backseat, unlocked one of the doors, and went inside. In the dim light he tore the Christmas wrapping off a few of the presents and stuffed them into a shopping bag, followed by a couple of other things he thought he could sell, then left, locking the door. He drove the car some distance away from the garages, turning into an office car park, where he abandoned it, running through the back alleys of Malworth toward home.

He was putting the shopping bag into his bedroom closet when he heard the front door open and close, and the click of his mother's heels on the floor. He knew it must be ten past nine; his mother did evening cleaning at the Riverside Family Center and always came home at exactly the same time. The heels clicked again and her voice floated up.

"Dexter? Dexter, are you in bed, love?"

Ryan heard her footsteps on the stairs, heard her open Dexter's bedroom door. He was locking the closet door when she came into his bedroom, and he turned to look at her.

Not forty yet, and she looked worn-out. Washed out. Her pale bare arms were hardly any wider at the top than they were at her wrist, and her elbows always looked to him as though the bones might start poking through, there was so little flesh between them and her skin. One day, he told himself, he was going to buy her a big house with someone to do her cleaning, instead of her having to do other people's; one day she would lose the worried frown that seemed almost permanent.

His dad had left home when he was four years old; all Ryan remembered of his parents' marriage had been tears and shouting just after Dex was born, and he had known it had something to do with Dex being black. He hadn't understood why it upset his father so much; he had thought the baby was a nice color. Much better than a silly pink baby. Now, he couldn't believe that his mother had actually waited until Dex was born before facing the music, but he supposed it was in character; she had a tendency to think that if she ignored things they would just go away. And, in that instance, his father did indeed go away.

After a while she had married Edward Gibson, Dex's father, and she was happy then. Ryan had liked him too; everything was fine until Edward went to work one morning and never came home again. He had told his supervisor he didn't feel well, and was clocking off to go home when he just dropped down dead. That had been five years ago, and his mother never really got over it.

There had been the odd man since, but nothing serious, and these days there wasn't anyone at all. Ryan wished there was; maybe then she would have something else to think about, and wouldn't come sailing into his bedroom whenever she felt like it. He should have somewhere of his own. Somewhere he could take girlfriends. Somewhere he could do what he liked. One day, he thought. One day it would happen.

One day he'd have a penthouse flat and she would have a house in the country and no problems at all. His dreams of that coming about were tempered a little by realism; he knew that more often than not he was the cause of his mother's problems, and he knew that his lifestyle was not one likely to produce penthouse flats and cottages in the country. But deep down he still believed it could all be turned around. One day.

She looked with deep suspicion at the locked closet door. "What have you got in there?"

"Nothing," he said.

"Why are you locking it, then?"

"It's private." He put the key in the coin pocket of his jeans.

"Ryan," she sighed. "Have you been up to something?" She advanced farther into the room. "Have you?"

"No!" he said, with the same injured innocence that he used in court. It depended on the magistrates whether or not it worked there. It never worked with his mother.

"You have. Have you been getting Dexter into bother? Where is he?"

"Why would I be getting him into bother?" Ryan asked, puzzled. "Isn't this Monday? He'll be at rehearsal for the panto."

All Dex wanted was to be an actor, to be in the movies. He'd joined the amateur dramatic society when he was ten years old, and he loved it. He'd even had publicity photographs done; he did a Saturday job with a photographer, so they hadn't cost him anything. He sent them out now and then to people who produced TV ads and things, but nothing had come of it yet. It would, though, Ryan thought. He was a good actor, and he could sing. Maybe Dex would get rich and famous and make everything happen.

"He isn't at the rehearsal. I saw that Marianne woman when she arrived at the center, and she asked if he would be well enough to get to their next rehearsal. He'd called her to say he couldn't go because he wasn't feeling well—she thought he might have this flu. I thought he must be in bed when he wasn't downstairs." She regarded Ryan with deep suspicion. "Have you had him out with you on some job? Is that it?"

Ryan sighed dramatically. She was convinced he was going to corrupt Dex. "He's not been with me," he said. "I don't know where he is." He frowned. It was a bit odd. But perhaps it wasn't that inexplicable. "Maybe he felt better and went anyway."

His mother picked up his mobile. "How do you use this thing?"

He told her, and watched as she dialed the number of the Riverside Theatre, listened as she asked if Dexter was there, and didn't need to hear the answer as she thanked whoever she'd spoken to and handed back the phone to him, so he could terminate the call. The look said everything.

"You had him with you, didn't you?"

Ryan shook his head, baffled. "What makes you think that?"

"If there's nothing wrong with him, he wouldn't miss a rehearsal unless you told him to. Where is he?" She came around the foot of the bed and stood looking down at him as he peeled back the Velcro of his trainers. "Answer me, Ryan Chester! Where is your little brother?"

Ryan reached past her for his new trainers. "I don't know where he is!" he said again. "He's not been with me."

"Did you run away and leave him?" Her hand flew to her mouth as a thought struck her. "Oh, my God, has he been arrested?"

Ryan had laces on the new trainers; he took some time to thread them, then looked up at her. "He's fourteen—if he'd been arrested they'd have contacted you, wouldn't they?"

He should know. He was always being arrested when he was fourteen. His way of life hadn't changed very much, but he was better at evading arrest than he had been; he hadn't been caught for over a year. His court appearances used to be constant.

He remembered the first time he'd been arrested after his seventeenth birthday. When he'd realized that the police weren't going to get his mum, that he was on his own, it had been a little bit scary. But he'd felt proud too. He'd grown up, reached the age at which he no longer needed an appropriate adult present. And he'd felt relieved. Now his mum didn't have to know every time he got into a little bit of bother, and he didn't have to hear her insisting that he tell the cops the truth. But Dex was still a juvenile. They'd have rung her at work if they picked him up. Besides, Dex didn't do anything like that.

"Dex isn't like me," he said. "He won't be in trouble."

"I hope not," she said. "But he's been a bit funny lately, Ryan. Secretive. He doesn't talk about what he's been up to, like he used to. It's not like him to be like that."

Ryan smiled. "He's fourteen, Mum," he said again. "He's not going to come and tell you everything that happens to him anymore."

"But haven't you noticed?" she said.

Ryan couldn't say he had, but then he was very rarely home. "He's okay," he said. "I don't think he's sniffing glue or anything, if that's what's worrying you."

"He's doing something," she said. "Something he doesn't want me to know about."

Ryan smiled. "What's the matter?" he said. "Do you think he'll go blind?"

"I wish I could believe that's all it is," she said. "You'd tell me, wouldn't you, if he was taking drugs or anything like that?"

"He's not taking drugs," said Ryan. "He's just growing up, Mum."

"Maybe. But I keep remembering you at his age. I was never out of the police station. And Barry takes drugs. He'll probably be spending Christmas in prison because of it."

"He smokes pot, Mum. It's not the same thing. And Dex isn't into any of that."

She frowned. "What did you put in the closet?" she asked.

Ryan had bought the lock after he'd found her going through the closet and then questioned him about what she'd found. He still had to put up with the questions, but at least she couldn't go into it anymore. "Nothing," he said as he finished lacing his shoes and stood up. "Nothing to do with you. Or Dexter."

"It had better not have anything to do with Dexter." She looked from the closet to him, and walked toward the bedroom door. "Why hasn't he come home? Is he scared to? If you've been getting him into trouble, you can just pack your bags now."

She didn't mean it, even if he had gotten Dexter into trouble—Ryan knew that, and so did she. And, as it turned out, her threat didn't have to be put to the test, as they heard the front door open and slam shut.

"Dexter? Is that you?"

Ryan shook his head. Who did she think it was, for God's sake?

"Mum?"

Ryan shrugged. "See?" he said. "He's not been arrested."

She turned to call through the open door. "I'll be right down, love," she said. "And I'll be going to the chip shop in a minute, so think about what you want." She turned back to Ryan. "I don't know about him," she said, "but you've been up to something. And if I have the police round here again, you can find somewhere else to live, because I'm not putting up with it anymore."

Ryan shook his head and walked past her to rattle downstairs with his mother following him at a more sedate pace. He stopped dead when he saw Dex. "What the hell happened to you?" he asked.

Dex looked away. "I fell," he said.

"You fell?" said Ryan. Dex's eye was almost closed; blood from his nose was drying on his face, and he had a bruised mouth. He gently held Dex's chin between his fingers, turning his head left and right, checking the extent of the damage. He had taken a beating from someone. "You fell on to someone's fists," he said. "Who did that to you?"

"Dexter?" His mother ran down to him. "Are you all right? Oh, dear God. Do you need a doctor? Who's been hitting you?"

"No one," Dex said, pulling his head away. "I fell down some stairs. I'm all right. I don't need a doctor."

"Why didn't you go to rehearsal?" she asked.

"I didn't feel well. Then I felt a bit better and I went out for a walk."

"A walk?" said Ryan. "It's chucking it down out there!"

"It wasn't. Not when I went out."

"Since when have you gone for walks?"

"I just wanted some fresh air."

"Leave him alone, Ryan," said his mother, putting a protective arm around Dex. "Oh, you're all wet." She unzipped his bomber jacket and began to take it off, as if he were a child.

Dexter caught his breath with the movement, then impatiently shrugged off her assistance and took the jacket off himself. Very carefully.

Ryan took the jacket from him.

"I was at the shops!" Dex said defensively, though Ryan hadn't said a word. "The pavement was wet and I slipped and fell down those steps by the hairdresser's."

The jacket was wet, as his mother had said, but there were no smears of dirt on the shiny green material. No scratches, no indication of a fall. There was some blood, and stains down the front. "Were you sick?" he asked, handing the jacket to his mother.

"A little bit," said Dex. "But I want chips," he added, anxiously.

Ryan wondered briefly if his mother was right—kids gathered at the shops to sniff glue. But his mother didn't seem to have thought of that, and he wasn't about to put the idea back into her head.

"You weren't well," his mother scolded him. "You shouldn't have gone out. Come and let me get you cleaned up. Are you sure you want to eat? Maybe you should just go to bed with a hot drink and aspirin."

Ryan watched as she shepherded Dex into the living room, and shook his head. Whatever he'd been up to, Dex had not fallen down any stairs. He followed them into the room, sitting down beside Dex on the sofa as his mother bathed his injuries and glared at Ryan as though it was his fault. If his mother went out again, he would have the opportunity to interview his little brother in circumstances in which he might find it easier to talk. Not that Dex was going to find it easy to talk at all with that swollen lip.

"Are you sure you want food?" his mother asked Dexter again. "You must be shaken up."

"Yes, I'm sure," said Dex, his eyes widening, alarmed that he might find himself going without his supper. "Burger and chips."

"Well, all right. Do you want anything?" she asked Ryan.

"No," he said. "I'm going out. I'll get something at the club."

"You're not going anywhere until I get back. You'll stay and keep an eye on your brother. He could have concussion."

He could, thought Ryan. He'd been hit hard enough. "Did you get knocked out, Dex?"

Dex shook his head. "I don't think so," he said.

Ryan performed perfunctory ringside tests; he passed a finger in front of him, and Dex's eyes followed it; he held up three fingers, and Dex didn't see six. "He'll be okay," he said, and ran a hand over his brother's short, tightly curled hair. "Won't you, champ?"

Dex nodded.

"Even so. He's not well. You just wait here until I get back." His mother picked up her coat, then put it down again. "On second thoughts, you can go," she said. "You'll be quicker than me." She opened her bag, taking out her purse, and selected exactly the right money. "Cod, beefburger, and a large bag of chips. Straight there and straight back," she said.

Ryan smiled. She used to say that when he was ten. "Cod, beefburger, and a large bag of chips," he repeated. "Are you sure you don't want to give me a note for the man in case I forget what I've gone for?"

"Less cheek. Just hurry up."

Ryan was back in ten minutes with the fish and chips, and helped his mother put them on plates, something only mothers ever did. "Keep an eye on him, Mum," he said. "If he looks drowsy or he's sick again, you should get the doctor." He saw his mother's face, the worried frown deeper than ever. "But I think he's okay," he added reassuringly. "Honest."

He went up to his room and retrieved the carrier bag from the closet, then rattled down again, popping his head around the door to say cheerio. He glanced at Dex as he went out, and Dex looked away immediately. But there would be another opportunity to talk to him.

"I told the officers who came earlier."

Tom nodded. "I know, sir, but I'd just like you to go over it again with me, if you wouldn't mind."

He was with Geoffrey Jones, the neighbor who had called the police. Everything about him, from the hair he'd combed over his bald patch and his horn-rimmed glasses, through his cardigan and slacks, right down to his nylon socks and polished shoes, instantly irritated Tom.

Mr. Jones gave a short sigh of resignation. "You'd better come in, then," he said.

Tom closed the front door and followed Mr. Jones into the immaculately tidy sitting room, where his wife, wearing a sculpted hairdo and a fussy blouse and skirt that quarreled with one another, was hovering anxiously as Mr. Jones moaned about the intrusion. Her face was pale and drawn, and her eyes red; Tom doubted that she had received much in the way of sympathy.

"I don't see why the other chap can't tell you what I told him. Why should I have to go through it all again?"

"Geoffrey," said his wife. "Estelle's *dead*."

"Well?" he said. "Telling umpteen policemen what I saw isn't going to bring her back to life, is it?"

Mrs. Jones looked hurt and shocked. Tom cleared his throat. "Detective Sergeant Finch, Stansfield CID," he told her, since her husband was clearly dispensing with introductions, and turned to Mr. Jones again. "I'm sorry we're taking up so much of your time," he said. "But if you could just tell me in your own words what—"

"In my own words? Whose words do you suppose I'm going to use?"

Tom produced something approaching a friendly smile, for which he felt he deserved a medal. "Well, perhaps you could just tell me what made you call us," he said.

"Sit down, Sergeant Finch," said Mrs. Jones. "Would you like a cup of tea?"

"Oh, for God's sake, woman! We're not running a café! We might have to have policemen all over the place, but you don't have to make them all tea into the bargain!"

"It's only polite."

Tom took a deep breath. "No, thank you, Mrs. Jones," he said, but he did sit down as invited. "Now, Mr. Jones, if you could tell me what happened tonight—it is quite urgent."

"I know it's urgent! How many break-ins have there been round here? And what have you done about them? Nothing, that's what!"

The evening paper had been running a campaign about the rise in the burglary statistics, complaining about police performance. Last year it had been street crime, and the Chief Constable had decided that street crime must be targeted. If you took resources away from one thing to deal with another, this was what happened. Next year it would be burglary they were targeting. And thefts from vehicles would go up.

"I can assure you we have been working on them, Mr. Jones, but if we could just get back to tonight . . ."

"Tonight, a young woman has died because of these . . . these animals! And it's all very well you and your colleagues coming here now—now that it's finally happened. The place is crawling with policemen when it's too late! Why didn't you try harder to catch these people in the first place? And why aren't you looking for that black lad instead of making me tell you all about him again?"

Tom was used to getting the blame for all the ills that befell mankind; it didn't bother him. In a way, it made him feel more comfortable with Mr. Jones; until now, he had seemed to regard the death of his next door neighbor as more of an irritation than anything else. But under all that bluster was someone shocked and frightened, and Tom knew if he didn't calm Mr. Jones down, he'd get nothing useful out of him. This wasn't his strong point; he would be much more at home with the burglar. He understood how to talk to lawbreakers and those suspected of having broken the law. Witnesses were different.

"Believe me, Mr. Jones, my colleagues are looking for him. But it would make a big difference if we had a little more to go on. And we find that if we ask people to go over what they saw, they sometimes remember a little bit more than they did originally. So, perhaps you could start at the beginning? I believe you were coming home from work?"

"From my place of business," said Mr. Jones, bridling once more.

Tom, with a slight movement of his hand, apologized for calling it something so lowly as work, and correctly guessed that Mr. Jones didn't work for anyone else. "You're in business for yourself?"

"I have a shop in the High Street. Toys and games. I was open late tonight, so I didn't get home until about ten past eight. I drove into the garage—"

"That's at the rear of the house?"

"Yes. There's a service road running along the back of these properties. The garages are at the rear, of course."

Tom nodded.

"And as I came back out I could hear an argument."

"Did you recognize the voices?"

"No. He was angry, and she was crying—it could have been anyone, really. He wasn't shouting—if anything, he was keeping his voice down. But he was very angry."

"Did you hear what was being said?"

"Just the odd word—mostly swearing. From him. And I heard noises. A scuffle or something, and what might have been blows. I heard her cry out."

"You should have gone next door, then," said Mrs. Jones. "If you thought someone was assaulting her."

"I thought it was her husband."

"And that would have made it all right, would it?"

"No, but—" Mr. Jones looked helplessly at Tom, appealing for some male support. "I would have done something," he said, "said something, if it had gone on for any length of time. But it didn't. It lasted a few seconds, that was all. Then it went quiet, and I thought it had calmed down. That's when I came into the house."

"Did you hear any of this, Mrs. Jones?"

"No," she said. "But I had the television on. I thought maybe that's what Geoffrey had heard, because they'd been having a row." She smiled a little. "Well, they always are in soaps, aren't they?"

"And that couldn't have been what you heard?"

"No, of course it couldn't! I know the difference between the television and real people. Besides, they don't use that sort of language in soaps."

"What sort of language?"

"Well, you know," said Mr. Jones, and lowered his voice, glancing apologetically at his wife. "I heard him call her a 'fucking bitch.' "

"You're certain it was from next door?"

"Well, I couldn't see anything, because of the hedge, but it was definitely coming from that direction—and it sounded as though they were outside. It certainly wasn't the TV."

"Right," said Tom. "Then you heard the glass breaking?"

"Well, I went upstairs and I heard it then. It would be about five or so minutes later, I suppose. I looked out of the back bedroom window to try to find out what was going on, and I saw this boy running out of Eric Watson's garden and off down the back road. Mr. Watson was in the garden—he shouted at him to stop, but he didn't, of course."

They hadn't been told that the first time around. All they had known was that Mr. Jones saw him running down the back road. But the back gates to the Bignalls' garden were locked, so jumping the wall into the neighboring garden would be the quickest way out. Was that how he had come in as well? The hoped-for evidence on the gate wouldn't be forthcoming if that was the case. And the bit about Watson shouting at the intruder hadn't been mentioned before either. But perhaps Mr. Jones was embroidering the story second time around, Tom thought.

"Can you remember exactly what he said?"

"I think he shouted, 'Come back here, you little bugger,' or something like that." Another glance in his wife's direction.

Mr. Jones clearly wasn't used to swearing in the house; he was almost enjoying the freedom that factual reporting had given him to indulge. And it seemed definite enough, thought Tom. Unless he was a pathological embroiderer of stories, it did seem that he'd heard Watson shouting.

"And from up there I could see the Bignalls' French window was wide open, and all the rain was getting in. And there was no light on, so obviously they didn't know. I didn't know it was broken, though. It's just one pane—it wasn't obvious."

"I made him go next door then," said Mrs. Jones. "To tell them about their French window being open."

"So I went and knocked on the front door, but I couldn't get a reply," said Mr. Jones. "The front bedroom light was on, but everywhere else was in darkness."

"He wouldn't phone you," his wife said. "He kept saying they were probably making up after the row and didn't want to answer the door, didn't you, Geoffrey?"

Mr. Jones looked a little embarrassed. "Well, you know," he mumbled. "They're that sort of couple."

"Oh?" said Tom. "What sort of couple?"

"Well—you know. Rows and things."

"Violent rows?"

"Oh, no," said Mrs. Jones. "Never. He was always trying to calm her down when she had one of her turns. She was just a bit—well, highly strung. Sometimes she got a bit depressed, you know. You'd hear her now and then, going on at him. She thought the world of him, really, but she was very suspicious—you'd hear her sometimes screaming at him that he didn't love her, that he just stayed with her for—"

"Christine!" said Mr. Jones.

Mrs. Jones looked mutinous. "Well, it's true!" she said.

"Just stayed with her for what?" asked Tom. This was getting very interesting, assuming it wasn't all just exaggeration.

"Her money," said Mrs. Jones. "But she didn't mean it—I know she didn't. She was always telling me how much she loved him, and how she wished she didn't say things like that, because she knew they weren't true."

"Was she the one with the money, then?"

"Well," said Mr. Jones, "I don't know about that, particularly. She had a nice income from a trust her grandfather set up for her. Poor girl lost her parents when she was very young. Her grandfather brought her up on his own—he lost his wife in the same accident. I think that's why she confided in Christine like she did. A sort of mother figure."

"How long have you known her?"

"They moved in when they got married," said Mrs. Jones. "Seven years ago, now. They're a nice couple, really." Her eyes filled with tears. "Well," she said. "You know. They were. But she made his life a bit difficult—she knew she did. They almost split up at one point, but they got over that. She would come and see me when she needed to get something off her chest."

"Yes," said Mr. Jones. "Like I say, they argued all the time, and then they'd make up. So that's what I thought they were doing."

"But I didn't think that was very likely," said Mrs. Jones. "There was the breaking glass and that boy running away and everything. And even if they were doing what he thought they were doing, they could still have been broken into, I said. So eventually he phoned you."

"Were you at home earlier in the evening, Mrs. Jones?"

"Yes."

"You didn't notice anything today about teatime, did you? We've been told that kids were making a bit of a nuisance of themselves."

She shook her head. "No," she said. "I've seen gangs of boys from the London Road estate here quite often, though. They're a bit rowdy, and they can make a bit of a mess, but they don't really do any harm."

"They're probably the ones doing the break-ins," said Mr. Jones. "Don't do any harm, my foot."

"Would you mind letting me see the view from the back bedroom?" asked Tom, getting up.

After a show of reluctance, Mr. Jones agreed that he didn't mind enough actually to prohibit it. Upstairs, Tom looked out of the window, getting the lay of the land. A six-foot-high wall ran along the rear of the properties on this side of the road, punctuated along its length by wooden gates to the driveways leading to the double garages. The high hedge between the Jones' garden and that of the Bignalls would have meant that Mr. Jones had no view of the Bignalls' garden, or of the French windows, until he came up to this vantage point. A low wall separated the Bignalls' garden from their neighbor's on the other side. Bricks were piled up neatly beside it; one pile, however, lay scattered on the ground, about halfway down. The intruder could have knocked them over in his haste to leave.

Tom could see reasonably well because now the lights at the rear were on, but that had obviously not been the case when Mr. Jones looked out of this window earlier. The back road itself was a short, unlit service road, and behind that lay a small wood, so no light was to be had there. He would have been able to see someone running through Watson's gate two gardens away, but it was hard to see how he had seen anything more definite than that on this rainy, starless, moonless night.

"It's very dark," he said. "How could you be sure the boy you saw running away was black?"

"Watson's got one of these high-power security lights," he said. "Goes on as soon as there's any movement, floods the place with light. I could see that boy as clearly as if it was daylight."

"Can you describe him?"

"He was black. I told you."

"Yes," said Tom, his patience once again severely tested. "Anything else? What he was wearing, perhaps? Did he have short hair, or dreadlocks, or what? Was he fat, thin, tall, short . . . how old would you say he was?"

"He was black," repeated Mr. Jones, with a shrug.

"Mr. Jones, can't you just tell me a bit more than that?"

Mr. Jones sighed again. "Definitely young, smallish—maybe a child, maybe a teenager. Wearing the sort of thing they wear."

The sort of thing who wore? Black people? Teenagers? Burglars, maybe. The newspaper cartoon image of a burglar complete with mask and striped jersey and his bag of stolen goods over his shoulder came into Tom's mind. He frowned as he realized something.

"You saw this boy immediately after hearing the window break?"

"Yes."

Tom didn't know what, if anything, was missing from next door, but he did know that the intruder had time to make the usual sort of mess. Drawers had been pulled out, cupboards opened, shelves disturbed, and it certainly looked as though items were missing from them. So if this youth had run away the minute the window was broken, it seemed more likely he was a lookout who had gotten cold feet rather than the actual burglar. Whoever was doing the actual burgling might still have been inside. If Mr. Jones hadn't wasted almost half an hour between hearing the altercation and phoning the police, they might have arrived with the intruder still on the premises. Or at least in time to save Mrs. Bignall.

"Was this boy carrying anything?" he asked.

Mr. Jones frowned, and thought. "No," he said eventually. "No, now that you mention it, I don't think he was. He was running very fast—you know? Arms going like pistons. He couldn't have been carrying anything."

Well, at least they could try finding the lookout, if only Mr. Jones could see past the color of his skin to give a decent description. Once they had him, there would be no problem. He was obviously already alarmed, and once he found out that his partner in crime had caused someone's death, he would be very eager to shift the blame.

Tom tried again, dredging up the interviewing techniques he was supposed to apply when dealing with honest, upright citizens who had inadvertently become mixed up in a criminal investigation. "Now that you've got a picture of him in your head, can you remember *anything* about what he was wearing? Anything at all about him?"

Mr. Jones was shaking his head slowly, but then he stopped and frowned again. "One of those bomber jacket things," he said. "Shiny. Green, maybe. Yes. Yes, I think it was green. But Mr. Watson might be able to give you a better description—he was much closer to him than I was. He was standing by his greenhouse, and the boy was at his gate."

Yes, thought Tom, looking over at the greenhouse. He would only be about ten feet away from the boy. The only problem was that Mr. Watson said he hadn't seen or heard anything or anyone at all, and he had once been a policeman himself, according to the uniforms. But while Mr. Jones might not be someone Tom had taken to readily, it seemed unlikely that he'd imagined all this, so Watson was definitely worth a visit.

"Thank you," he said, making his way back to the stairs. "You've been a great help. And I'm sorry if we've inconvenienced you."

"It's a terrible business. In this neighborhood too."

❦

Lloyd pulled up in the once-quiet street with its handful of well-to-do terraced houses, now alive with vehicles and urgency, and looked at Carl Bignall. "If you'd prefer to go to a neighbor or a friend," he began, "I can—"

"No." Bignall opened the car door. "No, I'm all right, thank you." He got out and walked slightly unsteadily toward the house.

Lloyd had driven him home because Bignall had received such a shock when he heard what had happened; he definitely wasn't all right. Lloyd caught up with him. "Dr. Bignall, if you could follow me, it might be as well," he said. "The SOCOs—the scene-of-crime officers—might want us to keep clear of any area they still need to examine."

"Yes," muttered Bignall, falling into step behind him. "Yes, of course. I understand."

They met Tom as he emerged from the house next door. "Ah, good," Lloyd said as all three reached Carl Bignall's front door. "Could you look after Dr. Bignall, Tom?"

Tom took Bignall into the sitting room, and Lloyd continued on to the kitchen at the end of the hallway, where Estelle Bignall's body lay. He was walking under streamers and holly; how sad it all looked.

"You can come in, sir," said the young constable who stood guard. "The SOCOs just finished in here."

Lloyd went in and looked at the small, slim young woman who lay on the floor, naked under her bathrobe, her hands bound behind her back with the belt, her ankles taped up. Hanging loosely around her neck was a man's tie, still knotted tightly at the back, and on the floor beside the body lay a rolled-up ball of material and a man's glove. The photographer was snapping away, impassively and efficiently.

"Did the FME remove the gag?" Lloyd asked. "I'm sorry—I don't know your name."

The young man stood almost to attention. "PC Gary Sims, sir. I removed the gag and got the material out of her mouth. I then attempted mouth-to-mouth resuscitation, but it failed."

Lloyd nodded, smiling a little. "I'm not a court of law, Gary," he said.

Sims relaxed a little. "I wasn't sure what to do, sir. I thought she was dead, but you know—you're told you mustn't assume that, you must try to preserve life, but you're told not to disturb a homicide scene, and I couldn't do both, so I just did what I thought I had to do."

"That's all you can do," said Lloyd, and looked down at the body again. "Was she still warm, then?"

"Not exactly warm. But not cold."

Lloyd nodded, and looked again at the victim. She was in her mid-twenties, fair, probably very attractive before this happened to her.

"Do we know who that glove belongs to?"

"No, sir. It was there when I found her. I didn't touch it."

"Why would he remove one glove, do you think?"

"Maybe he couldn't tie her up properly with his gloves on."

"But if you had to remove one glove to tie a knot, wouldn't you have to remove both of them?" It was a little puzzle, he thought. And little puzzles sometimes solved the bigger ones.

"Not if you used your teeth, sir. He would have been hanging onto her with his other hand while he tied her up, wouldn't he?"

Yes, presumably he would be doing that. So it wasn't a little puzzle after all, then. Who needed Judy? Everyone could point out flaws in his reasoning. Even little boys in police uniforms.

"There was one of these Sellotape dispensers on the table, and scissors," said Sims, nodding over to the kitchen table, on which lay a roll of Christmas paper. "Someone had been wrapping presents, I think. The SOCO took them."

Perhaps, thought Lloyd, the burglar had left a set of his doubtless already-filed fingerprints for them to find when he used the tape. And whether he had or not, Lloyd had every intention of having whoever did this behind bars before the holiday began.

Through the adjoining door he could see the crime scene technicians dusting the window and everything else that had been disturbed, examining the carpet, collecting samples of the mud that had been walked through from the garden into the dining room, carefully bagging up the broken glass that lay on the rain-soaked carpet, the brick that lay on the patio. He would wait until they finished before he went in.

Freddie arrived as he went back out into the hallway.

"Lloyd! We meet again. Good of you to let me fit in my game of squash before you called."

"She's in the kitchen, Freddie. Constable Sims is with her."

"Is Constable Sims male or female?"

"Male."

Freddie pulled a face. "Your police force is sadly lacking in talent at the moment, you know that, don't you? I think I'll report you to the Equal Opportunities people."

"Sir!" called Sims. "They've finished next door—they've moved out to the patio now."

"Thank you," said Lloyd, and left Freddie and Sims to their work, as he went into the large dining room, also decorated for the season. One of the Bignalls obviously made a big thing of Christmas. More garlands, balloons, baubles, and a tall Christmas tree whose lights changed color through the spectrum. Books lay scattered on one shelf, and the other shelves were empty save for a vase of flowers. It looked almost artistic—minimalist, Japanese. He had never been struck by the artistry of a burglary before. Tom came in from the hallway.

"Dr. Bignall's with PC Warren," he said. "He's pretty shell-shocked, but Warren's checking the rest of the house with him."

Tom had unloaded Bignall; Lloyd wasn't surprised. Victim support was not Tom's strong suit at the best of times, and with the new haircut, Tom looked exactly what he was: a tough, uncompromising detective sergeant. The curls had been disarming; people had let their guard down a little, were taken by surprise when he'd shown his mettle. Lloyd felt that he might have thrown away an advantage.

"Guv—I think there might have been two of them. Dr. Bignall says there were a lot of presents under the tree in here, and they're not here now." He nodded over to where the tree, slightly lopsided, sat in its tub, two Christmas-wrapped presents beneath it. "Someone else must have removed them, because this kid who ran away wasn't carrying anything. And I want to talk to the other neighbors, especially Watson. We're getting conflicting stories."

Lloyd listened to what had been overheard, to how Tom thought the burglars had gained entry to the property, and to the information he'd gleaned about the Bignalls' marriage.

"Right, Tom—you go ahead and talk to the neighbors. I'll try and find out what's gone missing."

"And one other thing," said Tom as they walked out together into the hall. "Jones said the disturbance sounded as though it was going on outside, and it was definitely before the window was broken. If it was the intruders, one of them was female."

Lloyd went into the sitting room to ask Carl Bignall if he could tell them what presents had been stolen. His reaction to Lloyd's question was predictable.

"Oh, for God's sake. Your sergeant just asked me that! Why on earth are you so bothered about what's missing? I told him—I don't care."

"It's just that it might help us catch whoever did it if they try and sell any of it. I believe you've had a chance to check out the rest of the house?"

"Yes—they don't seem to have been anywhere else." Bignall closed his eyes. "Sorry. I do know what some of the presents were, but I can't think. Some of them were wrapped, and some weren't. We always put them all under there until Christmas Day. Some of them had been opened—I just can't think what they were." He rose wearily. "Can I see her?" he asked.

"We will need you to make formal identification," Lloyd said. "But you might prefer to wait."

"No. I'd like to see her now."

In the kitchen, he nodded briefly. "I just had to see for myself," he said. "Or I'd have gone on thinking it was all a mistake."

Lloyd could understand that. Having someone tell you your wife had been killed during a burglary was something you could choose not to believe; seeing her would draw a line under it at least. He ushered Bignall into the dining room. It really was important to know what was missing.

Carl waved a hand at the shelves. "They've taken some ornaments," he said. "I can't really remember what was there." He looked down and frowned. "There's mud all over the carpet," he said.

"It might help us catch them," said Lloyd.

Bignall shook his head, and glanced over at the Christmas-decorated tree. "They've taken almost all the presents. I know that Estelle had got her—" He broke off, his eyes widening. "There was a portable stereo," he said, pointing to the floor beneath the tree. "It's gone." He looked at Lloyd, his face pale.

"Was it particularly important to you?" asked Lloyd.

"It . . . it was Estelle's present to me."

"I'm very sorry," Lloyd said.

One of the SOCOs came toward them. "Was it about so big?" she asked, spreading her hands. "Dark green?"

"Yes," said Bignall, nodding, his eyes wide.

"Then I've got some good news at least," she said. "It's gone to the lab, sir. We found it beside the open window, so we think there's a chance the intruder dropped it when he was disturbed. And he left a glove behind; there could be fingerprints on it." She smiled sympathetically. "It won't come to any harm."

Bignall nodded, still looking bewildered.

Lloyd went out to the garden where a crime scene officer was asking for the photographer. At least they'd found something to photograph, he thought as he made his way down past the bricks to the bottom of the garden.

"Got something?" he asked.

"The rain's been helpful," said the officer. "We've got footprints. We found one set on the patio, but these have been made by someone else. I'll be able to make a pretty good cast of them."

Footprints at the bottom of the garden tied in with Tom's theory regarding the means of entry. And the SOCO seemed to be endorsing his two-intruder theory. Now for his other one. "Is either set likely to be female?"

"Not unless she's got very large feet. I'd guess a size ten or eleven shoe here, and maybe a nine on the patio."

So the altercation the neighbors heard had probably not been between the intruders, Lloyd thought, unless there had been at least three of them, one of whom didn't leave footprints. It was perfectly possible not to step on mud, even crossing from one garden to the other, so there could have been a third intruder. But a disagreement followed by a death was always worth looking into. He looked back up the garden to the dining room and wondered.

It could, of course, have been one of the reportedly frequent quarrels between Carl and his wife that happened to occur immediately before Carl left the house. And it could have been coincidental to the break-in; a quarrel being the last contact someone had with the deceased before being suddenly bereaved was not at all unusual, and very guilt-inducing. But if it was the Bignalls whom Mr. Jones had heard, it had been different from usual: this one had apparently sounded violent.

So the question had to be asked, but he hadn't asked it yet. Lloyd didn't believe in asking questions when people expected him to ask them. Much better to catch them off guard, when they'd decided he wasn't going to ask at all.

Denis Leeward hadn't got drunk; he'd sipped his beer through the pub quiz, in which his team had come second, and gone home to Meg, who asked what he'd done to himself when he was unable to mask the pain he felt when he sat down. He'd checked; he didn't have any broken ribs. But they hurt like hell all the same.

"Walked into the proverbial door," he said, and smiled weakly. "I was leaving the treatment room just as the nurse was coming in. The door handle caught me right in the rib cage. No real harm done."

"How was Alan?" she asked as she went into the kitchen, and he heard the kettle being filled.

Alan? Oh, of course. "Oh, he's fine. Sends his love."

"Have you eaten?" she called through.

No. No, he hadn't eaten. And he was, now that she mentioned it, surprisingly hungry. "No—we just had a drink at the pub," he said. "Played in a quiz team, would you believe? I wouldn't mind some supper, if there's any going."

"There's cold chicken. Would you like a sandwich or would you rather have a salad or something?"

"A sandwich would be fine."

He sank down into the armchair and looked around his comfortable, somewhat untidy sitting room, seeing it for the first time in years. Through the kitchen door he could see Meg making his sandwich, making tea, and he was seeing her for the first time in years too. He loved Meg. He loved being a doctor. He'd risked it all, and for what?

He was halfway through his chicken sandwich when the phone rang, and he wouldn't, couldn't, answer it. Meg looked puzzled, but she didn't say anything. He always answered the phone. It was just one of those things that evolve over the years; if Denis was there, he picked up the phone. But not this time.

She waited just a fraction longer, then went out to the hallway.

"Oh, hello, Carl," he heard her say, and the mouthful of chicken sandwich he had just swallowed seemed to lodge itself in his throat.

Carl didn't tell Meg what had happened; she went to get Denis, and Carl tried to come to terms with what had gone on in here tonight. He didn't understand why this was happening to him.

Lloyd had shown him the glove the woman said they'd found, asked if it was his, which it wasn't, but he had the feeling that Lloyd hadn't believed him, and the more he denied all knowledge of it, the more he sounded, even to himself, as though he was lying. He understood why people confessed to things they hadn't done; if saying that the glove was his would stop Lloyd looking at him the way he was looking at him, he would very probably have done so. He had never felt so confused in his life.

The sergeant was a brisk, no-nonsense man with little time for finer feelings, and Carl could handle that; he felt at least that the sergeant believed him. But Lloyd—well, Lloyd didn't say much, but Carl felt as though every question he did ask was loaded.

After what seemed hours, Denis came to the phone.

"Denis," Carl began. "I don't quite know how to tell you this. There's . . . there's been a break-in here. Estelle—well, she . . . that is, the police think she surprised the burglar, and he—" Carl took a moment. "She's dead, Denis," he said. "They tied her up and gagged her. She couldn't breathe."

There was silence. For a moment Carl thought he'd been talking to thin air and was going to have to say it all again, but finally Denis found his voice.

"That's dreadful," he said. "I don't know what to say."

"There's nothing anyone can say," said Carl. "But I wondered if you could do me a favor."

"Anything."

"It's young Dexter Gibson. I've just had a call from his mother to say that he had an accident tonight, and she's worried he might be concussed. Perhaps you could go and check him out for me?"

"Of course," said Denis.

"She's probably worrying about nothing, but if you could go, I'd be grateful."

"Of course I will. Are you going to be all right?"

"Yes. Thanks. I—I'll talk to you later."

"Right. Look—if there's anything I can do, just say. I know it's a useless thing to say, but I do mean it. I mean—don't stay there on your own, will you? I know there's probably somewhere else you'd rather go, but there's a bed here for you if you'd like to stay with us. And don't, whatever you do, worry about work. I can handle everything."

"Thanks, Denis."

Carl hung up and went back into the living room. "Sorry about that," he said. "A patient wanted me to go out—Denis Leeward's dealing with it."

Chief Inspector Lloyd looked faintly puzzled. "You don't subscribe to one of these emergency night doctor units?"

"Yes, I do," said Carl. "But Mrs. Gibson cleans for us. That's why she called me direct."

"Your cleaner? Does she work here or at the surgery?"

Carl stared at him. Why on earth did he care about that? What did it have to do with the police? Or Estelle's death? "If it's of any consequence," he said testily, "she works here."

"Fingerprints," said Lloyd. "We need to eliminate any that have a right to be here. When did Mrs. Gibson clean here last?"

"Oh," said Carl, feeling foolish. "This morning, I imagine. She comes every day."

"If you can let us have her address? And we will need your fingerprints too. Not tonight, obviously, but if you could come to the station tomorrow perhaps?"

"Yes, of course. Sorry. I didn't mean to bite your head off."

"Oh, forget it. Now—do you think you could try to sort out what's missing?"

Sergeant Finch, young and fair-haired, with a crew cut that made him look like an American marine, asked Eric when he had heard the window break.

"I'm not sure. About ten, quarter past eight. Something like that."

"And you went out into the garden?"

"Yes. Like I said, I thought it was my greenhouse."

"I believe you have a security light that's activated by movement?"

"Yes."

"Did it come on when you went out, or was it already on?"

Eric didn't know how much Mr. Jones had actually seen; he might have told the sergeant that the light was already on. Though it went against the grain, he felt obliged to tell the truth. "It was on."

"So someone or something must have activated it before you went out to investigate the breaking glass?"

Eric shrugged. "I suppose so."

"How long does it stay on?"

"Three minutes, if it doesn't detect any further movement."

"And how close does the movement have to be? Would movement in the Bignalls' garden trigger it?"

"No. It did, but she complained, of course, so I had to change the setting."

"She?"

"Mrs. Bignall. Whatever I did, she complained. Anyway, now it comes on about a third of the way up the garden, I suppose. And from the side . . ." He thought about it. "I think it would come on if anyone got within a foot or so of the garage."

The young detective looked thoughtful. "So someone running diagonally from the Bignalls' house over the wall into your garden would trigger it when he crossed your driveway," he said, almost to himself. "But someone getting into the Bignalls' garden from yours probably wouldn't, because they'd probably stay near the back wall." He looked at Eric. "Does that seem reasonable?"

Eric agreed that in such a hypothetical situation, that would probably be the case.

"We have a witness who saw someone leave by your gate. You were in the garden at that moment, according to him, and your light was on. But you didn't see anything."

"No. I was checking out my greenhouse."

"Did you hear anything before that?"

"Like what?"

"Raised voices?"

Eric shrugged. "I doubt if I'd notice," he said. "That mad cow next door is always crying or yelling." He smiled. "You move to a neighborhood like this, you'd think you'd get a bit of peace, wouldn't you? Not with her next door, you don't."

"How long have you lived here?"

"Since February. These two next door are always shouting—and she has the nerve to complain about *me*," Eric added.

Sergeant Finch didn't seem too interested in his squabbles with his neighbors. "Did you hear anything later on?" he asked. "When you were checking out your greenhouse?"

"Like what?"

It was the sergeant's turn to shrug. "I don't know," he said. "Running feet, maybe?"

Eric's policy had always been to let the police find out things on their own and to give them no help whatsoever, even when he'd been in the job. Besides, the less you told them, the quicker they went away. "I didn't hear anything," he said. "I didn't see anything. I just checked the greenhouse and came back in."

"Then why did you shout to whoever it was to stop?"

If Geoffrey Jones had more to do with his time than spy on his neighbors, Eric reflected, he wouldn't be in this position. "Someone had broken a window or something," he said. "I just shouted."

"I'm told you shouted, 'Come back here, you little bugger,' " said Finch. "That isn't just shouting, Mr. Watson. That's shouting *at* someone."

"Buggers," said Eric. "Plural. It was kids breaking bottles against the wall, I thought. And nothing scares them off more than inviting them to come back and talk to you."

"And you didn't notice the Bignalls' French window standing open though the house was in darkness?"

"No."

"If you didn't see someone leaving your garden, didn't you wonder what had made your security light come on?"

"No."

Finch sighed. "For someone who was a cop and security conscious, you seem to have been very uninterested in what was going on."

"Wasn't my problem," said Eric. "My property was intact. I'm not in the job any more. And everyone round here's security conscious. Why do you think Bignall had his gates locked? There have been burglaries round here, Sergeant. Just like tonight."

"To be honest, I was wondering why he bothered to lock his gates, since it's so easy to get on to his property via yours. And you don't keep your gates locked."

"I do if I'm leaving the house empty. A bloke up the road had his house broken into a month ago and the thieves backed a bloody van up his driveway and filled it up with his belongings. We don't have to make it that easy for them."

"And yet," said Finch, "you hear a window breaking, come out to find your security light on, and don't notice an intruder in your own garden?"

"I'm sorry if I don't come up to scratch as a witness, Sergeant."

"And you don't notice that your neighbor's French window is wide open with the rain getting in?"

"I'm not the bloody neighborhood watch! As long as it isn't me, I don't give a bugger who's been turned over."

"So you did see something."

Eric shook his head and smiled. "All right, yes. I saw the French window open, and I just didn't give a shit. But I saw nothing else, and if you sit here until hell freezes over, you can't make me say I did. I've got better things to do with my time than sit around the bloody magistrates' court waiting to give evidence against some kid who'll get off with a smacked wrist anyway. My time's money."

"What do you do for a living these days?"

"I'm a photographer. I've got a studio in Welchester."

The sergeant looked interested. "What got you into that?"

"I was a police photographer, but they civilianized the job fourteen years ago. I didn't fancy being back in the front line, so I left and started up a business."

"You've done all right, then?"

"Can't complain."

"The thing is, this'll be going further than the magistrates' court." Finch was watching him closely as he spoke. "This is manslaughter, at the least."

"Manslaughter?" Eric repeated. "I thought it was just a break-in. Who's been killed?"

He could see the sergeant try to work out if it was genuine surprise or not, but it didn't really matter what he thought. With the police, all that mattered was what you said. And that only mattered if they'd cautioned you.

"I'm sorry," Finch said. "I thought someone would have told you. Mrs. Bignall was found dead."

"Bloody hell." He hadn't known there was anyone at home.

"Does her death change your mind about what you saw?"

Eric shook his head. "I didn't see anything," he said. "How can it change my mind?"

"Thanks very much," said Judy, who could have walked home by the time Marianne finally stopped flapping and left the theater.

During the day it was actually quicker to walk, especially since there was a shortcut through the park. Because not only couldn't cars use the shortcut, but the one-way system meant it was necessary to drive for a considerable distance in the opposite direction before finally making it into the center of Malworth where she lived.

"It's very good of you to give me a lift home," she said. "It's taking you out of your way."

"Oh, no trouble at all, darling!" Marianne started the car, and the windshield wipers cut two semicircles in the fine spray of rain on the glass. "We couldn't have you walking home through the park, not at this time of the night—I don't care if you are a police officer. A warrant card isn't a suit of armor, and there are some very funny characters about. And you couldn't really run, could you, darling? Not in your condition." She backed carefully out of the parking space, and that maneuver completed, the brief silence was over. But when she spoke, it was about neither of the things Judy expected to be exercising Marianne's mind.

It wasn't about Carl Bignall's sudden departure with Lloyd, despite the fact that Carl's car remained on the rooftop car park, something that must surely have been driving the ever-curious Marianne mad with a desire to know what was happening.

And it wasn't about the impossibility of mounting a production when Cinderella had the flu, her understudy had phoned to say the train had been delayed by at least fifty minutes and she wouldn't make it to rehearsal after all, and Buttons's under-understudy had to go rushing off on police business, unaccountably taking Buttons's actual understudy-cum-Ugly Sister with him. This had left Marianne with no Buttons, Judy's inadequate Cinderella, only one Ugly Sister, and no choice but to abandon that evening's rehearsal, but none of that seemed to be uppermost in Marianne's mind.

Indeed, for a moment after Marianne spoke, Judy had no idea what she *was* talking about.

"It's going to be very difficult," she said. "Both of you being in the police, having to drop everything at a moment's notice."

What was going to be difficult? Then it struck Judy that Marianne was still talking about her condition. She was beginning to realize the immense pulling power of babies, and consequently of mothers-to-be; other people seemed to be endlessly fascinated by the whole thing. She, of course, never had been, and still wasn't. Normally, she hated discussions of this sort. But at least she wasn't being pumped for information about Carl.

"It's not as difficult at the moment as it might be. I've been transferred to HQ—it's nine to five. And I'm working from home most of the time anyway."

"And will you still be doing that when the baby's born?"

"I'll be on maternity leave from next month. But even when that's up I can probably work mainly from home until next September," said Judy. "Then I'll be back in Stansfield."

"But still nine to five?"

"Basically," said Judy, not exactly truthfully, but she had no desire to discuss the pros and cons of working mothers, child care, nurseries, or anything else with Marianne.

The current canteen wisdom was that Lloyd would be offered early retirement and she would get his job, but there was a lot of time for them to change their plans between now and next September. And CID was nine to five, more or less. But circumstances had temporarily forced Stansfield CID to become a serious crime squad in all but name, expected to handle all serious crime committed in an area with a population of 300,000; as a result, its Detective Chief Inspector did get called out at odd hours. Come the reorganization, due to be revealed in March and in place by April, it was rumored there would be a small Serious Crime Squad based at Barton HQ, and if that happened, the Stansfield CID chief would have an easier time of it. The problem was, she would prefer to head up the serious crime squad.

"When *is* the baby due?" asked Marianne.

Judy was brought firmly back to reality. She was an expectant mother—if there was a police force on this planet that had ever entertained the idea of having their serious crime squad run by someone who had to breast-feed an infant, she didn't know of it. "Early February," she said.

"Aquarius! How wonderful! What are you?"

"Scorpio, I think."

"Ah! An unbeliever."

Judy smiled. "Lloyd's the one who believes in all that sort of thing," she said.

"Unusual," said Marianne. "Men usually pretend not to believe even if they do. You must let me do a reading when he or she is born."

"She," said Judy.

"Oh, did you ask what sex the baby was? Most people don't."

Judy gave a little shrug. "They asked me if I wanted to know, and I did," she said. The more she knew about what to expect, the better; that was why she'd gone to the relaxation classes. Why she had made Lloyd go with her. The ease with which he could assume the persona of someone to whom child-rearing was second nature had, as she had suspected it might, deserted him. Lloyd thought babies were women's work, whatever he said.

"Will you let me do a reading for her?"

Judy supposed she should, in view of her desire to know what to expect, and since she thought the whole thing was nonsense anyway, she might as well. She was just about to agree to Marianne's offer when Marianne spoke again.

"Is it true?" she asked.

"I'm sorry?"

"Someone said that Estelle had been found dead. I wasn't going to ask you about it, because I know you probably aren't supposed to discuss it with other people, but . . . is it true?"

Judy had thought Marianne was flapping even more than usual; she should have known that someone would have overheard snatches of the conversation between Lloyd and Carl, and passed the news on without delay. Marianne had been trying desperately to mind her own business; that explained her sudden interest in the baby.

And Judy wasn't sure what to do. But there seemed no doubt; if there had been any mistake, if it hadn't been Estelle Bignall, if it had been some sort of false alarm, Lloyd would have let her know by now. She watched rain bead the window, fragmenting the light from the street lamps, then get swept away by the hypnotic wipers, and decided it was going to be in the local paper tomorrow, so she might as well confirm it.

"I'm afraid it is," she said.

There was a silence as the car made its way over the river, passing the neo-Victorian lamp standards that lit the bridge. The wet tarmac gleamed, revealing unsuspected little dips and valleys in the apparently smooth surface.

"That's dreadful. Dreadful. Did you know her?"

"No. I never met her."

"I've known her since she was fifteen."

Judy hadn't realized. "Oh, I'm sorry," she said. "It must be a terrible shock for you."

Marianne signaled left, and the bypass bore them determinedly away from High Street, just half a mile away across the parkland that bordered the river. Shopkeepers had presented petitions; residents had made representations to the local council, which in turn had asked the county council, responsible for road planning, to reconsider the scheme. No dice.

"She was one of our leading lights," said Marianne. "She was very pretty, and good—but well . . . things changed, not very long after she married Carl."

Judy used her usual technique; she didn't speak after Marianne had spoken. Marianne would want to fill the silence, and what she filled it with would give her a clue to what Marianne wanted to tell her.

"It was six, seven years ago she married him, I suppose. Yes, it must be almost seven years. It seems like just the other day. She was an absolute picture on her wedding day. They both were, I suppose. He's so handsome. But she . . . well, she was radiant. So young, so in love."

Judy felt she was being prompted to inquire, so she did. "Was Carl equally in love?"

Marianne sighed dramatically. "Who knows? He's a darling, but he's very vain, you know. I think . . . I think Estelle looked the part, if you see what I mean. They made a very attractive couple, and he knew it. But he's ten years older than her, you know. And he was divorced. I'm not sure that was a good thing."

Judy smiled. "Lloyd's ten years older than me and divorced."

"Oh, that's quite different, darling. For one thing, Lloyd's an absolute peach—you only have to meet him to know that—and, well, you're not Estelle."

Judy stored that description away to tell Lloyd, and was torn between finding out why Carl wasn't an absolute peach and the other thing that puzzled her. She went with it first. "What was special about Estelle?" she asked.

"Well, she was eighteen when she married him. Eighteen and twenty-eight is different, you know, darling. I mean—you and Lloyd are both mature."

She had been twenty when she'd met Lloyd; not that much more mature than Estelle.

"Oh, but you would be, darling," said Marianne, when Judy pointed that out. "*Dexter's* more mature than Estelle."

"And Carl? Why isn't he as good a bet in the marriage stakes as Lloyd? Did he treat his first wife badly or something?"

"Oh, no—that just didn't work out."

"What, then?"

"Well, Carl—I mean he—" She brought her lips together. "No," she said. "No, I mustn't be bitchy about Carl, not when something as dreadful as this has happened. I just don't think he made her very happy."

"Do you mean he made her unhappy?"

"No!" Marianne took her eyes off the road to look accusingly at Judy. "Am I being interviewed?" she asked.

"Sorry," said Judy. "It goes with the job."

"I don't think he made her unhappy in any specific way," Marianne said, apparently unconcerned now about whether she was being interviewed. "I mean—I don't think there was another woman or anything. I don't think he *meant* to make her unhappy at all."

"But?" said Judy.

"But he did. Not immediately. But after they'd been married about six months, she became quite ill. Took to her bed at the least provocation, always thinking she had some imaginary illness or other. Got very nervy and depressed. Eventually, she seemed to get over that, but this year she's been very down again. She left the society—said she wasn't good enough, which was absolute nonsense."

Judy frowned. "And you think Carl was to blame for that?"

"Well, I certainly don't think he helped. I think once Estelle got to be a bother to him . . ." Again she shook her head. "No, I really mustn't say things like that."

Like what? Judy thought perhaps defending Carl might do the trick, since Marianne was desperate to be bitchy about him. "He did stay with her, though," she said. "Despite the way she was. Not all men would do that."

"Well, of course he did, darling. If he divorced Estelle, he divorced his second income."

"Second income?"

"Estelle has . . . had . . . a private income from a trust fund." There was a pause. "For her lifetime."

The line had been beautifully delivered. The mistake over the tense, underlining the fact that Estelle was now dead; the payoff timed to perfection. And Judy's line was obvious. "So what happens to it now?"

"The principal forms part of her estate."

And Judy learned of the accident that had robbed Estelle of all but her grandfather, of how he had made what Marianne called a "not inconsiderable" fortune from a chain of grocery stores in Welchester County, which he had in the end sold to one of the big supermarkets as local offshoots. Of how he had been unwilling to leave this money to Estelle, whom he didn't think was stable enough to handle it; he was afraid she would be conned out of it in no time, so he set up a trust fund for her from which she received a "not-to-be-sneezed-at" income. The principal would form part of her estate in order to benefit his presumed grandchildren, which, of course, had not materialized. Marianne had been the executor of his will.

"He died when Estelle was seventeen," Marianne said.

And Carl Bignall had married her when she was eighteen. Judy knew better than to jump to the conclusion that Marianne had set up for her, aware that Marianne could make a three act drama out of crossing the road. But it was interesting. And under all the theatrical delivery, Marianne was hurting, and angry.

"I was very surprised to hear she wasn't well tonight," Marianne said. "Her Monday nights are very important to her. I thought maybe she really did have the flu, or something, but—well, Carl seems to think it was just Estelle being Estelle."

The car made its way around the third side of the square it had been forced to follow, back to where it had come from, and this time was allowed to make the turn into High Street, where she was going to be dropped off. Judy had very little time left to find out what Marianne was trying to say now. "When did you see her last?" she asked.

"Just today. She came to see me this afternoon, and she was fine.

No sniffles. In fact, she's been much better for the last few weeks. Much happier in herself. She was still worrying about everything and anything, but she didn't seem so lonely, somehow." She smiled briefly as she drew up outside the greengrocer's store above which Judy had her flat and pulled on the hand brake. "I think that's why Carl failed to make her happy," she said. "He let her become very lonely."

She refused the offered cup of coffee, so the interview was terminated at 10:17, and Judy let herself in to the flat wondering about those imaginary illnesses. Doctors had been known to poison their wives; perhaps Estelle's illnesses weren't so imaginary. She had felt unwell again tonight, and now she was dead.

Or perhaps she was letting Marianne's melodramatic take on life affect her judgment, she told herself sternly. Off-the-wall theories were Lloyd's stock-in-trade, not hers.

Chapter Three

In a dark corner of the already dimly lit Starland, Ryan sat at a table with Baz and his customer, conducting a conversation at the top of his voice in the confident knowledge that no one else in the club could see or hear them.

"They're brand new. Look—some of them have still got the wrappers on. Ten CDs for thirty quid. Baz says your dad's got a market stall—you can sell them tomorrow for seven-fifty each."

Wayne, introduced to Ryan by Baz, looked through the CDs by the light of the ever-changing laser that played around the room. "I've never heard of any of them," he said. "I'll give you a fiver."

"It's jazz. People who are into jazz buy more CDs than anyone," Ryan said.

"What?" Wayne turned an ear to Ryan.

"I said you'll get rid of them in no time!"

"Ten quid," said Wayne.

"Twenty."

Ryan glanced at Baz as Wayne debated with himself whether they were worth it, and winked. Baz winked back, slowly.

"Fifteen," Wayne said.

"Okay, you're robbing me, but I'll settle for fifteen." Ryan had high hopes that a friend of Baz's could be parted from his money without too much trouble, and moved on to the next item. "Baz says your wife likes cats," he said.

"Likes what?"

"Cats!" Ryan's reply was bellowed into unexpected quietness as the DJ turned down the music in order to tell someone to move a car.

"Oh, cats. Yeah." Wayne nodded as the music blasted out again. "Got three of them," he said. "Dunno why. All they do is sleep and eat."

"Got her a Christmas present yet?" Ryan went into the shopping bag he had with him and pulled out the little ornament. "There," he said, putting it on the table. "Fifteen quid. What do you think?"

"It's green."

"It's jade, innit?"

"Cats aren't green. You don't get green cats."

Ryan sighed, shaking his head. "Ten quid, then," he said. "It's worth fifty of anyone's money."

"How would you know?"

"It's jade, I told you. It's semiprecious."

"It's green. If it was black or . . . or . . . white, that would be different. I'll give you five for it."

"Five?" repeated Ryan. "It cost me more than that."

"Or ginger," Wayne added. "One of hers is ginger. She wouldn't want a green cat. Five, tops."

"All right, five it is. How about this?" Ryan once again went into the shopping bag, put a black leather handbag on the table, and opened it, delving into the tissue paper to pull out the purse. "Matching purse and everything," he said. "Worth a hundred and fifty in the shops. What will you offer me?"

"I'll give you ten for it."

Ryan sucked in his breath. "I was looking for thirty."

"Ten. And that's final."

"All right," said Ryan, "You can have it *and* the CDs *and* the cat for half what the bag's worth on its own. Seventy-five for the lot."

Wayne shook his head. "I won't give you more than ten for the bag."

"That's all I'm asking."

Wayne frowned. "You said it was thirty."

"On its own, it's thirty. As part of the package, it's ten."

Wayne's frown grew deeper. "How come?"

"Okay," said Ryan. "I'll charge you separately for everything, *and* knock twenty off the bag, and you'll see I'm right. What did we just say for the package?"

"Seventy-five," said Wayne.

"Seventy-five. Knock twenty quid off the price of the bag, that's fifty-five, right?"

Wayne nodded.

"Add the fifteen we agreed for the CDs, comes to seventy, plus the fiver for the cat—comes to the same thing. Seventy-five."

Wayne checked Ryan's arithmetic, his lips moving. "Oh, yeah," he said.

"Is it a deal, then?"

"Yeah," said Wayne, reaching into his back pocket. Ryan pocketed the money just as he remembered that he had an urgent appointment.

Outside the pulsating club, Ryan and Baz stood on the wet pavement as Ryan counted three ten-pound notes into Baz's hand. Someone had to make sure he got his beer money.

"Thanks, Ry." Baz pushed the notes into his shirt pocket. "I'm going back in now that I've got some money. Did you see those two girls at the bar? I think one of them fancies me."

"Don't keep her waiting, then," said Ryan.

"Are you not coming back in? Her mate looks okay."

"No. I want to go home and have a word with Dex before he goes to bed. I'll see you, Baz."

Baz patted his pocket. "Thanks, Ry," he said again, and looked at him admiringly. "He didn't even want that cat, and you sold it to him. It's a pity we had to drop the price of everything so much, though."

Ryan grinned. "Yeah, Baz. Your mate drives a hard bargain."

"We always have my whole family here for Christmas—my sister and brother-in-law, and their kids, my mother and father, and my brother and his wife. We make a big thing of it. So there were a lot of presents—there was a rechargeable razor for my father, and an electronic organizer for my mother, loads of stuff for my nephews—computer games, and—" He shook his head. "I have to tell everybody what's happened," he said. "I can't take it in myself yet."

"Take your time, Dr. Bignall," Lloyd said automatically, as he tried to visualize what might have happened in here tonight. It didn't really add up.

"It's all right," said Bignall. "It just sort of hit me."

"I know," said Lloyd. "Can you remember what any of the other presents were?"

"Jazz CDs for my brother. They were remastered twenties recordings. And I got a handbag for Estelle."

"Can you describe it?"

"It was black leather. With a flap that folded over the zipped part. And it had a purse in it." He looked at Lloyd. "Is this all worth it?" he asked. "Do you really think they're going to turn up? I mean—who'd be stupid enough to try and sell anything after something like this?"

Most of them were stupid enough, thought Lloyd. But they probably had no idea what had happened to Estelle Bignall after they left her, so if these items had been stolen, someone would be trying to sell them. *If* they had been stolen. He wasn't happy about this. Not happy at all.

Bignall told him what he could remember of the presents, and then looked around the room, sorting out what was missing. "I think that's the lot," he said. "Oh—there was a little jade cat there." He pointed to a shelf on which books were scattered.

PC Sims added that to the list he had been making of the missing items as Bignall had noticed them, and handed it to Lloyd. Apart from the Christmas presents, there was a piggybank with loose change in it, a table lamp, a clock, and two candlesticks in modern wrought-iron. None of it was worth very much, as Bignall had pointed out, and everything was taken from the dining room. They were all small and portable; the other break-ins in the area had been more ambitious. Televisions, hi-fis, computers, even furniture.

"I believe you said that your wife had to cancel an engagement tonight?" Lloyd said.

"Her writer's group," said Bignall. "She joined it because—" He broke off. "Well, because she wanted to share my interest in writing. And she found she enjoyed it—she went every Monday."

"And who would know that the house was usually empty on Mondays?"

"Everyone who knows us, I suppose." He frowned. "You don't imagine it was someone we knew, do you?"

"No," said Lloyd. "But the more people who did know the house was empty, the more likely it is that the burglars got to hear about it."

Tom came in then, and indicated that he wanted to speak. Lloyd excused himself, asked Bignall to tell Constable Sims if he remembered anything else that should be there and wasn't, and went out into the hallway, where he got the gist of Tom's interview with Watson, and his opinion of the man.

"He's ex-job, guv. He was with the Welchester County force for eighteen years, but he seemed a bit iffy to me, so I checked him on the computer, and he's done time for actual bodily harm. Ten years ago, mind—and nothing since, but I'd swear he's lying. He says he saw nothing, and that he thought it was kids messing around because there were some here earlier on, but none of the other neighbors saw or heard them if there were. I think he's trying to put us off the scent."

Lloyd nodded. "I think there's more to this than we're being invited to believe," he said. There must be, he thought. His dictum that things were not always what they seemed usually had little effect on Tom, who was firmly of the entirely reasonable belief that mostly they were. He handed Tom the list of the missing items. "Get that circulated for the night shift. And show it to any of your informants who might prove useful. If any of these things turn up tonight, we need to know."

Tom went off again, and Lloyd knocked on the kitchen door, going in to find the body being zipped into a bag, and Freddie just packing up.

The body was taken out the back; Lloyd walked with Freddie to where his car was parked at the front. The rain was holding off, but everything was still gleaming in the streetlights. "Well?" he said.

"Well, she died from asphyxiation, and she died within the last two or three hours—say between six and nine P.M." Freddie beamed at him then. "But it's an interesting one," he said.

For once Lloyd didn't get the sinking feeling he usually got when Freddie spoke these words, because he had gotten that the moment he walked into the Bignalls' house. "You don't think she died as the result of being gagged," he said.

Freddie's face fell. "How did you know?"

Lloyd smiled. "Because if she had, then it wouldn't be interesting, would it? Simple logic, Freddie."

"You've spent too long with Judy Hill," grumbled Freddie. "Logic's her line, not yours—you're all flights of fancy and imagination. Why aren't you glowering at me Welshly like you usually do when I indicate that things could be less than straightforward?"

"Because I hoped you were going to find something interesting. Otherwise I think someone might get away with murder."

Freddie looked impressed, for once. Lloyd couldn't remember ever having impressed Freddie.

"You'll want to know my reasons for believing she didn't suffocate as a result of being gagged."

No, Lloyd couldn't say he did. He had to know, but that wasn't the same thing as wanting to know. He would happily live the rest of his life not knowing; he would be delighted simply to take Freddie's word for it. But he couldn't do that.

"I wondered a little when I saw the gag. I spoke to Constable Sims—asked him exactly what that handkerchief had felt like when he removed it from the victim's mouth. And he said it felt slightly damp. Now," Freddie said, looking as eager and enthusiastic as only Freddie could, "if someone stuffs something in your mouth and you are unable to breathe through your nose, you are automatically attempting to breathe through the obstruction. And that causes saliva to build up in the material, making it more and more dense—it thus becomes ever more difficult to get any air, and that's why you suffocate. And when the obstruction is removed, it is soggy. Not slightly damp."

"Right," said Lloyd, hoping that was as much detail as he'd be given.

"But of course, not having removed it myself, I'm not really in a position to draw any conclusions from that on its own. There are lots of ifs and ands. One man's slightly damp could be another man's wringing wet, she could have died very soon after being gagged, the handkerchief was lying on the floor for some time before I ever saw it, and so on. It's suggestive, no more. But . . ."

It was a full-blown lecture. Lloyd wished he could sit down.

". . . I can't see anything that would have prevented her breathing through her nose."

"Her husband said she had a cold in the head," Lloyd pointed out.

"Did he? I didn't see any evidence of that, but again, that isn't worth much on its own. Just a temporary problem with breathing through her nose could have done the trick."

All the same, thought Lloyd, it was interesting. If she didn't really have the sniffles, why did he say she had?

"She was facedown when Sims found her," Freddie went on. "That on its own could have given her a problem breathing, and panic plays a part the moment breathing becomes difficult. But I'm puzzled about *why* she was lying facedown—there seems to be no reason why she couldn't have rolled over onto her back in order to attempt to make breathing easier. Taken in conjunction with the slightly damp handkerchief, the accidental nature of her death begins to look a little suspect."

It was Lloyd's turn to be impressed. "All that before you've even opened her up," he said. "They'll be giving you a gold star."

"There's more," said Freddie. "The injuries to her wrists show that she struggled frantically to get free. But there are no bruises to her lower legs, which you would expect if he had to hold her down in order to tape up her ankles. And the gag—if he was stuffing something in her mouth, you would expect her to resist, move her head, try to bite him—he should have had to hold her still, exerted a lot of pressure while he got her mouth open, but there are only two small bruises on either side of her jaw, and none to her mouth or face. These inconsistencies all begin to add up."

"To what, exactly?"

"Exactly? Sorry—I can't give you a definite answer, certainly not tonight. I don't believe she died trying to breathe through that handkerchief. I doubt if she was conscious, or possibly even alive, when she was gagged or when her feet were bound. But unless she died some other way altogether, it's unlikely that I can prove that, and I could be wrong. It's a pity the gag was removed, or I would be on stronger ground."

"Are you saying you think she was murdered?" asked Lloyd. It was rare indeed for Freddie to go out on a limb.

"I'm saying it's possible she was asphyxiated in some other way. It might be an idea to collect any pillows, cushions—that sort of thing—for forensic examination."

"I'll arrange for that," said Lloyd, and then he thought about that. What if this intruder hadn't disturbed Estelle Bignall? What if he got into her bedroom with the intention of carrying out a sexual assault? Lloyd hadn't understood why Estelle Bignall had to be bound and gagged just because she'd interrupted the intruder. Perhaps the burglary was incidental and the real motive had been sexual. He asked Freddie about that.

"I've taken swabs, of course, but there's no reason to suspect sexual assault."

And there was the violent altercation that Jones heard; Lloyd wondered even more about that now. "Does it look as though she was physically assaulted at all? Slapped, punched, whatever?"

Freddie looked doubtful. "She struggled to get her hands free," he said. "He might have hit her to make her more cooperative, I suppose, but there's nothing obvious apart from the two bruises on the jaw, and they were more likely to be caused by someone holding onto her than by hitting her. No facial bruising, as I said. No body blows."

"Might she have bruised him—scratched him?"

"If someone heard a scuffle, she might have kicked him, but her feet were bare, so I doubt that she made much impression on him. She's small and slight—I doubt that she gave her assailant much trouble, even if she tried. We might get something from under her fingernails, but I doubt it. I think he tied her up before she had a chance to do any damage."

Lloyd sighed. Doubt was a word he could do without in an investigation, and pathologists used it all the time. Freddie had just used it three times in one utterance. "Anything else?" he asked.

"Mm. She was gagged with a matching tie and handkerchief. Very chic."

Lloyd groaned. "I'd like to think that you crack jokes in order to make your job bearable," he said. "But I think you crack jokes because you're enjoying yourself."

Freddie beamed. "I am enjoying myself," he said. "I've never made any bones about it. Or cartilage, or muscle . . ."

"Yes, yes," said Lloyd. "I've got it, thank you."

"But I wasn't simply cracking a joke about the tie and hankie. I was drawing your attention to something I thought you might find interesting."

"It's late, Freddie."

"Well, I don't suppose her assailant was wearing a matching tie and handkerchief, do you? In fact, if I think of all the men I know, I don't believe any of them wears a matching tie and handkerchief. We've all got them, of course, because at this time of the year we're knee-deep in them—"

"You're saying it was a present," Lloyd said, his eyes widening. "A present to Carl Bignall. And it would be under the tree in the dining room. So if the assailant removed it from the box, and left the box where it was, the SOCOs will have taken it, and his prints might still be on it." But wherever this struggle had taken place, it hadn't been in the neat, undisturbed kitchen. He frowned. "Why was she in the kitchen?" he asked rhetorically. Then a question to which he did want an answer. "Did she die in there?"

"She could have," said Freddie. "But she needn't have."

"Thank you, Freddie," Lloyd said.

"I'm sorry, Lloyd, but it's only in fiction that the pathologist can tell you that she was really killed in the orchard and her body was moved to the gazebo. If someone's been dead a long time before they were moved, the stasis bruising can sometimes indicate movement of the body, but in this case . . ." He shrugged. "If she wasn't killed in the kitchen, she was moved shortly after she died—and since she was *found* shortly after she died, that's not telling you very much. I might have something to tell you when I've opened her up—if she was strangled rather than smothered, for instance."

Lloyd frowned. "Wouldn't that have left marks on her neck?"

"Not necessarily. If he used his forearm, or something soft and wide. It could just possibly account for those little bruises on her jaw. It's a long shot. I'll see you tomorrow," he said. "But for the moment . . ." He smiled. "I'm going home."

Freddie's usually open-top sports car had its winter bonnet on; he had to open the door rather than jump over it, and Lloyd was entertained by the sight of Freddie folding himself into it. He roared off down the road, no doubt waking those residents who had finally managed to get to sleep, and Lloyd went back in to the house, asked someone to gather up anything in the way of pillows or cushions, then went into the sitting room.

He let Sims go back to his normal duties, apologized to Carl Bignall for the interruption, and tested Freddie's theory. "Can I ask, Dr. Bignall, did someone give you a matching tie and hankie set?"

"Yes," said Bignall, looking puzzled. "An aunt of mine sends me the same thing every year."

"And it was under the tree, unwrapped?"

"Yes. Why are you asking?"

Lloyd decided there was little point in sparing his feelings, which had already taken a bashing and would hardly notice another blow. "It looks as though that's what was used to gag your wife."

Bignall shook his head. "I don't think I can react anymore," he said.

"Dr. Bignall, are you sure you wouldn't prefer to go to friends or something? The scene-of-crime people are going to be here for some time."

Bignall looked as though he was about to insist on staying where he was, but instead he gave a little nod. "You're right," he said. "I can't stay here. Denis offered to take me in."

"I can give you a lift there, if you'd like."

"Thank you. I'll just call and let Meg know I'm coming."

Denis finished the tea that had been pressed on him and stood up. "He'll be fine, Mrs. Gibson," he said. "I'm sure he'll feel a lot better after a good night's sleep."

According to Dexter, he had fallen down a flight of steps, and his mother had apparently believed that. He hadn't fallen down steps, of course; Denis told Mrs. Gibson that in his opinion Dexter had been in a fight, or something. He had tried to discover the truth, but without success. It was more likely that Dexter had been beaten up, he thought, since it didn't seem he'd done much in the way of retaliation. He had spoken to Dexter and touched on the possibility of a racial attack, but the boy could not be moved. Dexter said he'd fallen down some steps.

Mrs. Gibson got up and saw him to the front door. "Is Dr. Bignall all right?" she asked. "When I called he sounded a bit odd."

Denis was about to fob her off with a noncommittal answer, but the woman worked for Carl and Estelle; he had to tell her what had happened.

She listened in shocked silence. "That's terrible," she said. "Just terrible. There was no need for that—what could she have done to them? She wasn't the size of tuppence."

Denis almost smiled at that description, coming as it did from someone who was hardly what he would describe as robust. "I don't think they meant it to happen," he said. "I think they were just trying to keep her from phoning the police, or running out to get help."

"I can't believe it," she said. "I can't."

No. Neither could he, until now. Now that he found himself actually telling someone.

Mrs. Gibson shook her head. "Please," she said, "if you're speaking to Dr. Bignall, please tell him—" She broke off. "I don't know," she said. "Just tell him I'm so sorry."

⁂

"Did you and your wife have a row tonight, Dr. Bignall?"

Carl felt as though he'd been slapped. The man was supposed to be giving him a lift, not questioning him. He'd been about to tell him there had been a bit of a scene, but what was he? Some sort of mind reader?

"Well . . . no. Not exactly. How do you know that?"

"The neighbors overheard."

That was impossible. They couldn't have overheard. But why would Lloyd lie about a thing like that? "They couldn't have," he said.

"Why's that?"

Carl felt bewildered. First the glove, now this. "It—It wasn't a row. Not really. More a discussion. And it wasn't like that—we didn't raise our voices."

"Oh? So what sort of discussion was it?"

He sounded much more Welsh than he had before. And Carl knew he didn't believe him. Again. He thought they'd had some sort of shouting match that the neighbors had heard. What on earth made him think that?

"It was—oh, I don't know what you'd call it. It wasn't a row. I really don't think the neighbors could possibly have heard us."

"And when did it take place, whatever it was?"

"Just before I left the house."

"Which was when?"

"Half past seven."

There was a silence.

Carl sighed. "And you're wondering how come I didn't get to the rehearsal until twenty-five to nine," he said. "Since the Riverside Center is twenty minutes away from my house."

"I would like to know where you were," said Lloyd.

"Driving around. I couldn't face going to the theater and dealing with Marianne's melodramatics about half the cast being absent—I just drove round to sort myself out a bit. And then I realized I was letting Marianne down, and I went to the theater."

"So this row was bad enough for you to feel obliged to cool off?"

"It wasn't a row," Carl repeated. "And I didn't have to cool off, as you put it. Estelle was—well, she was a very difficult woman to live with. She had mood swings and depressions, she was a hypochondriac, she—" He broke off. "Well—she was difficult. And tonight something happened that—that gave me a great deal to think about. That's all."

"What happened?"

"I'm sorry," said Carl. "I really don't think it's any of your business. It wasn't a row, and if the neighbors overheard people having a row, I can assure you it wasn't me and Estelle."

"No," said Lloyd. "Obviously not. The sounds they heard were of a few minutes after eight. So it couldn't have been you, could it? Not if you left at half past seven."

"I did leave at half past seven!" Carl said, his voice rising with indignation. Lloyd had been like this all evening; he was tired of not being believed.

"Please, Dr. Bignall, don't let these questions distress you. They must be asked, that's all. It's my job—I have to investigate what happened to your wife."

"Isn't it obvious what happened?"

"It's just the altercation that's bothering me, Dr. Bignall. The one the neighbors did hear."

"And you think it was Estelle and me, don't you?"

Lloyd shook his head. "It's a little puzzle, Dr. Bignall. And I like to get them cleared up as soon as I can."

Which meant he did think that it had been him and Estelle. Carl's head was spinning. This wasn't happening to him. He hadn't the faintest idea what had gone on at his house tonight, or who had been having this row the neighbors had heard. But every time he told the man the God's honest truth, he didn't believe him. He was very glad when they pulled up outside Denis Leeward's house and Lloyd wished him good-night.

❦

Eric had watched the last car make its way down the street, had waited until he was absolutely sure that no new cops were going to turn up, and now he went out to the landing, released the catch on the ceiling molding, and let down the ladder, climbing up a few steps to look in at the three men who were playing cards.

"Right," he said. "They've gone. You can leave now."

"Hang on," said one of the men. "I'm going to win this hand."

"I said you can leave. Now."

The other two were keener to leave; they picked up jackets and money while the other still complained. Eric stood at the bottom of the ladder as they emerged, then led them downstairs, through the house to the kitchen. "Keep the noise down," he said as he opened the door and they trooped into the garage in which their car sat next to his own. A moment later their car left his premises; he closed and locked the garage doors and went back into the kitchen. Bloody woman. What with one thing and another, he hadn't done half what he had meant to do tonight.

And he was going to have to move everything from up there and get it somewhere safe, just in case.

❦

"Hi," said Judy as Lloyd bent down and kissed her head. "How's it going?"

Lloyd had sort of moved in. Judy knew what he was doing; if they didn't find a house they could both agree on, he would by then have established that they lived in her flat, which was actually big enough for a couple with a baby. And, when she thought about it, it might not be a bad idea. Lloyd was still going on about gardens and things, but he'd never look after a garden, and she certainly wouldn't. There was the park just a quarter of a mile away, and she hadn't had a garden when she was growing up; she lived in a flat supplied by the university where her father lectured. She didn't think it had ever done her any harm. But she supposed that other people were the best judges of that.

"How we're getting on rather depends on how you look at it," said Lloyd, sitting down beside her on the sofa. "There's evidence to suggest that two people broke into an apparently empty house, and the lookout ran away while the other helped himself to the presents under the tree and a couple of other items. Mrs. Bignall heard the window break and came down to investigate, was overpowered, bound and gagged, and forced into the kitchen."

"Why the kitchen?"

"That's a little puzzle."

"And why was she bound and gagged at all?"

"That's another. And they're your department."

"Not my job anymore," she said, but she applied herself to that one anyway. There seemed little point in tying someone up and gagging them if you were only going to take a handful of Christmas presents. "Could the motive have been sexual?" she asked.

"That's what I thought, but Freddie says there are no signs of it. He's not happy that she died as a result of being gagged, though." Lloyd sat back. "How well do you know Carl Bignall?" he asked.

So, he had come to the same conclusion as Marianne, without knowing the background. "Why do you ask?" she said.

"Well, there's another little puzzle." He told her about the disturbance that had been heard at ten past eight. "Carl Bignall says he and his wife had words of some sort, but that he left the house at half past seven. It takes twenty minutes to get from his house to the Riverside Center, and you know when he got to the rehearsal."

"So there are forty-five minutes unaccounted for? Where was he?"

"He says he was driving around to sort himself out, whatever that means. How many times have we heard the driving round alibi in our careers? And how often has it been true?"

Judy told him then what Marianne had said. "She gave me the name of Estelle's lawyer, so you could check that what she told me is right," she said.

"Interesting," said Lloyd. "What's your impression of him?"

"He's on the committee, so I see him once a month," said Judy. "And lately when I've been helping out I've seen him every week. He's always exactly like he was last night. Bright and breezy and jokey. But I don't know him any better now than I did when I first met him."

"So you can't offer an opinion on the likelihood of his doing away with his wife?"

"Not really. But you might want to ask Freddie to test for drugs in her system."

Lloyd frowned. "Do you think she was a drug user?"

That hadn't occurred to her. "Maybe," she said. "But that wasn't what I meant, really. It's just that Marianne said Estelle changed after she got married, and was subject to unexplained illnesses. Marianne thinks they were imaginary, but . . ."

"Perhaps they weren't," he finished, yawned, and sat back, his eyes closed.

"And Marianne saw Estelle today," Judy said. "She says she was perfectly all right—no sniffles."

"Freddie was surprised she was supposed to have a cold," said Lloyd.

"So perhaps he was preparing the way for her having suffocated," said Judy.

"Perhaps," said Lloyd. "Or perhaps it was just someone who broke in. Freddie wasn't exactly definite about her having died some other way, and someone was seen running away, after all."

"Who saw him?"

"He was seen by one Mr. Jones, whom Tom has down as a racist, and apparently not seen by one Mr. Watson, whom Tom has down as a liar."

"Why does Tom think Mr. Jones is a racist?"

"Because the boy he saw running away was black, and every time Tom asked him to describe him, that was all he said. It irritated him." He grinned. "But then everything's irritating him since he got his hair cut."

"It's awful, isn't it?" said Judy. "He looks like Hitler Youth or something. At least he's not behaving like it, obviously." Then she felt a little shiver as she realized what Lloyd had actually said about the lookout. "How old was this boy?" she asked.

"Early teens, maybe younger."

She hoped she was wrong, but she couldn't not tell him. "Dexter's black," she said.

Lloyd's eyes opened. "If Jones is a racist, I don't know what category Tom would have you in," he said. "I take it you're not putting him forward because he's in possession of a black skin?"

She made a face. "His mother called to ask if he was at the rehearsal," she said. "After you and Carl left. So he wasn't at home with the flu, was he? And his mother obviously didn't know where he was."

"Even so," said Lloyd. "Aren't you jumping to conclusions just a tiny bit?"

"Not really," sighed Judy. "He would have expected the Bignalls' house to be empty, and Dexter Gibson's half brother is Ryan Chester."

Now Lloyd sat up. Literally. "Ryan Chester? Would that be burglar, car thief, too-clever-by-half, slippery-as-an-eel, more-trouble-than-a-barrel-load-of-monkeys Ryan Chester?"

"It might just be a coincidence," she warned.

"Has Dexter got a record?"

"No. He's never been in trouble."

"Well," said Lloyd, "it looks like he is now. Because the Bignalls' cleaning lady is a Mrs. Gibson. I didn't make the connection—I'd forgotten that was Ryan's mother's name."

Judy had hoped that she was wrong. Dexter was a nice boy, and so—in his way—was Ryan. She couldn't really see him doing something like this, certainly not for what had actually been taken. Of course, he might not think that tying someone up would do them any harm, and maybe he had intended taking a great deal more and panicked when he realized she was dead. And there was no maybe about his record; he was a burglar and a car thief, and all the other things Lloyd had said. Dexter thought the world of him, so he might have become apprenticed in the trade.

"It all begins to fall into place, doesn't it?" said Lloyd. "Dexter lets slip that the Bignalls' house is empty every Monday night, and it's too much temptation for Ryan. He persuades Dexter to go with him and act as lookout, maybe to make certain he doesn't blow the whistle on him, because it's reasonable to suppose that the lookout's heart wasn't in it, since he seems to have taken off the minute they gained entry."

Judy could see Lloyd moving into full-theory mode.

"Meanwhile, inside the house Mrs. Bignall comes down when she hears the breaking glass. Ryan trusses her up in the kitchen and carries on. What he doesn't know is that Mrs. Bignall has a cold and can't breathe."

"It seems a very strange thing for Ryan to have—" Judy began, but Lloyd wasn't listening.

"And Dexter's voice hasn't broken!" he said triumphantly. "So if he did get cold feet, and Ryan got angry—they would have an argument. In Bignall's garden. Before Ryan broke in. And Jones could easily think it was a man and a woman."

"Question," said Judy. "Why would Ryan call his brother a fucking bitch?"

"Ah," said Lloyd. "All right—the argument is still a puzzle. But the rest of it's okay, isn't it?"

"I can't see why the intruders wanted to tie Mrs. Bignall up if they were only going to take a few items," she said. "And, for what it's worth, I can't see Ryan tying someone up at all. Gagging them. If he was ever surprised by a homeowner, he might knock them over so he could get away from them, but that was all."

Lloyd smiled. "I'll forgive your truly appalling grammar," he said, "for solving this case so exceptionally speedily. I think we can forget Carl Bignall. Sometimes things really are just the way they seem."

"It's still all pure theory," she argued. "We don't even know that it's the same Mrs. Gibson. And even if it is, you can hardly go steaming in on the basis that a black boy whose description you don't even have was seen running away, and Dex didn't turn up for rehearsal."

"We'll need a touch more evidence than that," Lloyd agreed. "But I think it'll be forthcoming. Because unless Ryan Chester has changed his M.O. radically since I last had anything to do with him, he'll have tried to sell some of that stuff tonight. And I've got Tom on that."

Jimmy's nicotine-stained fingernail rasped over a three-day growth as he perused the list. "Aw, come on, Mr. Finch!" he said, looking up. "CD ROMs? Personal organizers? This sort of stuff's being offert roon' every night! Ye cannae tell where it came frae just by lookin' at it."

Tom smiled. "You find *out* where it came from, and if it's from a burglary that took place tonight, you tell me."

"Why me?"

"Because you're a stool pigeon, Jimmy. A grass. That is your job."

"Jimmy" was the inevitable name his informant had been given when he had arrived in Malworth. Despite living just ten miles from cosmopolitan Stansfield, which had become a home away from home for many nationalities and the Scots in particular, the citizens of Malworth still found the Scottish accent exotic and impenetrable, and the Scots themselves alarming. Calling them all Jimmy was their way of coping with that.

"No' sae loud, Mr. Finch!" Jimmy used his hands to reinforce his request, like a conductor during a quiet passage. "Ah'd no' be much use tae ye wi' ma heid bashed in."

Tom smiled again. "Jimmy, we're sitting on a damp bench on a bridge over a river in a very well-bred part of Malworth in the wee small hours. There isn't another person up and about for miles."

In the pool of light created by the fake Victorian gaslight, Jimmy looked around as though expecting mafiosi to loom out of the murky middle-class night at him, violin cases at the ready. "A' the same," he said, "ye cannae be too careful in ma position." He waved a dismissive hand at the list. "And that stuff's no' worth runnin' a risk fur. Ah'll tell ye that fur naethin'."

"It's worth more than you think. There's good money in it for you."

Jimmy pulled cigarettes and a throwaway lighter from his pocket and reconsidered. "How much?" he asked.

"That depends on what you give me. If you get offered any of this stuff—or see it being offered—I want to know. And I don't want some half-baked story. I want to know who's selling it and where I can get hold of him. Quickly. Got it?"

Jimmy looked at the list again, frowning, absently putting a cigarette in his mouth. "Whit's sae special aboot this lot?"

Tom wasn't about to tell him. Jimmy was no hero—if he thought he might be dealing with someone who had killed, however inadvertently, he would be off like a shot. "Mind your own business," Tom said. "Just do the rounds of the pubs and clubs and report back to me. Ring me. Whenever. I don't care if it's five o'clock in the morning."

"Why are you gettin' yersel' in a state aboot computer games and videos?" Jimmy spoke with the unlit cigarette between his lips. "Is it wan o' your pal's hooses that's been turned over?" He grinned. "Is it yer ain hoose?"

"Which part of 'mind your own business' are you having trouble with?"

"Is it like in the films?" said Jimmy, ignoring him. "This wee cat—is it stuffed fu' o' H or coke or somethin'?"

"Very funny, Jimmy. Just try and find it. It's hardly the sort of thing that's being offered round every night, is it?"

"Aye, aw right, Mr. Finch. Leave it wi' me." Jimmy removed the cigarette and grinned, showing crooked teeth. "Ah'll get back to you, as they say."

Tom got up and walked toward his car, opening the driver's door and looking back as Jimmy's face was lit up by the lighter flame.

"Oh, here, hang on a minute," Jimmy said, expelling smoke with the words. "Jade's green, is it no'?"

"It is."

"Big Baz was gaun on aboot a green cat. Ah thought it was wan o' thae cuddly toys, but maybe it wisnae."

"Baz Martin?" Tom closed the car door and went back to where Jimmy sat.

"Aye. A pal o' his sold it tae somebody in the Starland. Big Baz couldnae get over it, because the guy didnae want a green cat, but he bought it anyway. Said his pal could sell condoms to nuns. Said it aboot five times—he thought it got funnier the mair he said it. Ah telt him it wisnae funny in the first place, but that didnae stoap him." He took a drag and looked up at Tom. "But, aye, it was a green cat he was on aboot, right enough."

Ryan Chester was the pal, presumably. It had to be—Baz didn't work with anyone else but his smarter cousin Ryan. No one else would have him. "So where can I find Baz now?" Tom asked.

"He'll still be in there. He was tryin' to get aff wi' some bird." Jimmy looked expectantly at Tom. "So, Mr. Finch. Whit's that worth tae ye?"

"I don't know yet, do I?"

"Aw, Mr. Finch!"

"Don't worry, Jimmy," said Tom as he went back to the car. "If your information's sound, I'll pay out. Even though the risk to your health is what you might call minimal." Ryan and Baz were not about to leave Jimmy battered on the pavement.

"Ye'd better." Jimmy got up. "Oh—and Mr. Finch?"

"Yeah?"

Jimmy held up a greasy lock of his own hair and shook his head. "The barnet does naethin' fur ye."

Ten minutes later Tom pulled up in the empty taxi stand outside the Starland nightclub and winced as he walked into the smoky, laser-lit depths and the music assaulted his ears. He must be getting old; he used to like this sort of thing. Now he found himself automatically checking for iffy substances being peddled, and tutting under his breath at the way the girls dressed, at the overt sexual overtures being made by both sexes to both sexes, not necessarily in the conventional configuration.

And he couldn't help worrying about his own children, not that much younger than some of these girls, whatever the club policy was supposed to be, and how soon they would be exposed to this. Sex, drugs, and—well, whatever that music was. Not rock and roll, that was for sure. And not glam rock or punk or anything he could put a name to. This stuff would have some silly name that made it sound more like an estate agent's brochure than music. Garage, house—something like that. He didn't understand pop music anymore, and he had always sworn he would never get like that.

After a moment or two his eyes became accustomed to the half-light, and he made his way through the dancers to where he could see big Baz Martin trying and failing to perform the same actions to the music that everyone else was. Tom smiled as the overamplified sound resolved itself into a recycled pop song from his teenage years, and he watched them all doing the hokey-cokey, in effect. Now that he came to think of it, it was more like summer camp than Sodom and Gomorrah. But maybe that just made it more sinister.

Baz gave up and draped himself around the young woman he was dancing with instead, his tongue halfway down her throat by the time Tom reached them. At least she looked old enough to be out on her own.

"Sorry to break this up," Tom said.

Baz surfaced and looked at him, his eyebrows drawn together. "Who the hell are you?" he said, then his face cleared. "Sergeant Finch? What's happened to your hair?"

"A word, Baz," said Tom, steering him off the dance floor. "Excuse us," he threw over his shoulder at Baz's date, who looked less than impressed. Tom led the protesting Baz outside.

"I've got nothing on me, honest!"

"I should hope not," said Tom. "You're in court on Wednesday, aren't you?"

"Yes."

"Relax, Baz. I'm not looking for controlled substances. But I do want to know all about a jade cat."

"A what?" Baz craned his neck to see inside.

"A green cat. Your mate sold it tonight."

"It wasn't nicked," said Baz, his eyes still searching what he could see of the dance floor through the half-open door and the enormous bouncer. "Honest. He bought it. He said."

"Yeah? So who is this mate of yours?"

"I don't know his name."

Tom smiled. "A real close mate, is he? He wouldn't be your cousin Ryan, by any chance?"

"Ry? No." Baz shook his head, and turned away to see what was going on in the club. "I've not seen Ry for weeks. It was just a mate."

He looked back at Tom, his eyes imploring. "Look, Sergeant Finch," he said, pointing over his shoulder. "I'm on a promise. Can I go back in now?"

"No, I don't think so, Baz. I think you're going to have to come to the station with me and help me with my inquiries."

Baz's mouth fell open. "But Sergeant Finch—" he said, motioning toward the dance floor.

"Or you can tell me who your mate is. It's up to you."

"I dunno his name." Baz shook his head, and Baz was very stubborn. "Honest, I don't." He glanced into the club once more, and turned back, his eyebrows meeting with anxiety. "Sergeant Finch," he said, practically squirming with desperation, "I've got to get back inside."

Tom could have taken him in and spent the next two hours failing to worm Ryan Chester's name out of him in any form that could be called a statement, but he felt a carrot would be more likely to produce results than a stick. "Well, if you won't tell me who your mate was, you can tell me who he sold it to. Is the purchaser still in the club?"

Baz looked a little mutinous, which meant that he was. Now Tom knew he had some real bargaining power. "Let's go back in, then," he said. "Introduce me to him."

Baz's face, which had lit up with Tom's first statement, fell with his second. "You're joking, aren't you?"

"No. Either you tell me who bought it, or you don't go back in at all."

Baz was seeing his hoped-for night of passion slip away. "But I can't do that," he said. "I'm not a grass."

"I thought you said it wasn't nicked?" Tom said. "That's not grassing, Baz. Just point him out to me, and you can get back to what you were doing. Or you can spend the night with me. It's your choice, but you might be banged up come Wednesday, so it could be your last chance for a while. I know which I'd go for, if I were you."

Baz struggled with his conscience, and his libido won. "Okay," he said, diving back into the club so fast that Tom was left standing. He caught up as Baz nodded through the gloom to an older man who sat at a table with a group of people. "He's the one with the tie on," he said. "His name's Wayne. Don't tell him I told you."

Wayne, once the situation had been explained to him, and the word death had been introduced, proved more than willing to come to the police station voluntarily to help Tom with his inquiries.

Half an hour later Tom saw him off the premises and looked at his bowdlerized and sanitized statement. Wayne had, of course, bought the items in good faith, and was only too happy to hand them over. He wouldn't normally buy things in a drinking establishment, but he had assumed they would be the vendor's to sell, Baz being someone whose judgment he trusted, and it being Baz's cousin Ryan who was selling them. Tom smiled. Wayne must be the only man in Malworth who trusted Baz Martin's judgment, but given that Baz and Wayne's combined IQ fell short of double figures, it might even be true.

So Jimmy had earned his money, and now Tom had to plan a surprise visit for Ryan Chester.

Chapter Four

A dawn raid. Long before dawn, actually; it was only just getting light now. Ryan had never been the subject of one before, despite his calling; he had been woken in what seemed like the middle of the night by Detective Sergeant Finch telling him to get out of bed, demanding that he open his locked closet. At first he hadn't recognized Finch; the last time he'd had dealings with the detective, his hair had looked a bit like Dex's, only blond. Now he'd had it cut so short it didn't curl.

"It doesn't suit you," he had said.

"Your opinion doesn't interest me very much," Finch replied. "Get up."

He and his colleagues had searched his room, and when they found the candlesticks he was going to give to his mum, they arrested him on suspicion of burglary and manslaughter, which left Ryan open-mouthed with disbelief. He had hoped for quite some time that he was dreaming, but he was beginning to accept that it was reality. The really surreal bit was that they'd arrested Dex too, as soon as they saw him, which Ryan didn't understand at all.

Dex had been in bed when he'd gotten home, his mother having called the doctor just in case it was worse than Ryan had thought. The doctor had sent him to bed, so Ryan had to wait to talk to Dex. And he hadn't exactly been given the chance this morning, so he was none the wiser about who had beaten Dex up, or why, and now Dex had been arrested, just as his mother had predicted.

His mother had been in tears, and blaming him, of course. Saying she knew he'd been up to no good, knew he'd been getting Dex into trouble, and that had not helped his case with Finch. Then, when she realized they were saying he had killed someone, she went right off the deep end. Her son would never do a thing like that—the whole bit. Finch just raised his eyes to heaven and ignored her.

Ryan had been asked if the shoes he was wearing were the ones he'd worn last night, and he said yes.

"No, they're not," his mum said. "You wore those other ones early on."

"Mum!"

She had come up to him then. "Did you kill someone last night?" she asked.

"Of course not!"

"Did you burgle a house?"

"No."

"Then let them look at your shoes. Let them look at anything they want. Let them prove you didn't have anything to do with it."

Now, sitting in the cell, Ryan tried to get his head around it all. "What about Dex?" he asked Stan Braithwaite, the solicitor who had been doing his best to represent him since he was fourteen years old.

Stan shrugged. "Your mum said she wanted Dex to tell the police everything they wanted to know, and that he wouldn't need me there to do that."

Ryan closed his eyes. "Well, let's hope he wasn't burgling this house. Because I wasn't."

"Are you being straight with me, Ryan? You really aren't involved in this burglary?"

Ryan nodded. "But Dex was up to something, Stan. Have you seen the state he's in? Someone gave him a right going-over last night."

"Are you honestly saying you can't tell me anything at all about what went on there last night? The police are playing their cards very close to their chest—they haven't told me what they've got on you."

"I know nothing about any burglary," Ryan said. "And I've no idea what Dex was up to."

"In that case, you say no comment to every question they ask, or you'll make my job very difficult when your mum decides that Dex does need a solicitor after all."

"Okay."

It was Lloyd and Finch who were doing the interview. Ryan knew Lloyd; he hadn't had much to do with him lately, but they had sat opposite one another when he was a kid and Lloyd was a DI, and Ryan wasn't too keen on being questioned by him. Finch was okay—he was straightforward, but Lloyd was up to every psychological trick in the book. It was Finch who led the questioning, and that didn't surprise Ryan. Lloyd nearly always let his co-interviewer do that.

"All right," said Finch. "Where were you at eight-fifteen yesterday evening, Ryan?"

"No comment."

"And where was Dexter?"

"My client doesn't have to answer that," said Stan. "To quote the Good Book—he is not his brother's keeper."

"As I recall, it was a murderer who said that," Lloyd murmured.

Thanks, Stan. Ryan glared at him.

Sergeant Finch produced, much as Ryan had himself, the jade cat, the handbag, and the CDs. "I am showing Mr. Chester evidence bags marked TF1, TF2 and TF3," he said. "Do you recognize these items, Ryan?"

"No comment."

"I have a statement saying that you sold these items for seventy-five pounds in the Starland club last night." Finch looked impressed. "You're a good salesman, Ryan. I'd have reckoned thirty or forty pounds at the most. But then your customer isn't the brightest thing on two legs, is he? Not just as dim as Baz, of course. But close."

"No comment." Trust Baz to have mates who grassed you up. He really must stop using Baz. For anything.

"These items were removed from number 4 Windermere Terrace during the course of a burglary which took place last night."

Ryan could practically hear Stan's blood pressure rising. Finch sat back a little. "Number 4 Windermere Terrace is the home of a Dr. and Mrs. Bignall," he said. "Mrs. Bignall died as a result of treatment she received at the hands of the intruders."

Ryan stared at him, his mouth open. He hadn't recognized the address. And did he just say that Mrs. Bignall was dead? "What—What happened to her?" he asked.

"She was left bound and gagged. She couldn't breathe, and so she died."

"Your mother cleans for the Bignalls, doesn't she?" asked Lloyd.

Ryan looked helplessly at Stan, who was tight-lipped and angry, then looked back at Lloyd, nodding.

"So how did these items come to be in your possession?"

Ryan's mind was racing. "No comment," he said.

Lloyd shook his head, smiling a little. "Ryan, you and I have met before. I know you. You're a bright lad." He tipped the seat back slightly.

Ryan had seen him do that before. It was when he thought he had you.

"You know, it's said that if criminals weren't stupid, we wouldn't catch any at all," Lloyd said, rocking gently as he spoke. "And I have to be honest with you—there's a lot of truth in that. Most of them are very stupid, and that is how we get them. But you're not stupid, Ryan. We haven't seen you here in over a year, and I don't suppose that's because you're sticking to the straight and narrow. It's because you use your head." He let the chair fall forward. "CDs, Ryan. You must know that the cases are the perfect surface for fingerprints. A fingerprint expert would use Perspex if he wanted to demonstrate how fingerprint identification works. And these," he said, picking up the bag, "are going off right now to be fingerprinted. And since you know that your prints must be all over them, you would never be stupid enough to think you could get away with denying all knowledge of them."

"I think my client would probably like a word with me, Chief Inspector," said Stan through his teeth.

"Ryan?" said Lloyd.

"All right, all right, I sold them," said Ryan, seeing little point in having a word with Stan, despite the sharp kick his leg was given under the table. "But I never burgled anywhere."

Finch now produced the candlesticks, and everything he'd stashed in the garage. His mum must have told them about it, true to her belief that letting the police see everything would prove his innocence. It hadn't been used for a car—at least, not one his mother knew about—since Edward had died, and the rent for it was lumped in with the rent for the house; he thought she'd forgotten it existed. Unfortunately, she hadn't.

"And these?" said Finch. "I'm showing Mr. Chester evidence bag TF4, containing two candlesticks recovered from a closet in the home of a Mrs. Janet Gibson, and evidence bag TF5, containing items recovered from a storage garage in Ellis Street rented by the same Mrs. Janet Gibson. Your mother was unable to account for these items being in her closet and her garage, Ryan. Can you?"

"I put them there." He was kicked again, harder. Well, bloody hell, he had to admit it was him. He wouldn't put it past them to charge his mum with handling.

"Now we're getting somewhere," said Finch. "And how did you get hold of them?"

"I found them."

Lloyd was smiling broadly. "You found them," he repeated. "Well, why didn't you say that in the first place?"

"Chief Inspector," said Stan. "I really must ask you to allow me to speak to my client in private."

Lloyd raised his eyebrows inquiringly at Ryan, who shook his head and turned to Stan. "It's okay," he said. "I did find them."

Stan sighed deeply.

"You know," said Lloyd, "I've been a policeman since long before you were born, Ryan. Do you know how much walking I've done in that time? And in all those years, I have never once come across so much as one candlestick lying in the road. But you and your colleagues only have to step out of your front door and you find yourself tripping over microwaves, stubbing your toes on stereos, wading through bundles of cash, offensive weapons, credit cards, wallets—it's odd that, isn't it?"

"I found them," repeated Ryan. "They were in a sack."

"A sack?" said Finch. "Did you find a couple of reindeer while you were at it?"

Ryan closed his eyes. "A black plastic sack," he said. "A bin bag. You must have found it too—they were still in it."

"Did you keep the rechargeable razor for yourself?" asked Finch.

What was he talking about? Ryan frowned. "What rechargeable razor?" he asked.

"That's the only item known to be missing from 4 Windermere Terrace that we haven't recovered," Finch said. "Where is it?"

Ryan shrugged, and looked down at his hands.

"Someone answering your brother Dexter's description was seen running away from the vicinity immediately after the window was broken," Finch went on.

Oh, God, no. Ryan didn't react visibly, but inside he was terrified. What the hell had Dex been doing there? How had he gotten himself mixed up in this?

"Was he supposed to be acting as lookout? Were you initiating him in the art of burglary?"

"My client is not obliged to—"

"Dexter was nowhere near the place!" As soon as the words were out, Ryan could feel Stan give up on him. That question required no comment if ever a question did.

"Are you admitting that you *were* there?"

"No comment."

"Look, Ryan," said Lloyd. "I know that whoever carried out this burglary didn't mean Mrs. Bignall to die. So if that was you, believe me, this whole thing will go a whole lot better for you if you make a statement."

"But it wasn't me. I didn't burgle their house," said Ryan, finding himself close to tears. "I didn't tie anyone up."

"Did Dexter?" asked Finch.

Ryan lifted his head. "No!" he said.

"How do you know? I thought you didn't know where he was?"

Ryan shook his head. "I don't," he said. "But he wouldn't do anything like that."

"Well, if it wasn't you and it wasn't Dexter, that just leaves your mother."

Ryan jumped to his feet, to find Stan restraining him and Lloyd shouting at him to sit down.

"Chief Inspector, I think we can do without Sergeant Finch trying to provoke my client," Stan said.

"I think Sergeant Finch felt that he was offering the only other possible explanation," Lloyd said, and looked at Ryan. "How did these items come to be in your possession? The truth, if that's at all possible, Ryan."

"I found them. And that's all I'm saying."

"Very well," said Lloyd. "We'll see what Dexter has to say about it, shall we? Interview terminated at 9:23 A.M." He stood up. "And if I were you, Mr. Braithwaite, I would indeed have a word with my client. Make him see sense."

Back in the cell, Stan rounded on him. "How in hell am I supposed to represent you if you don't level with me?" he said. "You swore to me you had nothing to do with that burglary, and I find that the entire proceeds are in your possession! You do realize how serious this is? For God's sake, it's manslaughter, Ryan."

Ryan looked up at him. "I never killed anyone."

"Ryan, Ryan. Use your head. Even if it was accidental, it's still manslaughter because it's against the law to tie people up and gag them—or maybe you don't know that?"

"I never tied anyone up! I never burgled anybody! I found that stuff!"

"But don't you see? You've admitted handling it—what are they going to believe if you *can* prove it wasn't you who stole it? That Dexter did! That *he* tied the woman up! He's the one who was seen, not you! Now, for God's sake, tell me what you know about it!"

"Nothing! I know nothing about it!"

Stan shook his head. "All right," he said. "But—unless you want to land Dex in it, you say no comment to everything—and I mean *everything*—when they call you back in."

Ryan ran a hand through his hair. "All right," he said. "Sorry, Stan."

Denis had never seen Carl like this: pale, nervy, nibbling at a bit of toast only because Meg had insisted that he eat something. He shook his head at himself as he thought it; how did he expect the man to look after something as dreadful as what had happened to him? And yet he couldn't not be surprised to see the self-assured, urbane, clever Carl brought so low. He looked ill. Poor Carl, who always aimed for the moon, who had had such plans and dreams, looked as though everything he had lived for had gone.

Denis had never aimed for the moon, never been very ambitious; he had always been the junior partner in any practice he'd worked in, and this one was no exception. It was the young, handsome Carl who set up the practice and had to take on a partner because he was so popular. Denis smiled tiredly. He could see the disappointment on the women's faces whenever he took a surgery that Carl had intended taking. Half of them had nothing wrong with them, but then, that was true of patients in general.

As Denis had understood it, Carl's relations with his wife were all but nonexistent, physical or otherwise; all he had wanted when he married her was someone who looked good on his arm, and someone whose private income was his to spend as he pleased. Her psychological problems might not have been a result of his indifference, but that certainly hadn't helped her. But perhaps he had been wrong to believe Estelle. Looking at Carl now, starting when the mail came through the letter box with a noisy flop onto the mat, Denis had to rethink all that. Estelle must have meant a great deal more to Carl than he had ever suspected.

And before last night, he had been jealous of Carl. Jealous of his looks, of his personality, of his charisma. But Carl had nothing that he needed, or even wanted. Carl didn't even want to be a GP. He wanted to be a playwright, an actor, a producer—whatever. He behaved like a film star. He had his clothes tailored and went to London for a haircut; he bought the latest gadgets, whether for work or fun, then tired of them and gave them to him. Carl changed his car the way he changed lightbulbs—indeed, Denis had fallen heir to one of Carl's cast-off cars, which Carl had told him he could regard as his own. No money had changed hands; Carl just gave it away. And that sheer extravagance had seemed somehow glamorous to Denis.

But being jealous of him had been crazy; Carl's life was all style and no substance, a substitute for happiness, whereas he had everything he wanted: a happy marriage, a comfortable home, grown-up successful children, two happy, healthy grandchildren, a job that suited him down to the ground. And if he had indeed been crazy, Denis knew he wasn't anymore; it was just a great pity it had taken something quite dreadful to bring him to his senses.

Dexter Gibson sat beside his mother, his face badly bruised, his eyes scared, and his hands clasped in front of him. Lloyd sat beside Tom Finch, with whom he'd had to have a word about trying to needle Ryan into violence. Tom had protested that he had merely been trying to get Ryan to admit the truth.

"You do it, sir," Tom had said. "Saying things to provoke a response."

It was something Lloyd had always liked about Tom; the mixture of defiance and deference. He never took anything lying down, but he usually remembered to tack on a "sir" when challenging a senior officer.

"A response, Tom," said Lloyd. "Not a black eye. I backed you up in there because I think that's important, but don't expect me to do it again."

So it was a peeved Tom conducting this interview, and he was getting more peeved by the minute, as Dexter steadfastly refused to say who had given him the beating, insisting that he had fallen down some steps.

Tom had moved on to the burglary, explaining, as he had to Ryan, exactly what had been found when the police arrived. Dexter reacted, as they had expected him to, with scared, shocked surprise, and, Lloyd fancied, considerable sadness.

"Someone answering your description was seen running away just after the window broke. Was that you, Dexter?"

"No comment."

"Don't you start that!" shouted his mother. "That's your brother that's taught you that! Answer the man!"

Dexter looked away. "No. It wasn't me."

"Then where were you at about ten past, quarter past eight last night?"

"Walking."

"Why would you want to be out walking on a cold, wet night?"

Dexter shrugged.

"Where were you walking?"

"Round."

"Were you in Windermere Terrace?"

"No."

"Were you in Eliot Way?"

Dexter looked haunted. "Where's that?"

"It's the service road that runs behind Windermere Terrace," said Tom, with commendable patience, in the circumstances, since Dexter knew exactly where and what Eliot Way was. "A teenage boy wearing a shiny green bomber jacket was seen running down Eliot Way. Was that you?"

Dexter opened his mouth, then closed it, shaking his head.

Lloyd looked at him for a moment, then got up and strolled around the little room, keeping well away from the boy and his mother. Someone had once accused him of intimidation when he had gotten too close, and that wasn't what he was after at all. He just liked to be able to catch nonhardened suspects off guard with a question. He liked to see their expression just before they managed to rearrange it. And if they thought he was paying no attention, it sometimes worked.

Lloyd stood on tiptoe to look out of the window at the gray skies and the rain beading the cars in the car park, sneaking a look at Dexter now and then as Tom continued to work patiently on his resilience; Mrs. Gibson was allowing Tom a long leash, but Dexter's answers, though they passed muster with his mother, might as well have been "No comment."

Tom was talking about Estelle Bignall and what Dexter had known about her habits on a Monday night. Dexter had gone very quiet, looking down at his hands, and Lloyd could see a tear in the corner of his eye, which he blinked away, swallowing hard.

"Did you like Mrs. Bignall, Dexter?" Lloyd asked before he could recover, turning as he spoke.

Dexter looked up at him, his brown eyes wide with anxiety, nodding dumbly as a tear trickled down his face.

"A lot?"

"She was really nice," he said miserably. "She was good fun."

Not according to her husband she wasn't. She had mood swings and depressions and was very difficult to live with, according to him. Lloyd thought it wouldn't hurt to pursue this for a moment.

"In what way was she good fun?" he asked.

"Oh—just good fun. When she was in a good mood. She could be really funny—she would do impressions of Marianne, make everyone laugh. It made Marianne laugh too," he added, obviously worried that Lloyd might think she was being cruel behind Marianne's back.

"But she wasn't always in a good mood?"

"Sometimes she got cross, or she would be upset, and cry. But she was still a nice person."

"When was the last time you saw her?"

"We did a musical in the summer."

"What part did she play?"

Dexter shook his head. "She wasn't in it. She didn't really like being on the stage anymore. She helped with the costumes and that."

"And you haven't seen her since then?"

"No. She left. She wanted to do something else."

Lloyd nodded. "Did you miss her?"

"Yes."

It was perfectly obvious that the last thing Dexter would do was take part in a burglary at Estelle Bignall's house. So what was he doing there? Lloyd wondered if his fondness for Estelle Bignall might be the explanation. "Did you go to see her last night, Dexter? Is that why you were there?"

His eyes immediately dropped from Lloyd's. "I wasn't there."

The brief moment of openness was over; Dexter was back to telling uncomfortable lies. Lloyd tried a different tack.

"Does your brother Ryan know the Bignalls?"

"Not really." Dexter wiped away the tear with the heel of his hand.

"Is Dr. Bignall not his doctor too?" asked Tom.

"Yes," said Mrs. Gibson. "But Ryan never goes to the doctor. The only time he sees Dr. Bignall is if he gives Dexter a lift home from rehearsals."

"So he won't feel the same way about them as you do," Lloyd said to Dexter.

"S'pose not."

"You know what I think happened, Dexter?" Lloyd sat down opposite him again. "I think you found out Ryan was going to burgle their house. I think you told him he shouldn't do that, and he forced you to go along with him, to make sure you couldn't tell on him. When you got there, you argued with him, and he knocked you about."

He saw Mrs. Gibson take an indignant breath, and shook his head, hoping she would understand what he was doing. He didn't actually think that at all; Judy had pointed out the rather large flaw in that theory.

"No!" Dexter shouted. "Ryan wouldn't ever hit me! And anyway, he wasn't even there!"

Lloyd couldn't help feeling smug. He sat back. "But *you* were there, weren't you, Dexter?"

Dexter nodded, and Mrs. Gibson's mouth fell open. "Dexter!" she said. "What are you saying?"

He turned to look at her. "I didn't burgle anywhere! I was just there, that's all."

"Did you break a window?" asked Lloyd

"No. I heard it break, and I ran away."

"Why were you there in the first place?" asked Mrs. Gibson. "Did you go to see Mr. Watson?"

"No."

Dexter was shaking his head all the time, twisting around as he answered his mother and Lloyd. Now Tom chipped in.

"Do you know Mr. Watson?"

"Yes. I work for him on Saturday mornings."

"So he knows you—did he see you?"

"Yes. He shouted at me to stop, but I didn't."

"Why not, if you hadn't done anything?"

Dexter looked at Tom and shrugged. "I didn't think he'd believe me."

So Watson had simply been unwilling to give Dexter's name to the police, Lloyd thought. That would explain why he had lied about it, why he had spoken about boys from the London Road estate having been there.

"So why *were* you there?" Tom was asking.

"I went for a walk. I told you."

Tom made a disbelieving noise. "That area must be an hour's walk from where you live," he said.

Dexter shrugged again.

Lloyd sat back. "All right, Dexter, we'll accept that, for the moment. You were out for a stroll in the rain and cold, and you found yourself in the vicinity of Windermere Terrace. Where were you when you heard the window break?"

"Where he said," said Dexter, looking down at his hands. "Eliot Way."

Lloyd leaned forward a little. "We know that's where you ran to, Dexter," he said. "But where did you run from?"

Dexter looked away. "Nowhere. I was in Eliot Way all the time."

"But Mr. Watson's security light came on, didn't it?"

"Yes."

"So how did it come on? Was it when you ran across his garden from the Bignalls' garden? Is that why you didn't stop when he shouted? Because you didn't want to have to explain what you'd been doing?"

"No."

"There are some bricks piled up in the garden of number 4 Windermere Terrace," Lloyd went on. "Some of them had collapsed. If someone running out of the Bignalls' garden into the one next door had climbed over the bricks and they gave way, he might have hurt himself quite badly when they collapsed."

Dexter frowned slightly.

"Is that how you hurt yourself, Dexter?"

"No. I wasn't in their garden."

Lloyd sighed. He had hoped to get Dexter cooperating a little more than this, because if he was there, he might have heard the scuffle that Jones heard, might even have seen who it was. Perhaps he saw something he shouldn't have seen, was frightened to tell anyone about it. "Did you see who did break the window?"

"No."

"Did someone do that to you to keep you from telling?"

"No one did it. I fell," Dexter said, looking down again. "I fell down some steps."

"What steps?" Lloyd spread his hands. "There aren't any steps there, Dexter."

"On my way home."

"And where were these steps?" asked Tom.

Dexter's voice was barely audible. "Can't remember." And now he really began to cry.

"We'll take a break," said Lloyd, before Mrs. Gibson, practiced as she was in the art of being an appropriate adult, called a halt herself. She wanted to get at the truth as much as they did, but not, Lloyd was sure, at the expense of her son's self-control.

Outside in the corridor, Tom shook his head. "How was that different from what I did, sir?" he asked.

"How was what different?"

"Saying you thought Ryan had beaten him up. You never thought that. How was that different from me asking if Mrs. Gibson had burgled the house?"

Lloyd wasn't sure; he just knew there was a difference. "Style?" he suggested. "I'm less aggressive, perhaps."

"Guv, the kid's in there crying his eyes out!"

Lloyd smiled. "That's because he wants to tell us who beat him up, and he's afraid to," he said. "He's confused and frightened because of what happened to him—not because I was aggressive."

"Well, you wouldn't be, with a fourteen-year-old boy who's never been in trouble," said Tom. "It was Ryan Chester I was interviewing. Sir."

That was true. And it was Tom's usual way of interviewing regular customers, or those he felt could rattle—asking quick-fire questions, stinging them into a response that might need a bit of explaining away. Lloyd wasn't sure why he had felt the need to warn him about his technique this time. It was because of Ryan's reaction, he supposed, but he wasn't sure why what Tom said had made Ryan so angry—he must have known Tom wasn't seriously accusing his mother of the crime, that Tom had said what he did to indicate how ludicrous the alternative was. So why *had* Ryan taken such deep exception to it? After some further consideration, Lloyd thought he knew.

"I think," he said, "the difference is that what you could get away with when you had a halo of golden curls you can't get away with now. Is there any chance you'll let them grow back?"

Judy was finding it increasingly difficult to get into the confined space behind the desk that had been set up in her living room; she was eternally grateful to the Assistant Chief Constable for suggesting that most of the work on the LINKS project could be done at home, and she didn't have to look ungainly in front of Joe Miller. Not that her public image was his reason for making the suggestion; he was hoping that her maternity leave might be less disruptive that way, because with luck she would just give birth and carry on working, like Russian peasants were once popularly supposed to do.

She booted up the computer to begin her day's work, and logged on, feeling, as she always did, that the new rank she entered every day was a little fraudulent. The DCI rank had been part lure and part forward planning on the ACC's part. She knew that it had not gone down well with her colleagues, particularly those who had not even been considered for this cushy number. But those were the breaks, she told herself. She had spent her first twenty years in this job being passed over because of her sex; if it had now become politically expedient to promote a token woman within CID while removing her from any chance of actually heading up a major inquiry, why should she worry?

At the moment, the Local Information Networked Knowledge System was just an idea in the Assistant Chief Constable's mind, but they had asked everyone to input as much detail as they could from the crimes committed in various divisions in order to get an idea of how it would work in practice. It was voluntary, which meant they weren't getting a lot to work with.

At the suggestion of the ACC, Joe himself had been collating information gleaned from various local papers about antisocial behavior in which the police hadn't become involved. He had gone back to the beginning of the year and entered anything he could find about noisy neighbors or bullying in schools—anything that reflected badly on anyone, basically, on the principle that if they indulged in one kind of antisocial behavior, they might indulge in another, more criminal kind, and a connection might be made.

Lloyd, predictably, had muttered things about Big Brother and the freedom of the individual when Judy told him what Joe was doing. He really shouldn't have been a policeman, thought Judy. He would have been much more at home heading protest marches than policing them. He had wanted to know if the Data Protection Act covered it, and Judy pointed out that for the moment, it wasn't being networked—no one but she and Joe could read it. If and when the system was made available, not only to Bartonshire, but to the neighboring county forces, they would ensure that it complied with the law.

Lloyd had made a disbelieving noise.

"It's all public knowledge anyway," she had said. "He's getting these things out of newspapers, Lloyd!"

"Even so," said Lloyd. "What you're saying is that if some rapist, say, is heard to whistle a particular tune, and you find out that someone drove his neighbors mad playing the same tune at full volume over and over again, we'll descend on him and accuse him of rape."

"We'd need a bit more than that," Judy had argued. "But if the rapist was seven feet tall with blue hair, and so was the neighbor from hell—yes, we would probably think we had our man. And he wouldn't have been on police files, would he?"

"It's sinister."

"No, it's not! It's something about the community that the bobby on the beat would have known. We're just making his beat a little more wide-ranging, that's all."

Lloyd had gone through the roof then, telling her she was even speaking like the ACC now. And she had indeed been quoting his defense of the strategy. But she still thought it was a good idea.

And Tom Finch could always be relied on to input all his data from investigations, something that had surprised Judy. The man who hated paperwork so much that he sometimes didn't even go near his desk for three days at a time had no problem with sitting down at a computer and filling in the spaces in the questionnaire that she and Joe had devised to try and pick up on the things that didn't find themselves in a collator's report.

She would have thought Tom would regard it as a waste of time inputting details of people and incidents that had nothing to do with the actual crime, but apparently not, which was interesting. Last night's shout, as he called it, had been entered already, right down to complaints about gangs of youths from the London Road estate making nuisances of themselves. Presumably he actually found it easier to work with the computer, which gave the system some chance of success if everyone thought like he did.

The part that was to make it work—the cross-referencing that ought to mean that anything chiming with another report elsewhere would be highlighted—was the program they would eventually have installed at great expense if her committee recommended it and if it was, to quote the ACC again, street-legal. She had avoided using that expression when telling Lloyd about it. But in the meantime they were trying to find out whether the system would be of use by checking each piece of information, every name, individually. It was slow, painstaking work, and entirely unexciting until she got it to seek Eric Watson. The ABH was there, of course, but there was more than just that.

Up came a copy of a letter from the Malworth Borough Council, informing the police purely as a precaution that they had had a complaint about Eric Watson taking photographs of his next door neighbor, Mrs. Bignall, as she was sunbathing in the garden. It wasn't against the law, and it wasn't something the council could actually do anything about, but if an officer could perhaps have a word with him, it might keep matters from escalating. The officer in question had not seen fit to input his or her findings, so Judy didn't know who had been sent.

And Joe's search of the newspapers found something else: he had scanned in a cutting from a local paper in a neighboring county, with the headline BARELY CREDIBLE, about a raid by Welchester County on the West End Photographic Studio in Welchester. *Officers, acting on information that pornographic magazines were on sale to youngsters, descended on Eric Watson's studio only to find that all that was on offer were* photo*graphic magazines. Looks like someone's handwriting could do with polishing up!*

Or, as Joe had pointed out in a note, that an ex-colleague of Watson's had tipped him off about the raid.

She e-mailed Tom Finch with the information; it might not mean anything, but you never knew.

❦

The phone was ringing when Carl let himself into the house; he had been in such a daze of confusion last night that he had taken only his immediate needs, and of course Meg was insisting that he stay over Christmas. He let the machine answer it, and heard someone say how horrified he had been to hear what happened.

He stooped to pick up the Christmas cards, then walked along the hallway, glad of the Leewards' offer; he had no desire to stay here now. He would sell the house as soon as he could. But there were things he needed to do; bureaucracy demanded certain things of him, as did society; he had a lot of phoning, a lot of letter-writing, and a lot of form-filling to do.

He needed clothes, underclothes, his address book, insurance policies—dozens of things. At least it would give him something to do while he was under orders to stay away from work. Something that would make the well-meaning Meg leave him alone. He'd had the excuse this morning of having to pick up his car from the Riverside Center, and let the police have his fingerprints, but he had the whole holiday to survive, and there would be very few chances to get out of her clutches. He was sure that keeping busy would be approved of.

He stopped at the telephone table and played back the messages, ignoring them all but one: Janet Gibson, who, after offering her sympathy, begged him to return her call, which he did. He thought she wasn't going to answer the phone, but just as he was about to hang up, it was answered by a breathless Janet.

"Oh, Dr. Bignall, thank you for calling back. I just got back from the police station."

Carl sighed. Other people were being dragged into this, and it wasn't fair. "Oh, yes," he said. "They asked me for your address. They only want your fingerprints so they can eliminate them. I gave them mine this morning."

There was a silence before she spoke again. "Don't you know what the police are saying?" she asked.

"No," said Carl warily. What the hell was Lloyd doing now? If he was accusing Janet Gibson of some sort of complicity, then he would have the man removed from the inquiry. This was intolerable. "What are they saying?"

"They've arrested Ryan and Dexter," she said. "Oh, I know Ryan's no saint, Dr. Bignall, but I swear to you, he would never have done anything like that to Mrs.—" She broke off in tears, then pulled herself together and continued. "They think I just won't face facts, but I know him. He wouldn't *do* a thing like that. And you know Dexter! He's never been in any sort of trouble."

Carl was still trying to take it all in. "Calm down, Janet," he said. "Please, take a deep breath." He waited a moment. "Now," he said. "Have they told you why they think it was Ryan and Dexter?"

He listened as she told him what she had learned from the police interview with Dexter, his eyes growing wider as he heard what sounded like a very good case against the boys. And Dexter had apparently fallen, or been beaten up, depending on whether you believed every word he said or none of it. Apparently Denis hadn't believed him, and he would know the difference between a fall and a beating, so that meant Dexter had been up to something.

Carl had no idea what to say to Janet. He found himself mumbling things about it being early yet, and not to worry too much, and the investigation still had a long way to go, and other equally useless platitudes. And then a thought struck him.

"Janet—did Dexter say why he was here?"

"He wouldn't give them a proper answer. Just kept saying he was out walking. That's what he told me and Ryan, but Ryan didn't believe him. They asked him if he'd gone to see Mrs. Bignall, but he said no. And I thought he might have gone to see Mr. Watson, but he just keeps saying he was out for a walk."

"Watson? Why would he be visiting him?"

"He works for him," said Janet.

No. Surely not. Carl had dismissed it, had put it down to Estelle's fevered imagination.

"Dr. Bignall? Are you still there?"

"Er . . . yes. Look, Janet, try not to worry. There's probably a perfectly simple explanation. Fourteen-year-old boys are always up to something."

He said his goodbyes and put down the phone, feeling more confused than ever. Someone had been in here last night, and for all he knew, it was Dexter and his brother. He had never done more than nod to the fabled Ryan, but Dexter talked about him all the time; if Ryan had suggested breaking in, perhaps Dexter would have gone along with it. He was easily led. But that seemed very unlikely, and Estelle had told him something that he had dismissed as paranoia, as fantasy, and perhaps it wasn't. He might know why Dexter was here last night, and he would have to tell the police what she told him; he had no option.

The doorbell startled him; he wasn't here, officially, so somehow he'd assumed everyone would know that. But, of course, they didn't. He opened the door and, with a sinking heart, saw Marianne.

"Carl, darling, I can't tell you. This is just so dreadful."

He nodded, and stood aside to let her in. He could hardly close the door in her face.

"Are you managing all right, darling? You don't look very well. Do you need anything? You know, you'd be more than welcome to come to me."

He nodded again. "Thank you," he said. "But I'm actually staying with Denis and Meg—my partner and his wife. I'm just back to pick up some things."

"Oh, you poor darling. You must be distraught."

"To tell you the truth, I just feel confused." He might as well tell the truth. He kept thinking that eventually everything would fall into place and he would understand. Until it did, he couldn't really think about how he should be feeling.

"Oh, I know," she said. "I know. Have you eaten?"

"Yes," he said quickly, before more food was forced on him. "Meg made sure of that." They were all fussing over him as though Estelle had been some sort of solid prop rather than the exhausting, mercurial, and unpredictable woman she had been. Marianne, of all people, knew what she was like. He realized then that under all her gushing, Marianne must be feeling Estelle's loss. "Oh, dear," he said. "I'm being very selfish. This must have been just as much of a blow for you."

Marianne looked dramatically torn. "Yes, and no," she said eventually. "I read her palm once, you know, and the lifeline . . ." She finished the sentence with a small shrug. "I didn't say anything to her, of course."

"Of course," said Carl. When did etiquette allow you to open the door and get rid of flaky condolence callers?

But she wasn't that flaky. He could see her sharp eyes taking in the hallway and as much of the rooms off it as she could see through their open doors. "They don't even seem to have taken very much," she said.

"No. Just the presents under the tree and some small items from the dining room."

"Oh, it's just too dreadful." She looked at him, her head tilted to one side. When he was little, he'd had a dog that did that when it wanted to go out. He hoped it meant the same thing with Marianne, but apparently it didn't. "Would you like me to stay, darling, while you get your things together? I don't like to think of you here all alone."

"No, thank you Marianne. It's very kind of you, but I'm fine. Really." Now, surely, he could move to the door.

"Do you think I could use your loo, darling?"

She was like the dog, after all. Carl stood aside and waved a hand at the stairs, watching her as she went up. But he knew that she had no pressing need to use his facilities; she had a pressing need to see whatever there was to see. And he had no reason to stop her, though, much like Lloyd, she seemed to think he might have. He felt a little sick, especially about Dexter. He wanted everyone to leave him alone and let him sort all of this out.

She was taking her time, he thought as the minutes passed. Having a good look around, no doubt. As soon as he heard the toilet flush, he was on alert, and was right on cue as she came back down. "Thank you so much for coming, Marianne," he said, walking purposefully to the front door, opening it as she hit the bottom tread. "It was much appreciated."

"Not at all," she said. "And you know if you need anything—"

"I know," he said, "and I'm very grateful." And, heaving a sigh of relief, he closed the door with Marianne firmly on the other side.

He shook his head, went into the dining room, opened the boarded-up French window, and went out into the garden, bringing his notepad with him. He'd see what needed to be done out here before he put this place on the market, and the fresh air might help him think how best to approach Chief Inspector Lloyd about his thoughts on Dexter.

❦

Eric Watson watched as Carl Bignall came out into his garden and walked around, making notes in a pad, picking his way carefully through the neat piles of bricks that he had only yesterday spent all afternoon creating.

The bricks had been delivered at lunchtime, the whine of the hoist attracting Eric's attention as it lifted the pallet above the wall. He'd watched with amusement as the driver, with the entire garden to choose from, carefully deposited it right in the middle of Bignall's driveway. When Bignall arrived home about an hour later, he had to leave his car on the street and manhandle the polythene-wrapped bundles into a wheelbarrow to be carted over to the existing wall. One of the piles must have been dislodged; the bricks had broken free from their polythene, and Bignall was piling them back up as Eric watched.

Eric doubted that the wall would even be built now, because he'd seen people doing this sort of thing before. Checking on what needed straightening up before they got someone like him in to photograph the place. If he didn't miss his guess, number 4 was going on the market, and it would be quicker to get the bricks taken away than to build a wall. Or perhaps there would be a special offer—free bricks to wall up your neighbor included in the purchase price.

Dr. Bignall wasn't exactly prostrate with grief, then. There he was, taking care of business, and rightly too, in Eric's opinion. He was well rid of that crazy woman. Worse than Geoffrey Jones for meddling and interfering and watching people through the curtains, and completely loony into the bargain. Bitch. All he'd done was photograph some blue tits using his bird feeder, and the next thing he knew, he had a bloody copper on the doorstep.

Oh, she'd been very polite. It wasn't against the law, she'd said, but it was important to get along with one's neighbors, or these things could escalate. Once he'd established what it was he was supposed to have done, he tried to explain that he hadn't been taking photographs of Mrs. Bignall, that he had at no time pointed the camera at her, and that he had indeed barely been aware of her presence.

The policewoman had been very understanding, but suggested that he try to ignore the blue tits when Mrs. Bignall was sunbathing.

"I'll try," he'd said, "but let's hope she doesn't take to sunbathing topless on a cold day. . . ."

The policewoman, who had a triple sense-of-humor bypass, said it was that sort of attitude that could get him into trouble.

ϕ

"And it turned up where?" asked Tom, holding the phone to his shoulder with his chin as he used both hands to leaf through the papers on his desk. He was in the incident room, where those assigned to the Bignall case were busy sifting through statements and receiving calls from the public as a result of the appeal for witnesses to the youth running away. They had put out the appeal before Dexter admitted it was him, but it might turn up something about Ryan.

"In a stolen car found in an office car park," said Sims. "The car was reported stolen at half past eight last night, and the traffic police spotted it this morning. They told us, and when I went to check it out, I found a rechargeable razor still in its box, under the backseat. We'd been told to watch out for one being offered for sale, so I thought I'd better call it in."

Tom looked at his list, and asked Sims for the make. "It's the one," he said. "At least, it fits the description exactly. What did you do with the car?"

"I arranged with Inspector Saunders to get it taken to Forensics, because it was too early for anyone to be around in CID," said Sims. "I waited with it until Forensics came. I've informed the owner that it's been found and it's in good nick, but that he can't have it back just yet. And I got his prints for elimination in case they found anything in the car."

"And the car was taken from where, exactly?"

"From outside a house on London Road. On the other side of the wood from the service road behind Windermere Terrace." Sims gave Tom the name and address of the owner, who had been visiting at the house in London Road when his car was stolen.

"Great," said Tom, beaming. He wondered if Sims had ever thought about CID. They could do with someone like him.

"He's a representative of a credit agency," said Sims.

"A debt collector, in other words?"

"Yes—he was making calls on reluctant payers. He reckons he couldn't have been in the house five minutes. Came out, and his car had gone."

Oh, that sounded like Ryan, all right. He could steal ten cars in five minutes. "Here's hoping they do find prints," said Tom, "because I can save them an awful lot of time if they do. Thanks, mate."

He looked at his monitor, which was telling him he had e-mail, but he wanted to talk to Forensics first. He hit the rest, and dialed out, impatiently listening to the ringing tone. "Dave? Tom Finch here. Any luck with that car you took in this morning from Malworth?" His face lit up when he heard the answer. They had indeed found something—prints on the steering wheel that didn't match the owner's. "Right," Tom said. "Get them checked against Ryan Chester's prints. Do you want to place a small wager on it?"

Dave didn't, and Tom grinned, bringing up his e-mail with a triumphant click of the mouse. Among the boring stuff was one from Judy Hill, which was a little less boring, but it didn't seem all that important. Gary Sims had said that the Bignalls were about to build a higher wall between their house and Watson's, and now they knew why. Watson might be a bit of a voyeur, and possibly a porn merchant on the side, but he wasn't in the frame for Mrs. Bignall's manslaughter. That was down to Ryan Chester, whatever anyone said. Still, he'd better do what Judy asked, Tom decided, and at least let her have the rest of the info on that incident.

It was while he was trying to find out who had dealt with it that the call came through from Forensics.

"You were right," said Dave. "They are Ryan Chester's prints. No question."

"Yes!" Tom metaphorically punched the air, having had one too many pained looks from his Chief Inspector when he did it for real. Though he'd seen Lloyd do it himself, when he thought no one was looking. Just like some other things Tom could mention. Whatever it was, it was all right for Lloyd to do it, but Lloyd gave him grief if he did it. Lloyd could be a pain in the ass sometimes.

It didn't take Tom long to track down the WPC who'd gone to see Watson; he knew her, having worked with her when he arrived at Stansfield. She was based in Malworth these days, and he dropped in to see her on his way to interview the owner of the car that had been stolen. What, he asked, had she thought of Watson?

"He was a bit creepy," Sarah said. "But to be fair to him, I think he was just photographing the birds. He's got photographs of birds all over the walls."

Yes, Tom had seen them. "A bit creepy how?" he asked.

She grimaced. "I don't know," she said. "He sort of looked at me a bit—you know. As if I was a stripagram or something."

Tom grinned. "Maybe he thought you were," he said. "Kept waiting for you to rip your uniform off and sing 'Happy Birthday' to him."

"He'd wait a long time," she said, with an involuntary shiver. "He's got this big garden. It's lovely, mind you—he's a really good gardener. But he showed me where he was standing when he was using the camera, and how she couldn't have thought he was pointing it at her, and all the time he was telling me about all these flowers, and saying this one was very good up against a wall, or that one preferred being in a bed with lots of others, and stuff like that. All nudge-nudge wink-wink stuff. Creepy."

"Did he say anything about Mrs. Bignall?"

"Well—he cracked a joke about cold weather and blue tits, but other than that, he just said he didn't know why she'd got it in for him. Maybe she just found him creepy too. I wouldn't blame her if she did."

"Did you know he had a record?"

"No," she said. "I didn't think to check—it was just a neighbor's dispute, really. If I'd known, I'd probably have taken someone with me. What sort of record?"

"Well, the only thing that might qualify as creepy was a report that he was selling pornographic literature to minors in his Welchester studio," Tom said. "If he was, he got rid of it before the raid."

"Doesn't surprise me."

Tom nodded. "But you believed him that he hadn't tried to photograph her?"

She nodded. "I don't think he knew what I was talking about at first. Did he have something to do with what happened to her?"

"No," said Tom, his voice thoughtful. "I doubt it. But—thanks."

He was sure Ryan Chester had burgled number 4 Windermere Terrace, but Lloyd thought there might have been a sexual motive, and burglary and sexual assault did often go hand in hand. If there was, it would eliminate Ryan as a suspect, because he was no sex offender. Watson wasn't either, of course, but he seemed to be a bit iffy from that point of view; Sarah wasn't the sort to get the jitters just because a man made suggestive remarks.

The things that had been taken weren't the usual souvenirs of a sexual assault—it was more often than not underwear and other personal things, but Lloyd was always saying that things weren't always how they looked, and you never knew. If they got nowhere with Ryan, it might be worth keeping Watson in mind.

In the meantime, he was going to have a word with the owner of the car that Ryan Chester had appropriated.

Reg Hutchinson was not the muscled heavy Tom was expecting when he'd been told of his calling; he was fortyish, small, rotund, with a shiny face, gelled fair hair, and a three-piece suit. He was less than pleased about the police holding on to his car; as luck would have it, he was on holiday beginning that day, but he would have to rent a car if he didn't get his own back after Christmas.

"How long have you been doing this job?" asked Tom.

"Three and a half years now," said Hutchinson.

"And what did you do before that?"

Hutchinson looked suspicious, but he answered, after a fashion. "A bit of this and a bit of that," he said. "Why do you want to know?"

"Oh, just making conversation," said Tom.

Hutchinson shook his head. "My car gets nicked, and I get a detective sergeant wanting to know what I did for a living three and a half years ago? That's not making conversation. What's going on? And why can't I have my car back?"

Tom had checked up on him; Hutchinson didn't have a record. But he behaved as though he did. "I'm afraid part of the proceeds of a burglary were found in your car," he said.

"Oh, you're kidding me." He sighed. "I'll never get the bugger back, will I? It's the break-in where that woman got killed, right?"

"I'm sorry, I can't comment on that," said Tom.

"Do you think I had something to do with it?" he asked.

Tom shrugged. "Anyone can report a car stolen. If you can tell me where you were at around eight-fifteen, I'll be out of your hair."

"Eight-fifteen?" Hutchinson looked ill at ease.

Tom grew interested. "*Can* you tell me where you were?" he asked.

Mrs. Hutchinson walked past the small room, which had been turned into an office, where Tom and her husband were talking. Hutchinson got up and closed the door. "Well, I could," he said. "But we promise our customers confidentiality."

"It's up to you," said Tom. "But your car seems to have been involved in a serious crime, so I can't cross you off until I know where you were when that crime was committed, can I?"

Hutchinson sighed. "I suppose I have no choice." He opened the briefcase that was lying on the desk, pulling out a clipboard with a printed sheet on it, handing it to Tom. "The names and addresses, the time and duration of visit, and the amount paid," he said, running his finger along the top of the sheet. "You can see where I was all day." He looked shifty. "Will you have to check up on me?" he asked.

"I don't know," said Tom, who'd had no reason to think he should until Hutchinson had said that. "I might. Why—does that bother you?"

"No," he said. "Not really. Just try not to alarm them. I call on them because they're behind with their repayments—my relationship with them is important if I'm to get any money out of them. And I do all right with the softly-softly approach, so I don't want anyone messing it up for me."

Tom frowned. "Why would I alarm them? It's you I'd be checking up on."

"These people are in debt up to their eyebrows. If they see you walking up the path, God knows what they'll think you're there for."

It took Tom a moment to work out what the man meant. He wasn't used to producing this reaction in people; he had wanted a harder image, but he wasn't at all sure he liked it now that he'd gotten it.

"Look . . ." Hutchinson went over to a small safe, opened it, and took out a leather bag. "This is the money I collected," he said. "You can count it—check that it tallies, that I really did call on all these people. I'd rather you did that than you went out and talked to them."

"No," Tom said, handing back the schedule. "I'll take your word for it. That's fine, thanks."

Back in his car, he looked at himself in the mirror. Who was it who wrote a poem about seeing yourself as others saw you? He thought he looked all right. It was true that when he'd gotten home after having his hair cut his wife asked when he was getting the swastika tattoo, and he'd had to put up with remarks of a similar nature from his colleagues, but he'd put that down to people having to get used to the new look. The trouble with that theory was that Hutchinson had never seen the old look.

And that worried him.

Chapter Five

"At 10:10 A.M.," said Sergeant Finch. "Present are Detective Chief Inspector Lloyd and Detective Sergeant Tom Finch. Also present is Mr. Stanley Braithwaite."

Ryan couldn't believe the time. They'd gotten him out of bed at six o'clock this morning, and he felt as if it must be lunchtime. Was it really only ten past ten?

"Mr. Chester, I must remind you that you are not obliged to say anything, but it could harm your defense if you do not mention now something which you later rely on in court." He put a bag on the table. "I am showing Mr. Chester evidence bag GS 1," he said. "Do you recognize this item, Ryan?"

Ryan looked at it. It was that rechargeable razor he'd been talking about earlier. "No comment," he said.

"Have you ever seen it before?"

"No comment."

"You have already admitted having in your possession items which were stolen during a burglary on number 4 Windermere Terrace,"

Finch said. "This was the only item which had not at that point been recovered from that burglary. I'll ask you again. Have you seen it before?"

"No comment."

Lloyd, true to form, was wandering around looking as though he was deeply interested in every poster, every dog-eared booklet that hung from the notice board, every crack in the plaster. Ryan knew that he was waiting for the moment when the interview took a turn he felt he could exploit. That was why making no comment was important.

"Would you like to know what we've found your prints on, Ryan?"

"Well, you haven't found them on that razor," Ryan said, despite himself, and received a gentle nudge from Stan.

"A car," said Finch. "A car that was taken and driven away without the owner's consent from London Road last night at half past eight. And would you like to know where we found that razor? *In* the car that was stolen from—"

"Yeah, all right," said Ryan. "I've got the picture. The razor must have fallen out when—"

This time it was no gentle nudge, and Stan's foot caught him right on the anklebone.

"Are you admitting that you took the car?" he asked.

"No comment."

Carl had spent the morning calling people to acknowledge their phone calls, to tell them what had happened, and to find out what happened next.

He still had to talk to the registrar and Estelle's solicitor, and to this end he was sorting through the bureau drawer that contained birth and marriage certificates, insurance documents, wills, and the rest of the papers that documented a person's life.

But his mind kept going back to what Mrs. Gibson had said. The problem was that Estelle could very easily have known that Dexter worked for Watson, and woven a fantasy around that fact; he had no wish to set the hounds after some innocent hare. But it might be true, in which case something clearly had to be done about it.

Okay, he thought, sitting back. Here's the deal. As long as the police continued to think that Dexter and Ryan had something to do with the break-in, he needn't do anything. Watson wouldn't be active while the police were taking a deep interest, not only in Dexter, but in him as a witness. But if they came to the conclusion that Dexter had not been involved, then he would have to tell them.

That seemed a reasonable compromise, he told himself. He would only be setting the police on Watson if he was absolutely forced to, and then even if Estelle had invented the whole story, he wouldn't feel so bad about it.

No comment, no comment, no comment. That was all Ryan Chester was saying, and Tom was growing more and more frustrated. He'd had his wife moaning at him first thing about his never being home, received a bollocking from his chief inspector, was accused of looking like a loan shark's muscle by a debt collector, of all people, and had now had more than enough. Proper procedure was all very well, but why did only one side in this game have to stick to the rules?

That's all it was to people like Stan and Ryan—a game. Like having to answer questions without saying yes or no. Keep saying no comment and the chances are they won't even be able to charge you: that was the advice people like Stan gave to their clients. A woman had died in that burglary, and he was sitting here playing this stupid game with this yob and his legal adviser. Well, all right, if they wanted to make a game of it, that was fine by him.

He smiled. "All right, Ryan, I'll ask you the easy questions—the ones you don't have to phone a friend about."

Ryan looked wary; Stan glanced at Lloyd.

"By my reckoning, London Road is about a ten-minute walk through the wood from the rear of Windermere Terrace. With your knowledge of the area, would you agree?"

Ryan sighed. "Yes."

"Very good. Now, if you were running instead of walking—what do you think?"

"Five, six minutes." Ryan looked uneasy, but he had answered, which was something.

"I agree. So let's see how you do on this one. Five minutes from eight-thirty?"

"Eight twenty-five," said Ryan in a bored tone, looking down at the table and tracing the pattern on the Formica with his finger.

"And at around eight-fifteen last night, someone broke into number 4 Windermere Terrace, bound and gagged Estelle Bignall, and threw a few things in a black plastic bag. That needn't have taken more than about ten minutes, need it? She was very small and slim—it wouldn't take very long to deal with her. So if that someone left number 4 Windermere Terrace at about 8:25 and ran, they would arrive in London Road at about eight-thirty. Right?"

Ryan shrugged.

"Now, Ryan—take your time. Your brother was seen running away from the scene, and has admitted being there. You have admitted selling items stolen from the house. Most of the rest of it was found on premises rented by your mother, and one item was found in the car that was stolen from London Road at eight-thirty. Now, you don't have to answer the next question, but listen to it and the four possible answers before you decide."

"Chief Inspector," said Stan.

Lloyd could hardly accuse him of being aggressive this time, Tom thought, looking at Lloyd. And if he was in trouble again, he didn't care. He'd had enough of this whole business.

"Yes, Mr. Braithwaite?" said Lloyd.

Stan sighed and shook his head. "Forget it," he said wearily, and gestured with his hand for Tom to carry on.

"Thank you," said Tom. "The question is, Ryan, did you break into number 4 Windermere Terrace? Is the answer: A, Yes, I did; B, No, but my brother did and asked me to stash the gear; C, No, the man whose car I took must have done it; or D, No, my mother did it?"

He saw Ryan glance at Stan, but he had outlined his reasons for offering that as a possibility; Ryan couldn't complain about that. Stan let it pass, but predictably advised Ryan not to answer.

"Okay, Ryan," said Tom. "You've used your phone-a-friend lifeline. But before you decide what to do, don't forget you've still got your fifty-fifty. Would you like me to take away two wrong answers? C is wrong because we know exactly where the owner of the car was all evening, and D is wrong because your mum was out doing an honest evening's work, unlike you."

This time Stan cleared his throat and tried to look important, but failed miserably. "Chief Inspector Lloyd, are you going to allow your sergeant to continue to make a mockery of this interview?" he asked.

Lloyd knew Stan as well as Tom did. Stan wasn't offended by the tone of the interview—he much preferred it not to get heavy. He just liked to break up the questioning when he could. But Lloyd had said he wouldn't back him up again if he stepped out of line; Tom sat back and waited to see what he did.

Lloyd seemed to bring his thoughts back from the other side of the world, and smiled in a vague way at Stan. "Sergeant Finch's style may not be mine," he said, "but the answers are perfectly valid explanations, either one of which your client is at liberty to offer, if he chooses not to take your advice."

"But how can I pick one when the—" Ryan broke off. "No comment," he said.

Shit. Ryan's ankle would be black and blue at this rate, thought Tom. He'd make sure they were sitting a lot farther apart in the next interview. "Is that your final answer?" he asked. "You've still got a lifeline left, Ryan."

Ryan looked up, his face faintly amused. "Ask the audience?" He shook his head. "No thanks, Mr. Finch," he said, then nodded toward Stan. "He doesn't believe me any more than you do, so I know what the answer would be."

"You've got a fourth option, Ryan," Tom said. "You can tell the truth."

"I have told the truth. I found these things. But you want to get someone for killing Mrs. Bignall, and you've got me and Dex, so that's all you care about."

"All right, Ryan," Tom said. "You tell me where you found the proceeds of the burglary, and in what circumstances, and I'll listen."

Ryan looked back at him for a moment, unsure of what to do; he knew all the interviewing techniques, and was rightly suspicious of any sudden change of tack. But after some consideration, he nodded briefly. "All right."

"Ryan, you might want to—" began Stan No Comment Braithwaite, but Ryan waved his advice away.

"I found them in the wood. In a black plastic sack. I couldn't believe it. A sackful of Christmas presents. Some of them were even wrapped. It was like you said—I was looking round for Rudolph to turn up. Thought it must be one of these TV setups or something."

Tom didn't believe him, but he humored him. "And what were you doing in the wood, Ryan?"

"I was just out for a walk."

"Ryan," said Lloyd, his voice quiet, forestalling Tom's angry response, "Sergeant Finch has said he'll listen to you, so you listen to me. We are not going to sit here and be told nonsense. Whatever you were doing there can't possibly be as serious as what you are suspected of doing, so do yourself a favor. Forget the habit of a lifetime and just tell us the truth."

Ryan glanced at Stan, who shrugged.

"Okay," Ryan said. "I was after a car. I'd been asked to get hold of a Saab, and I spent all day trying to find one. I finally saw one parked in Eliot Way."

"The service road behind Windermere Terrace?"

"Yes."

"So we pull up at the end of the road—"

"We?" Tom said.

Ryan sighed. "A mate was driving me round."

"Who? Baz?"

Ryan ran a hand through his hair, and had an argument with himself about how much of the truth he should tell. "Yeah, all right, it was Baz. He drove me. But that's all he did. He didn't know what I intended doing."

"Oh, right," said Tom, grinning at the official wording Ryan had used. "He thought you were just—what? Taking a tour of Malworth?"

"Yes. That's not against the law, is it? When I saw the Saab, I said I had something to do and he should just go home. So he did."

Tom shook his head, giving up on that. "Go on, then," he said.

"I'm just about to break into the Saab when I hear a noise, and then a light comes on—some sort of security light. So I hid."

"What sort of noise?" asked Lloyd.

Ryan frowned. "I'm not sure," he said. "Like—Like rubble being moved, or something."

"Could it have been a pile of bricks collapsing?"

Ryan's face cleared. "Yes," he said. "It could."

"Where did you hide?" Tom asked.

"In the wood. And I hear someone get into the car, and after a couple of minutes it drives off. So I come back out of the wood, and that's when I found the sack. I fell over it."

Tom threw his pen down in disgust. "Oh, right," he said. "And you expect us to believe that? Someone else conveniently burgled the house for you and dumped the proceeds at your feet?"

Ryan shrugged. "No. I knew you wouldn't believe me. But it's what happened."

Lloyd seemed to be taking it seriously. "Are you saying the sack wasn't there when you went into the wood?" he asked.

"I don't know. It could have been. I didn't see it—I fell over it, like I said. It was tucked under a sort of bush thing. I looked through the stuff, saw the Christmas presents and things, and—well, I reckoned if someone was chucking them away, I might as well have them. I walked through the wood, and that's when I saw the car I took from outside the house in London Road."

"You're admitting that you took that car now?" asked Tom.

"Yes. You said you wanted the truth, and that's what you're getting."

But this was the bit that didn't quite add up, and he could prove that the little sod was lying. "You took this car at half past eight," he said.

Ryan shrugged. "If you say so. I don't know what time it was."

"We know what time it was. It was only parked there for five minutes, from 8:25 to eight-thirty. So you would be about to break into the Saab at about what time in relation to when you stole the car?"

"Ten, fifteen minutes or so before that."

"Around quarter past eight." Tom leaned toward Ryan. "Dexter was there at around quarter past eight. He says he was in Eliot Way when he heard the window break. And he saw the light come on, just like you did. The problem is—he says he didn't see you. How could he miss you?"

Ryan tried to rub the tension from the back of his neck. "He's just saying that, Mr. Finch! He's not going to tell you if he saw me trying to break into a car, is he?"

"I'll tell you what I think," Tom said. "I think the reason Dexter didn't see you breaking into a car is that you're making all that up. When that light came on, you were inside the Bignalls' house helping yourself to the presents under their tree. A sort of Santa Claus in reverse. And when Mrs. Bignall caught you and threatened to scream the place down—"

"No! I never went near Mrs. Bignall! I was trying to nick a Saab—it was a four-year-old 9000 turbo, and I can tell you the number, even. I was looking at it long enough."

"Then tell us," said Lloyd. He jotted it down, and looked up. "All right," he said. "I think we could do with a break, and I suspect that Mr. Braithwaite might want to discuss your position with you, Ryan. Interview suspended 10:50 P.M."

Tom stopped the tape, furious with Lloyd for suspending the interview just then. You were always in with a shout when they disregarded their solicitor's advice, and he'd gotten Ryan rattled before Lloyd had let him off the hook.

Out in the corridor, Tom took a deep breath so he wouldn't say anything he would regret, and when he spoke, it was through his teeth. "Sir, why did you do that?"

Lloyd smiled. "Do you know you only call me sir when you really want to call me something much worse? You forget to do your TV cop act when you're really fed up. No guv, no boss—it's 'Sir, why did you do that?' It's a bit of a giveaway." He started walking toward the dispatch room.

"So why did you?" Tom demanded, catching up to him as he got to the door. "I was just getting somewhere with him."

"Because," said Lloyd, "I want to check the number Ryan gave us. I think Carl Bignall was still there at eight-fifteen." He held up the piece of paper on which he'd written the number. "This might prove it." He disappeared into the dispatch room.

Tom shook his head. Ryan Chester was as slippery as they came; they hadn't been able to pin anything on him for over a year, despite the fact that he was very active indeed. He wouldn't take his word for anything.

Lloyd came back out. "I think the row that Geoffrey Jones reported was between Bignall and his wife," he said, "and it wasn't coincidental to her death, because if it was, why did he lie about when he had left?"

"You haven't got the registered owner yet," Tom reminded him.

"It'll be his. Do you want to bet? Carl Bignall put the finishing touches to the so-called burglary by breaking the window, and Dexter saw him."

"Why didn't Jones?" asked Tom.

"It would take Jones a moment to get into his bedroom and look out of the window," said Lloyd. "By that time Dexter was at Watson's gate, so Carl Bignall could certainly have left by his."

True. Tom thought about that. Ryan ran into the wood, and Bignall came out of his gate, locked it, threw the sack into the wood, got into his car and left for the theater. He supposed it made sense of a sort.

"He didn't get to that rehearsal until twenty-five to nine, and I'd bet my pension that the burglary was staged. You saw it, Tom! Drawers pulled out and upturned for no reason at all that I could see. Two artful presents left beneath the tree—the portable stereo, obviously dropped when the intruder was disturbed. I was looking at a stage set, not a burglary!"

There was a big stumbling block, though. "You've got no evidence, sir," Tom said.

"I've got a witness, if this car is Carl Bignall's."

"Ryan Chester?" Tom's voice almost disappeared out of the top of his head with disbelief. "Ryan Chester is a liar, sir. And a burglar. And he had the stuff in his possession—he *sold* some of it!"

"I agree that Ryan isn't the most credible witness in the world," said Lloyd. "But we might have another one. Watson was there too, remember."

Tom made an exasperated noise. "Guv—that's not a whole lot better. He's got a record, and Judy Hill thinks he might have been overinterested in Estelle Bignall, remember. If he tried something on with Mrs. Bignall, and she knocked him back, he could be in the frame for this himself. He spooked Sarah Brightling, and I know her, guv—she doesn't get the vapors because some guy makes suggestive remarks. And I told you I didn't think he was giving us the whole strength about what was going down there last night. Anyway—how does an ex-cop who didn't even get his thirty years in wind up living in a place like that?"

Lloyd grinned. "That's better," he said. "You've gone back into telly-cop mode. And I agree—Watson's a suspect, even if he is an outside bet. But I think even you will admit that it would be quite a coincidence if he thought up the same lie as Ryan Chester."

A WPC opened the dispatch room door. "Sir—that number you gave me? It's a Saab 9000 registered to a Carl Bignall."

Lloyd beamed at her, and she went back in. "Well?" he said to Tom.

"Ryan didn't see it, guv. He's just trying to give us someone else to suspect—Bignall gives Dexter lifts home from rehearsals, remember. So Ryan would know the number."

He had just produced what he thought was his best rebuttal of Lloyd's theory, but Lloyd was beaming at him in much the same way as he'd beamed at the WPC.

"*That's* why Dexter was there," he said. "He must have overheard Ryan and Baz arranging to steal Bignall's car. He went there to try to stop them."

There was something wrong with that, but Tom couldn't put his finger on it. He frowned. "I don't know, guv."

"It's possible," said Lloyd, continuing toward the CID suite. "And one thing's for certain—Dexter saw something while he was there that he's afraid to tell us about. Now, I'm sure he wouldn't tell us in a million years if he saw Ryan doing something criminal, but I don't think he'd be frightened. And he is. So, I'm going to have a word with Watson. If he agrees that Bignall's car was there . . ." He lifted his hands by way of finishing the sentence.

"And meanwhile Ryan Chester's being given lots of time to think up a better story," Tom grumbled as he pushed open the door to the incident room and Lloyd went off to his office. Lloyd would never accept that things were sometimes just not that complicated.

"Forensics have checked up on the bin bag, Sarge," said DC Marshall, in his slow Glasgow drawl. "They say it came from a roll of bin bags in Bignall's kitchen. The perforations match up exactly. So that's no help. And we've had the results on the shoe prints, but you're not going to like them either."

Tom learned with mounting disbelief and irritation that neither Ryan's nor Dexter's shoes matched the shoe prints found at the scene. He hadn't been able to let rip at Lloyd, but he could and did at Marshall. "I don't want to hear this, Alan! Ryan Chester knows how to get rid of evidence. He'd throw away the shoes they were wearing if he knew they'd left foot marks!"

"Ryan's a size ten," said Marshall stolidly. "Dexter's a size seven. The shoe prints were left by a size eleven and a size nine."

"One's too big and one's too small? I feel like bloody Goldilocks!"

"Well, at least you don't look like her anymore, Sarge."

"Very funny." Tom ran his hand over his shorn hair. "What about the fingerprints?"

"No match there either. The fact is, Sarge, there's nothing that places Ryan or Dexter in the house or the garden."

Tom sat down at his desk. "I don't get it," he said. "Just how many people *were* there breaking into Bignall's property last night?" He sighed. "About the fingerprints—how soon can they start checking them against known villains?"

These days the process was computerized, and if there was a match to be found, it didn't take too long to find it. Providing someone started checking them.

"They say they'll do it as a matter of urgency," said Marshall. "But there's a backlog," he warned. "They're not all in the computer yet. Still—we might get lucky."

"We'd better. We're back to square one with this."

Marshall nodded, went back to his desk, then turned. "You know, Sarge—I think you were more philosophical when you had your curls."

Tom threw an eraser at him, but it missed. He'd better let Lloyd know what was what, he thought wearily. He would be smug.

"See?" Lloyd said, when Tom told him what Forensics had—or more to the point had not—found. "Sometimes things *aren't* the way they seem."

Tom looked exceedingly disheartened. "Last night I thought I had this whole thing sewn up. I was up all night—and for what? So I could prove that Ryan Chester is guilty of theft by finding?"

"And taking and driving away without the owner's consent," said Lloyd, offering mock encouragement. "Why don't you pay Watson another visit? See if he'll admit seeing Dexter this time. And perhaps he can tell us if Ryan really did see Bignall's car."

Tom sighed and nodded, and walked to the door, then snapped his fingers and turned back to Lloyd. "Got it," he said.

"The breakthrough? Or just the answer to the riddle of the universe?"

"What's been bothering me, guv. You said Dexter might have been there because he overheard Ryan and Baz planning to steal Bignall's car, and went to try and stop them, but why would he bother? As far as he knew, Bignall's car wouldn't be there. Dexter would think he'd be at the rehearsal, wouldn't he?"

Lloyd grinned. "You've been taking lessons from DCI Hill," he said. "Another theory shot down. Well—perhaps it's just as he said. They were cruising round, and spotted it."

"Or perhaps he's lying his head off, guv."

Meg had rung to see if Carl had gone to the surgery; she was worried about him because he went to give the police his fingerprints at half past eight and he still wasn't back.

Denis glanced at the clock above his door; it was twenty past eleven. Carl was a grown man; it was up to him where he went and what he did, but he understood Meg's concern, because the Carl who had sat at their breakfast table was not the Carl they knew.

He was sure Carl wouldn't be contemplating throwing himself in the Andwell; people didn't, not even people who had lost loved ones in this particularly horrific way. Somehow, people just picked themselves up and got on with their lives. That was probably what he was trying to do. And Denis knew Meg; she was kind and well-meaning, but she could be a little smothering. It wouldn't surprise him if Carl was just keeping out of her way.

He would be busy, he had told Meg. There was a lot to do; death was a very bureaucratic business.

It was the American marine again. Eric didn't like this one bit. Once again he showed Sergeant Finch into his sitting room.

"I think I told you everything I could last night," he said.

"I thought your memory might have improved since then," said Finch. "You were in your garden after you heard the window breaking. Did you see anyone?"

Eric sighed. "Is this too difficult for Bartonshire's boys in blue, or what? I must have said this ten times. I went out to check my greenhouse. So that's what I was doing. I didn't see anyone at all."

Finch nodded, and looked out of the window. "Your greenhouse has got very large panes of glass, hasn't it?" he said.

"Most greenhouses have," said Eric, puzzled about the observation.

"I'd imagine one of them would make a hell of a noise if it got broken."

"Probably," agreed Eric. "Do you run a protection racket on the side, or something?"

Finch smiled. "It's just that next door's French window has got small panes. A foot square or so, wouldn't you say?"

"Something like that—I can't say I've measured them."

"Seems a bit odd that you thought it might be your greenhouse. I mean—how much noise would a little pane of glass like that make?"

"Enough, apparently. What are you getting at?"

Finch shrugged. "Seemed odd, that's all," he said.

"Well, if that's everything, Sergeant Finch . . ."

But Finch hadn't finished. "You employ a schoolboy named Dexter Gibson, don't you?"

Eric stiffened. "What about it?" he said.

"The description we were given of the boy seen running away fits Dexter."

"Yeah? Well, I didn't see anyone."

Finch raised his eyebrows slightly. "What do you think of Dexter as an employee?" he asked.

Eric shrugged, not sure where this was going. "He's a good kid," he said.

"So if you had seen him last night, you wouldn't tell us?"

"I might have told you, if I had seen him. But I didn't see him."

"Did you see anyone?" asked Finch. "I'm not talking about anyone in your garden. Did you see anyone or anything on the road when you were checking your greenhouse?"

Eric wasn't sure what Finch was getting at. "Like what?"

"Like a person or a vehicle. Or both."

"No, but I wouldn't." He jerked his head toward the back window. "See for yourself," he said. "You can't see the road—the back wall is too high."

Finch wasn't going to catch him that way. Watson had chased Dexter almost to the gate, but the kid had been too fast for him, haring off down the road, leaving him standing. And there hadn't been anyone else there, but he couldn't have known that if he'd just been checking his greenhouse.

"Do people ever park on that road?"

"Not usually. Visitors tend to park at the front of the houses, and the people who live here park in their own driveways or drive into their garages. Bignall's car was parked there earlier, because some idiot driver dumped a load of bricks on his driveway, but it wouldn't have been there when the window broke, because he'd left by then."

"You saw him leave? Would you know what time that was?"

Eric smiled. It sounded as though Bignall might be a suspect, and, now that he thought about it, that was hardly surprising. He'd been married to the mad cow—anyone unlucky enough to be in that position might want to do away with her. "Half seven," he said. "Same time he always leaves on a Monday night."

Finch looked pleased with that, but Eric wasn't too happy with the situation—it sounded as though they'd gotten Dexter despite his best efforts to keep his identity quiet, and God knew what he'd be telling them.

❦

"Oh, darling, I'm so glad I caught you in."

Since Marianne knew perfectly well that she was working from home, she would have been very unlucky not to catch her in at ten to twelve in the morning, Judy thought. But she'd been hoping for a call from Marianne; she felt there was more information to be gleaned from that quarter. Marianne had said what she wanted to about Carl, but there was something about Estelle that she had perhaps been more reluctant to divulge, and Judy wanted to know what it was.

"I wondered if you might like to have lunch with me," Marianne said. "There's a wonderful restaurant that opened in Chandler Square—too expensive for most people, which is why they had a table at this time of year. I've booked it, so you must say yes."

Judy hadn't actually said anything but her name and number so far, and she did indeed feel a little like a prisoner of war about to be interrogated, because she was sure she would be. But she could hold out against Marianne's interviewing technique, and she might find out exactly what Marianne had been hinting at so heavily last night.

"That would be lovely," she said. "What time?"

"I've booked the table for one o'clock. I'll meet you there, darling."

She wasn't sure how Lloyd would feel about her conducting her own private investigation into this business, but her lunch hour was her own time, Marianne was her friend, and there was no rule that said police officers couldn't have lunch with a friend.

What harm could it do?

Chapter Six

When he got back to Stansfield, Tom bought an evening paper; in the days leading up to Christmas, it appeared earlier and earlier, and Tom had never worked out why.

The headline screamed WOMAN LEFT TO DIE BY BURGLARS at him, and he read the item, more or less a rehash of the press release, but with more descriptive color than the press officer was allowed.

As he walked into the incident room, he got bombarded from all sides with information, almost all of it negative. There were no prints on the tape dispenser. The empty box that had probably contained the tie and handkerchief had Bignall's prints and someone else's—presumably his aunt's, because the unknown ones didn't match either the prints found on the door between the dining room and the kitchen or the ones found on the window frame. All the unidentified prints found at the scene, including these, had been checked against known felons, and they had drawn a blank.

Estelle Bignall's bathrobe had no foreign fibers on it, so they had nothing on what her assailant had been wearing.

Two things that were of some interest: the mud that had been walked through the dining room into the kitchen contained brick dust from the garden and glass from the window, and the muddy shoe prints on the patio did not. Therefore the person on the patio had probably not entered the house. Which, Tom thought ruefully, fitted nicely with Dexter being a lookout and running away, except they weren't his shoe prints.

The other thing—the one that had distinct possibilities—was that someone had called to say that he'd seen a van parked on the main road, at a bus stop between the entrances to Windermere Drive and Eliot Way, at about eight-twenty. He had written down the number because of the burglary in which a van had been used, and the driver, a heavily built young man, had run back to it and driven it away as he'd done so. And it was the number of Baz Martin's van. Of course, Ryan said he'd been there, but he said Baz had gone home before anything happened, and clearly Baz had not.

He'd let Ryan have his lunch while he went to have a word with Baz, and then interview him again, now that he knew he'd been lying about both that and seeing Bignall's car. In fact—he'd take him his lunch himself, and let him look at the paper.

That might make him come to his senses.

Officially, Lloyd had to assume that Estelle Bignall's death was the result of the treatment she received at the hands of burglars, because so far that was what the evidence suggested, but he still didn't believe it. And neither did Freddie, so he had hoped that the full post-mortem might produce something they could go on, but as Freddie said, it had been a long shot.

"No evidence of strangulation," he said. "I think she was smothered, but not necessarily by being gagged. The vaginal swabs were positive, though, which might be of assistance to you. They've gone off for DNA analysis."

Lloyd's eyebrows rose. "Really? I thought you said you didn't think there had been a sexual assault?"

"I think I said there were no external signs of sexual assault," said

Freddie. "And I don't recall saying anything at all about sexual assault just now."

Lloyd sighed. Pathologists were so pedantic. "So what are you saying?"

"In my opinion there are three possibilities. One, the sex was consenting, and coincidental to the subsequent violence; two, she submitted to sex before any violence was done to her—possibly in the hope that violence *wouldn't* be done to her; or three, she was raped when she was no longer able to offer resistance."

"Do you mean after she was dead?"

"Or unconscious. She would lose consciousness quite quickly if she was being smothered. If it was an assault, it wasn't violent, and she didn't put up a fight, that's all I'm saying."

"So what would you be prepared to say in court?" asked Lloyd.

Freddie sucked in his breath. "What I've just said about the sexual activity is what I would say in court," he said. "And as far as her death goes, I would be prepared to say that in my opinion the findings are not consistent with accidental smothering due to being gagged. That the bruises on either side of her jaw are consistent with someone having held her by the back of the neck, which could suggest deliberate smothering. But the defense would have no trouble finding someone to say exactly the opposite."

"So how would they account for the non-soggy handkerchief?"

"They could point out that she, suffering from some sort of upper respiratory problem, could well have panicked and died very soon after being gagged."

"But you said you could find no evidence of an upper respiratory problem," said Lloyd.

"No. But even if we discount the head cold, we don't know how the tie was used to hold the gag in place—it was very tight, and could have obstructed her nostrils. The tie could also account for the bruising on the jaw. Sims obviously just pulled it away—he didn't note its exact position."

"And your belief that if she had been alive when she was gagged she would have rolled herself over so that at least she wasn't facedown?"

Freddie shook his head. "The self-preservation thing is opinion at best, but even if it was an established fact that someone would do everything in their power to facilitate breathing, we only have Sims's word for it that she was facedown when he saw her. We don't have a photograph to prove it."

"It wouldn't be enough on its own anyway," said Lloyd.

"No. And even if it was, Sims is young and inexperienced and was in two minds about what to do," Freddie went on. "He was in something of a panic himself—a good defense barrister would tie him in knots. By the time he was finished, Sims wouldn't be able to say for certain if she was lying facedown or dancing the polka when he saw her."

The lack of injury to her mouth seemed to Lloyd to be the best bet, but Freddie, professionally able to see the facts from both the prosecution and defense points of view, shook his head.

"If she interrupted the intruder, the first thing he would do would be to try to keep her from making a noise," he said. "A hand over her mouth would be the quickest way, and he could have told her that if she allowed it to be done, she wouldn't get hurt. Only after that does he start tying her up, and only then does she start to struggle, *because* she can't breathe. She passes out from lack of air before he tapes up her ankles."

It was possible, thought Lloyd. But it certainly didn't sound like Ryan Chester's style.

"Any or all of these things could mean that she died exactly as it looks as though she died," said Freddie. "I just don't think she did. It's an opinion. No more than that."

Lloyd didn't think she had either; time for Judy's suggestion, he felt, and offered it.

Freddie smiled. "She thinks the doctor was putting arsenic on his wife's porridge?"

"Well, she did have mysterious illnesses. He says she was a hypochondriac, but perhaps she wasn't. So if we can find evidence of any previous attempts to do away with her . . ."

"Sure," said Freddie. "I can test for all the usual drugs. But from what I've seen of her organs so far, she seems to have been in very good physical health. I mean," he said wickedly, "just look at this, for example."

Lloyd didn't.

Carl left Estelle's solicitor, feeling a little more in control than he had been. It was up to the coroner, apparently, to release Estelle's body in order that funeral arrangements could be made, and he wouldn't do that until the police investigation had reached a stage at which they knew they no longer needed it, and then only if any criminal proceedings did not require the defense to be able to carry out their own autopsy. It meant he couldn't lay her to rest in the foreseeable future, and he felt that only then would he be able to draw a line under his life up to that point and start again. But at least he knew what was what.

As to the other things, they were as he'd believed them to be; Estelle's will was straightforward, and he already knew that the death certificate would be issued as soon as the cause had been determined. Dexter's possible plight was still nagging at him, but for the moment he was in no danger, so there was little point in worrying about that now.

And he had managed to spend the whole morning away from Meg Leeward's watchful and concerned gaze, which made him feel a little better in itself. But she would undoubtedly have search parties out if he didn't go back now, so he drove toward the village where the Leewards lived, still confused, still anxious about how it was all going to turn out, still aware that Chief Inspector Lloyd was deeply suspicious of him, but definitely a little more in charge than he had been.

"He's still not back."

Denis had come home for lunch, though it was something he didn't usually do, purely to see how Carl was, and even he was now bothered by Carl's prolonged absence.

"He looked ill this morning," she said as she began preparing a meal without even thinking about what she was doing. "I just hope he's all right."

Other men's wives might find it irritating if their husbands came home unexpectedly in the middle of the day expecting to be fed; not Meg. She was barely aware of what she was doing as she produced his lunch; she'd been born to look after someone. He had taken it for granted, even allowed it to get him down at times. He had never meant to have the kind of wife who stayed at home and looked after the house and him, and, when he married her, Meg hadn't seen herself like that either.

But children had come along, and she left work and brought them up; he didn't have a lot to do with it. He had resented that; he knew that now, though he hadn't been aware of it at the time. She was the one who had bathed them and put them to bed and told them stories; he would look in on them and kiss them good-night. Often they were asleep before he had the chance.

Carl would confide in him about Estelle; how unpredictable she was, how exhausting. But even that seemed glamorous to Denis; a wife who could fly into a rage, slip into a depression and be the life and soul of the party all in one night might be hard to live with, but it wouldn't be monotonous.

The doorbell rang, and Carl was back, apologizing to Meg for having been out so long, explaining that he had just wanted to get all the legalities sorted out as soon as possible so they weren't hanging over him. Meg sat them both down and served lunch, and Denis looked at Carl, much more like himself now, and realized that he probably needed a bit of monotony, a bit of Meg, to help him through all this.

And there was a beneficial side effect as far as he was concerned; while she had Carl to wait on and worry over, she wasn't doing it to him.

❦

Eric had gone over and over everything Finch had said, and the more he thought about it, the more he felt that Dexter had probably kept his mouth shut. He didn't know how they had got on to Dexter so quickly, but if Finch had known anything, he wouldn't have left without trying to find out a little more.

As it was, all that seemed to be bothering Finch was when Bignall left last night, so things were looking pretty good.

Judy didn't have to look for Marianne when she got to the restaurant; no one ever had to search for Marianne in a crowd. She was out of her seat, waving, scarves flying everywhere, as soon as Judy stepped over the threshold.

"Oh, I'm so glad you could make it, darling—I thought you might be too busy with all this dreadful business."

Judy sat down. "I'm not actually involved in the investigation," she said.

"Oh, I don't understand who does what in the police. I just wondered how it was going. I heard that two boys had been arrested—is that right, or aren't you allowed to say?"

"I don't honestly know, Marianne," said Judy. Which was true. She had accepted Marianne's invitation to lunch in the hope that Marianne was going to tell her something, not the other way around. She took the menu from the waiter and glanced at it. She never ate lunch; she wasn't all that interested in anything. Which was just as well, because she found that Marianne was ordering for both of them.

"You must have the sole, darling, it's absolutely divine. Isn't it wonderful these days? Real restaurants everywhere! Even in Malworth. This one costs the earth, but it's worth it."

Judy had just seen the prices, and felt that if the sole wasn't solid gold, they'd be cheated. But it was a lovely restaurant, so she supposed they had to pay for the surroundings.

"And what will you have to start?" asked Marianne.

"Oh, nothing, thank you. The sole will be fine."

Marianne ordered a starter, and handed the menus back to the waiter. "I eat," she said. "When anything unsettles me or upsets me, I eat. And I hate to eat alone. That's why I dragged you away from your work. But you do have a lunch hour, don't you, darling?"

Judy agreed that she did have a lunch hour, refused white wine, and parried questions about the investigation until Marianne's starter arrived, and with it came the real reason for Marianne's invitation to lunch.

"Do they think those boys did it?" she asked. "Or are they just hauling in likely suspects?"

Judy smiled. For someone who claimed to know nothing about police methods, Marianne's guesswork was very close to the truth. But not this time. This time they really did think they'd done it, or at least they had when she last heard. But Marianne didn't, and she wanted to know why.

"As I said, Marianne, I'm not on the investigation. They might just be witnesses of some sort."

"It's just that—well, if poor Estelle was just the victim of some vicious thugs, then there would be no need to bring up anything personal, would there?"

"Is there something personal you think should be brought up?"

Marianne demolished the rest of her starter, and drank some wine. "If I talk to you," she said, "that's not official, is it? I mean, you said you weren't involved in the investigation."

Which Marianne had known perfectly well all along. Judy waited until the waiter had taken Marianne's plate away before she spoke. "It's not quite like that," she said. "If you tell me something that has a bearing on the investigation, I'd have to act on it."

"But if it didn't," Marianne persisted, "I mean—if that lovely, lovely man of yours came home and said they'd confessed and it was all wrapped up, you wouldn't have to make an official report or anything like that, would you?"

"Marianne, all I can say is try me. If I don't believe that there's any reason for the investigation to know, then obviously I wouldn't make it official. But a confession from someone about the burglary wouldn't necessarily mean your information wasn't relevant. You'll have to trust me. Or not tell me."

The sole came then, and it was, as Marianne had promised, delicious. Judy hadn't known about this place. She knew Lloyd would love it. She might bring him here as a treat for being her lovely, lovely man. Which he was, mostly. When he wasn't being exceedingly irritating.

Marianne ate in a totally unnatural silence for a few moments, then came to her decision. "Estelle was having an affair," she said. "But, I mean—if this was just a burglary that went horribly wrong, then it has nothing to do with anything, and it might have nothing to do with it anyway, come to that. But I told you she'd been much happier lately, and—" She laid down her knife and fork. "I did a terrible thing."

Judy too laid down her knife and fork. "Marianne, if you are going to confess to a crime, please don't do it here," she said.

"No—not a crime. Well, yes, I suppose it was. I suppose it was stealing, really. Except that I'm giving it to you, so—"

"Stop there." Judy had been joking. Now she leaned forward and spoke in an urgent whisper. "You know if you go on, I am going to have to act on it, whatever it is."

"It's up to you, darling."

Oh, God, what had Marianne done? Lloyd would hold her personally responsible. "Can we go somewhere else?" she said. "Somewhere more private?"

"No one's listening," said Marianne. "And we haven't finished our lunch."

Judy looked around; the diners did seem engrossed in what they were eating and in one another; the hum of conversation and the civilized spacing of the tables precluded overhearing. The waiters weren't likely to come to the table for a little while. "All right," she said. "What have you done?"

"I went to see Carl this morning," she said. "Actually, he's staying with his partner, but he was at the house."

Oh, dear. Carl was being investigated by Marianne. Much scarier than being investigated by the police.

Marianne, who claimed clairvoyance, correctly guessed, or simply knew what she was thinking, and looked offended. "I just wanted to see if he was all right," she said. "Anyway, I had to go to the bathroom while I was there, and I couldn't help seeing the bedroom—the door was open and the bed wasn't made, so it caught my eye, because the house always looks immaculate. There were no pillows on the bed—any of the beds, come to that—is that significant?"

Judy didn't reply. Her sole was growing cold; Marianne was eating hers.

"And I saw Estelle's diary on the bedside table," she said. "I recognized it from the pattern on the cover. It was a real diary, not an appointment diary. I'd seen her with it lots of times."

Judy felt as cold as her sole. "And?"

"And I went in and had a look at it."

"Oh, Marianne," groaned Judy.

"It wasn't like on the telly, darling. They didn't have the room closed up—there wasn't any of that crime-scene ribbon over the door or anything—I wouldn't have gone in if there had been."

That was reassuring. Marianne finished eating and put her knife and fork together before continuing, leaving Judy in a state of near panic.

"I looked at the entry for the previous Monday night—I told you her Mondays were important to her, and I doubted that it was some writer's circle that got her so excited. Sure enough, she had been writing about this man, and I thought—well, it could be evidence. And since the police hadn't removed it, and anyone could go into that room—well, someone else *could* have removed it. Someone who wouldn't have brought it to you." She dipped into her bag and produced the diary, placing it on the table, then gave a little shrug. "So I took it first."

Judy closed her eyes.

"I mean, if Carl knew about the affair, well—it could be evidence, couldn't it, as I said?"

It seemed unlikely to Judy that it was evidence; Carl would hardly have left it lying on the bedside table if he'd known it could incriminate him.

"Is that stealing?"

Marianne was looking theatrically perplexed, but Judy was used to Lloyd, who could look any way he chose, and she wasn't fooled. Marianne had known exactly what she was doing when she took that diary.

"Well, it belongs to Carl," Judy said. "And you had no right to remove it, so—technically, yes."

"But I've brought it to you, darling. You're the police."

"And what am I supposed to do with it?"

Judy hadn't opened it. Hadn't touched it. She wished Marianne's supernatural powers could transport it back where it came from, beside Estelle Bignall's bed. But, a little voice at the back of her head was asking, *why* was it beside her bed? Surely Estelle hadn't kept it there? Had Carl Bignall found it and confronted her with it? Judy picked it up and put it in her own bag; it could indeed be evidence. But she couldn't invent some story to account for its now being in the possession of the police, which was clearly what Marianne wanted her to do.

"Marianne," she said, in what Lloyd called her nanny voice, "if it is evidence, we have to say how it was obtained. I have to give it to the investigating officers, and I have to tell them how I got it. Which means I have to tell them how you got it."

Marianne thought about that, then flicked one of her scarves over her shoulder. "Oh, well," she said, and smiled. "All I could think when I saw it was that it shouldn't be left there for just anyone to pick up. If they clap me in irons, at least it'll be a new experience, and I love new experiences."

Ryan, alone in a cell, was only too aware of the seriousness of his position; he hadn't needed the evening paper to tell him, though that was obviously why Sergeant Finch had so thoughtfully provided it. A woman had died, and the police thought he, Ryan, had brought about her death. They were doing everything in their power to find evidence to charge him with manslaughter. And, possibly for the first time in his life, he had thrown himself on their mercy and told the truth.

But Dexter hadn't. What had he been doing there in the first place? Surely he wasn't involved in something like this? And he'd lied to them about what he'd seen. Why? He'd never asked Dex to lie for him, never once. Contrary to what his mother apparently thought, he had never involved Dexter in anything. But what Dexter had said had made it look as though he'd made everything up.

When the interview had been abruptly suspended, he'd begged Stan to get Dexter to tell the truth, but Stan said it would do no good; the police would say he'd told Dexter what to say. He couldn't interfere with a witness, and he didn't represent Dexter.

So Ryan was reduced to trying to send a telepathic message to his brother. Please, please, Dex, tell the truth. There was no way Dex was involved in anything like that, and whatever he was doing there, it wasn't because he was burgling the Bignalls' house, so there was no reason for him to lie except to protect him. All Dex had to do was tell the truth—naturally, the police still wouldn't believe him, but they would have to take it into account.

But he knew his little brother. Lying didn't come easily to him, so once he'd made up his mind to lie, that's what he'd do. With all the conviction that a good actor had at his disposal. If Dex had decided he didn't see Ryan breaking into a car, then that's what he would say. For the rest of his life, if he had to. And by the time he realized that he wasn't helping, it would be too late to change his story.

Ryan picked up the evening paper again. How the hell could he convince them that he had had nothing to do with it? He turned the pages, trying to take his mind off it, and found himself reading something that brought his eyebrows together in a frown of concentration.

By the time the interview began again, Ryan couldn't wait to talk. Stan had called to say he'd been held up in court and would be there as soon as he could get away, and Ryan waived his right to have him present. He didn't need him present.

"Look," said Ryan, as soon as Finch had finished all the messing about with the tapes and the caution. He jabbed a finger at the paper. "That traffic jam. I was in it." He looked at Lloyd, and pushed the paper across to him. "Read it," he said. "The lights came back at 8:28, and I was there when they did. And the traffic was at a standstill for ten minutes before that. So I couldn't have been burgling a house out in the sticks at eight-fifteen, could I?"

Finch read it and looked up, his face amused. "Nice try, Ryan," he said.

Ryan's heart plunged. "What? What do you mean?"

"You read about a traffic jam and suddenly remember you were in it? Do me a favor. You didn't nick the car until half past. Twenty-five past at the earliest. That's how long it was there. And we know you've been telling us porkies, Ryan."

"What about?" said Ryan.

"About seeing a Saab. About sending Baz home."

"I did see a Saab! I tried to break into it."

"Not according to Baz," said Finch. "I've just been talking to him. He had no idea what I was talking about."

"Oh, come on—you know he would say that!"

"And his van was seen, Ryan. At twenty past eight. He was seen, running back to it. You and he were there to burgle the Bignalls' house, weren't you?"

"No!"

"Well, he didn't drop you off and leave, did he?"

Oh God. Ryan took a deep breath. "No—all right, he was waiting to make sure I got the Saab. Only that never happened. And when I found myself with all this stuff in the sack, I rang him to come and pick me up, but he didn't answer. That's why I legged it through the wood and nicked the car. And then I did get hold of him. And that's when I told him to go home. He'd been out of the van for a pee—that's why he was running back to it."

Finch was grinning.

"It's true! And I was in that traffic jam!" He looked at Lloyd. "I was, I swear it. I was in it for the whole ten minutes—that's the God's honest truth. There were kids singing Christmas carols—I can even tell you which ones they sang!"

"Did anyone see you?" asked Lloyd.

Ryan stared at him. He had never been in this position before. He had always told lies or said nothing whenever he'd been brought to a police station for questioning. Somehow, he'd thought the truth would do the trick, but it wouldn't. It couldn't. He didn't have any proof. Then he remembered.

"Yes!" he said. "Someone did see me."

"Oh, yeah?" Finch, of course. "Who?"

"I don't know."

"Oh, this gets better."

"No, I mean I didn't know who she was, but she knew me. She spoke to me."

Finch sighed. "All right, Ryan, I'll buy it. What did she look like?"

And that was when Ryan realized he had no chance. No chance at all. He closed his eyes.

"Come on, Ryan. It's not a difficult question. If you say someone saw you, I'm prepared to try and find her. What did she look like?"

"The Pink Panther," said Ryan miserably, his eyes still closed, and sighed. "She looked like the Pink sodding Panther."

Chapter Seven

"Are you going to check it out?"

"Oh, come on, guv—he must think we're idiots! I should never have left him the paper."

"Probably not," said Lloyd. "But you never know—Ryan could be covering up for someone. You thought that yourself at one point. At least, it was one of the answers you offered him to choose from."

"But you said that Dexter would never have broken into Estelle Bignall's house, and I agree with you—he thought far too much of her to do anything like that."

"But Baz Martin didn't. He's Dexter's cousin, remember—Dexter might accidentally have given him the information that the house would be empty. And Ryan could be covering for him."

Tom thought about that. Baz was certainly stupid enough to have bound and gagged someone for no reason, but he had never been violent in his life. If Ryan was unlikely, Baz was even more so.

"Perhaps Ryan wasn't there at all," Lloyd went on. "It's Dexter and Baz who were seen there, not Ryan. And if he really did get caught in that traffic jam—" Lloyd sat down on the edge of Tom's desk. "—then eliminating him could point us in the right direction."

Tom wasn't sure what to do with a senior officer who had a fixation. "Carl Bignall's direction, would that be?" he asked.

"No," Lloyd said. "Unlike you, Sergeant Finch, I'm keeping an open mind."

Tom gasped. "Since when?"

Lloyd grinned. "Since you told me Watson confirmed that Bignall did leave his house at half past seven—though that doesn't mean that Bignall didn't go *back* again, of course."

"No—it means that Ryan Chester was lying," Tom said, doggedly determined. "I reckon it's just the way it looks." He hit the newspaper. "This is just a story he's concocted after reading this."

"But we can't place Ryan in the house or the garden, and what happened in there just isn't his style—especially not if she was sexually assaulted, which she might well have been."

"Baz is even less likely, guv. He's got no record of violence at all—at least Ryan's been known to take a pop at someone in his time."

"But if Ryan's lying about Bignall's car being there, he might be lying about being there himself. And he might be telling the truth about the traffic jam."

"How?" said Tom, perplexed. "He didn't take Hutchinson's car until half past eight—the traffic lights had come back on by then."

"What if he didn't take Hutchinson's car at all? What if he was doing what he says he was doing? Stealing an upmarket car to order? Couldn't *that* have been what he was driving when he got caught in the traffic jam?"

Tom tried to hang in there.

"Just suppose," Lloyd said, "that while Ryan's peaceably going about his business, stealing a car from wherever, his cousin Baz is going in for a spot of private enterprise with someone else—that would explain why we've got two sets of footprints that don't belong to anyone we know of yet. And what if the one he teams up with is both stupid and violent? Dexter realizes what they're up to and tries to stop them. The language used was *about* Mrs. Bignall, not to her."

This was beginning to make sense, Tom thought, and carried Lloyd's hypothesis further. "Dexter's no match for the violent one," he said. "He gets a beating, runs as soon as they're busy breaking the window. They go in, and are interrupted by Mrs. Bignall. The other one assaults her, Baz realizes it's all getting too heavy for him, takes fright, and runs back to his van. The other one leaves with what he's got and runs through the wood. *He* takes Hutchinson's car."

Lloyd nodded. "And then Baz rings his cousin Ryan, tells him they've got a stolen car full of stolen goods, and will Ryan help them out? Naturally, he doesn't tell him they're the proceeds of an aggravated burglary, or Ryan wouldn't have taken anything to do with it. Ryan goes to meet him, getting caught in the traffic jam, and once he's free, drives to where Baz has the car, and goes to his mum's lock-up garage in it—leaving his fingerprints—and hides the booty. Then he drives the car to the car park where it was found, and he and Baz go to the Starland club to sell some of the stolen goods."

Tom thought about that. "So Ryan doesn't know until we tell him where the stuff came from, or that Estelle Bignall died as a result of what Baz's mate did to her." Tom had to admit that Ryan really did seem in the dark about all of that, and trotting out the hoary old story of having found the stuff indicated that he'd had no time to prepare for questioning. "He's caught on the hop, and he's trying to protect Baz, so he makes up a story about being there and seeing Bignall's car to throw suspicion on Bignall himself." Tom was nodding now that he could see the logic of this. "But that backfired because of Dexter, and now he's stuck in a cell trying to work out how he can get out of this without shopping Baz," he said. "That's why he said Baz was working with him, because if he can prove *he* wasn't burgling the Bignalls' house, we might leave Baz out of it too."

Lloyd smiled at him. "It's perfectly possible," he said.

Tom smiled back. "I like it, guv. We can get them to check the prints against Baz Martin's at least. And we should have no trouble finding his mate when they check the other ones." He backtracked slightly. "Assuming he's known to us and *was* known to us long enough ago," he said. "Do you know they've got unindexed prints going back two years? No wonder the little sods don't mind leaving their prints everywhere."

"Quite," said Lloyd. "So, if you can find the Pink Panther and eliminate Ryan, we might get a step closer to finding out who *did* break into the Bignalls' house."

Yes, thought Tom. It would be worth checking out.

Lloyd stood up. "But, as it happens, I agree with you," he said, turning to go. "It's a fiction. Because I still think Ryan was trying to break into Bignall's Saab."

Tom made a good-humoured V sign at Lloyd's retreating back.

"I've got eyes in the back of my head, Sergeant Finch," he called over his shoulder.

Lloyd was very good at theories, and Tom knew that he had a tendency to accept them as gospel. Lloyd knew that too; he said that Judy always found the flaw in them, and that Tom took them too seriously. That was why Lloyd had laughed that one off at the end.

But Judy said there was always something in Lloyd's theories. It was instinctive; he didn't know himself what it was. The trouble was, Tom knew he couldn't sift through the nonsense to find the nugget of truth the way Judy could, so he would just have to do it the hard way, and check out Ryan's story.

He picked up the paper he had confiscated and read the report, swearing under his breath as he reached the part about how charity workers had made the most of the traffic jam "with Sylvesters and Donald Ducks and Pink Panthers all descending on the becalmed drivers," and how "the frayed nerves of the frustrated drivers were soothed by the St. Anne's School choir singing Christmas carols." Ryan had almost certainly got the whole thing out of the paper. He was probably just trying to make a fool of him. Still, it wouldn't hurt to make inquiries. Ryan need never know he'd taken it seriously, even for a moment. He glanced at the number, rang it, and asked to speak to the editor.

"Yes, Sergeant Finch, how can I help the police?"

Tom explained how he could help.

"Oh, sorry," he said. "Our collectors weren't in costume. But dozens of people were organizing collections and bringing the money to us—that little girl has really touched Malworth's heart."

He even spoke in journalese. Tom sighed. "I don't suppose you know which organization wore costumes?"

"I don't even know which organizations were doing it."

"But if I find out who was registered—"

"I think you'll find most of them were spontaneous, Sergeant. Our appeal is properly registered, of course, but as I said—everyone is collecting. Shops, offices, you name it. We had a steady queue of people bringing in bucketfuls of money, but—really, I don't think many of them were doing it on an official basis."

"I wonder where they got the costumes?" Tom asked, thinking aloud.

"There's a firm that rents that sort of thing—I know it lent them for the day as their contribution to the cause. They'd know who they lent them to, I suppose, but I doubt if the organizers themselves will know exactly who wore what. And, well—I saw at least three Pink Panthers all at once yesterday. I don't fancy your chances of finding a particular one."

What he was saying, thought Tom, was that anyone at all could have put on a Pink Panther costume and rattled a bucket at people in order to relieve them of their money. And even if Ryan was telling the truth about being in the traffic jam, then that's what any friend of his would be doing. Ripping people off. And he wasn't very likely to find her, in that event. But he could approach this from a different angle; he would have another word with Baz Martin.

And he was beginning to think he'd let Watson off too lightly—he still wasn't being straight with them about last night, and it might well be worth having another go at him.

The fax suddenly came to life with the report on the broken pane of glass, and Tom read it, his brow furrowing. The writer was puzzled about exactly where the glass had gone when the window was broken. There were what he called spicules of glass in the curtains, which he had expected to find, as the curtains were apparently closed at the time of the incident. However, he went on, the glass itself had scattered two feet beyond the curtain, which didn't really make sense, as a closed curtain would have had the effect of containing the glass, and it would have scattered only an inch or two out on reaching the ground. On the one hand, the curtains appeared to have been shut, and on the other, they appeared to have been open.

"Another little puzzle," Lloyd said when Tom arrived in his office and he read the report on the glass.

"I know," said Tom. "What's a spicule?"

Lloyd grinned. "A small spike, I expect," he said.

"I think these guys can get too clever for their own good. I mean—you smash a hole in a window on a windy, rainy night—what's going to happen? The curtains'll billow out, won't they? So they wouldn't necessarily have contained the glass."

Lloyd nodded. "Good," he said. "No puzzle, then."

"Do you think we should give Watson a pull, guv? Maybe he *was* taking photographs of her. Stalkers have got to live somewhere—and next door to your target would be very handy. That might be why he moved there. There is something a bit creepy about him—even I've noticed."

"Perhaps," said Lloyd. "But I don't think it's that kind of murder. If it was, I don't think he'd have faked a burglary."

"All the same," said Tom. "We've got shoe prints and fingerprints we can't account for, and he was there. She made a complaint to the council about him—and he's holding out on us about Dexter. It wouldn't hurt to talk to him again, would it? Maybe check his shoes?"

Lloyd thought about that, then nodded. "You're right," he said. "It's time we really did have open minds about this."

They had come and invited him to help them with their inquiries, and had asked for the shoes he was wearing yesterday; he had thought it better to cooperate with them, but had contacted his solicitor as soon as he'd been brought to the station. He knew all about police stations. You went voluntarily and never came out again. Dexter had been talking, after all, but it didn't matter, he told himself. It would be his word against that of someone who was seen running away from the scene of a crime.

"I wonder if you feel like telling me when you last saw Mrs. Bignall alive, Mr. Watson?"

The question came from Detective Chief Inspector Lloyd, no less. Whatever they said, Eric could see they had graduated him from witness to suspect, from lone sergeant to two-handed interview team, and it was a DCI leading the questioning. He shook his head. "I can't really remember."

The bitch had come to his door saying she knew what was happening and if he didn't stop she would go to the police, whatever it took. Mad cow. What the hell did what he was doing have to do with her? But it didn't matter what Dexter had told them about that—the woman was mad. She had accused him of everything under the sun, and he could prove that.

"Perhaps you remember that Mrs. Bignall made a complaint about your taking photographs of her when she was sunbathing in her garden?"

"Yeah," said Eric. "That's right. But I didn't take photographs of her. I didn't even notice her. The woman was barking mad. Saying I was spying on her and God knows what all. I don't really see how I can help you with any of this, Chief Inspector. I told the constable who came originally and the sergeant here everything I know about this business."

"Did you spy on her?" asked Finch.

"No, of course I didn't! Why the hell would I want to spy on the woman?"

"Maybe you fancied her."

That nutcase? Finch must be joking, so he laughed. It was only polite.

"Perhaps you'd like to tell us again what you were doing at eight-fifteen last night," said Lloyd. "We've had two versions already—might there be a third?"

What had Dexter told them? Not much, or this wouldn't be a voluntary visit to the station. But enough.

"I heard the window break, went out, checked my greenhouse, and went back in. On my way back I saw that their French window was standing open, and one of the panes was broken."

"And did you do anything about that?" asked Finch.

"No, as I've already told you, I didn't. Why should I have done anything about it? It was their lookout if they'd had their window broken."

"And you still reckon you couldn't tell the difference between a foot-square pane of glass being broken and the sort of noise that would be made by one of the panes of glass in your greenhouse smashing?"

"I heard breaking glass, that's all. It sounded pretty loud to me."

"Is my client a suspect in this inquiry, Chief Inspector?" asked Watson's solicitor.

"Let's say we're keeping an open mind about that," said Lloyd.

"Why did you ask for the shoes my client was wearing yesterday?"

"We've taken photographs and casts of shoe prints at the scene, and we will compare your client's shoes with those impressions. It will be of great assistance to us, if only for elimination purposes. We're very grateful to your client for his cooperation."

"But he has denied having been on the scene of the break-in."

"Yes, I'm aware of that," said Lloyd. "But you see, we don't think that Mr. Watson has told us the whole truth about last night. For instance, he has said several times that he saw no one." He turned back to Eric then. "Do you have any comment to make on that, Mr. Watson?"

"No. I didn't see anyone at all."

"Come on, Mr. Watson," Finch said. "Dexter Gibson has admitted being there, and he says you saw him and shouted at him to come back. You wanted to know what he'd been up to, didn't you?"

So that was it. Watson shrugged. "He's a good kid," he said. "And I didn't see him breaking into anyone's house."

"But you did see him running away?"

Watson sighed. "Yes, all right," he said. "I saw him. I didn't want to get the kid into trouble, that's all. He works for me—he's never given me any trouble."

"Where was he when you saw him first?" Lloyd asked.

"At the gate."

"But he was in your garden, rather than on the road?"

Watson shook his head. "No, he was just outside the gate. For all I know, he was just going past."

Finch frowned. "But your security light was on when you went out," he said. "And someone running past your gate wouldn't activate it, would they?"

"No. Someone was on my property, all right—but that someone doesn't have to have been Dexter. Kids that age run if they think they might get into trouble, whether they had anything to do with whatever's happened or not."

Lloyd terminated the interview then. Eric felt pleased with himself; Lloyd had swallowed whole the idea that he had been reluctant to give them Dexter's name because he worked for him. Which, now that he thought about it, was precisely the case.

"Oh—one more thing, Mr. Watson. Would you have any objection to giving us a blood sample for DNA testing?" asked Lloyd.

Eric's eyes widened. What the hell was going on? "What for?" he asked.

"We believe that Mrs. Bignall may have been sexually assaulted," said Lloyd. "Again, we would like, if possible, to eliminate you from the inquiry."

Eric looked at his solicitor.

"It's up to you," he said.

"Well, I think I'd like you to eliminate me too," said Eric. "Yes, you can have a blood sample."

Now he had to wait until the doctor could get here to take it.

Ryan had been charged with theft, taking and driving away, driving without insurance, everything they could think of—but not, he was very relieved to discover, manslaughter—and he had been given police bail.

"Come on," said Stan, who had arrived when it was all over and his services no longer required. "I'll give you a lift home."

"What about Dex?"

"They've released him pending further inquiries," said Stan as he got into the car. He leaned over and opened the passenger door.

Ryan got in and sat back, his eyes closed. "What the hell was he doing there, Stan? Who beat him up? How come he's got himself involved in all this?"

"How come you've got yourself involved?"

Ryan opened his eyes, sat up and looked at Stan. "I swear to you," he said, "I found that sack in the wood."

"Oh, yes?"

"Well, if you don't believe me, what chance do I stand with them? Am I off the hook for manslaughter?"

"For the moment. I wouldn't count on staying off it, though. So far, you seem to be their only tangible link with this burglary. And a woman died, so they're under pressure from the press to make an arrest this time. Who do you think they're going to fall back on if all else fails?"

Judy, waiting in Lloyd's office, rehearsing how she was going to tell him about the diary, jumped when he opened the door. She always had; he didn't know how to open a door other than suddenly.

"When's the appointment?" he asked, looking at his watch. "It's only ten past three—I thought you said it was this evening."

"Relax," she said. "That's not why I'm here."

He sat down. "To what do I owe the pleasure, then?"

"I don't think you're going to like it very much," she said, going into her bag. She took out the diary and placed it on the desk.

Lloyd frowned. "What's that?"

Judy took a deep breath. "Estelle Bignall's diary."

Lloyd looked at it much as she had; like her, he neither picked it up nor touched it. "Why is it on my desk?" he asked. "Or don't I want to know?"

"You don't want to know, but you're going to. Marianne Mackintosh gave it to me." She told Lloyd how Marianne had gotten it.

"Oh, great," he said. "And am I right in assuming that you wouldn't have left your lair to come here if you hadn't thought it important to my investigation?"

Judy nodded. "I suggest you read the entry I've marked."

"How the hell did Warren miss her diary?"

"Warren?"

"PC Warren took Bignall round the house to check if anything was missing—he must have been in the bedroom. And you're telling me this was just lying there for Marianne Mackintosh to pick up?"

Judy was glad that someone other than she was getting the blame for this unorthodox acquisition of evidence, but she did feel that Warren was being judged harshly. "Presumably he had no reason to suppose he was dealing with anything other than a burglary gone wrong at the time," she said. "And there's nothing to suggest it's a diary, is there?"

"There's nothing to suggest it isn't! Young Sims would have had a look, that's for certain—he takes the job seriously, which is more than Warren seems to do." He shook his head, picking the diary up, and sighed. "Oh, it's me I'm angry with, really. I should have thought about looking for a diary—I was the one who suspected there was more to it than met the eye." He put on his glasses and began to read, his eyebrows rising. "Does she give him a name anywhere?" he asked.

"According to later entries, she calls him 'Papa,' and he calls her 'Nicole,' so that's not much help. He's married, and older than her, and that's about it in the way of clues."

The diary started in October, which was when Estelle had joined the writing group, and at first she had written in it every day. Then one Monday in November she had announced that she had a lover, and after that wrote in the diary only on Mondays. She seemed to have been reluctant to embark on an affair, but whoever it was had told her it was just what she needed.

"She had a novel way of dealing with the guilt," Judy said.

Lloyd read a few entries and looked up. "Do you suppose Papa knew that he was a Carl substitute?" he asked.

Judy shook her head. "I doubt it," she said. "I imagine if he'd had the slightest idea of her state of mind he would have been off like a shot. She picked the wrong men, all right."

"Unlike you," said Lloyd, with a smile. "If you were paranoid about the man next door taking photographs of you sunbathing, I hope I'd build you a higher wall before December."

Judy laughed. "You wouldn't know how to go about building a wall at all," she said.

"True." Lloyd read a few more entries, and closed the diary with a sigh. "I take it she was entertaining Papa when she was supposed to be at her writer's group?"

"Yes. I spoke to the group leader—she says Estelle came for three weeks and then didn't come back." She anticipated Lloyd's next question. "And no, they didn't lose any other member at around the same time. Besides, they're all women."

Lloyd turned the pages. "Damn," he said. "There's no entry at all for yesterday."

"No," said Judy grimly. "I don't suppose she got the chance to write it up."

Lloyd nodded, and closed the diary. "How long do these evening rehearsals usually last?"

"I've only been to a couple," said Judy. "One lasted about two hours, and the other about three, I think. Last night's broke up, of course. I think it depended on what they were doing, and on Marianne, of course. I believe she made them all stay until about midnight once, whereas sometimes she decided she was too fatigued to carry on after an hour. Once she sent them all home as soon as they got there."

"So Papa had no way of knowing how long he had before Carl came home," said Lloyd, tipping his chair back. "It's reasonable to assume he would arrive very shortly after Carl left and that he wouldn't stay too long, just in case. He doesn't sound overly considerate of Estelle, from what I've read. Half an hour would be about my guess."

Judy agreed, but she could feel one of his theories coming on, so what it was reasonable to assume would have very little to do with it.

"I think she entertained Papa last night," he said. "And Carl Bignall knew that she would be doing just that."

Judy listened as he told her of Freddie's findings, about Ryan's insistence that he saw Carl Bignall's car there. Even she had to concede that Lloyd had every reason to theorize this time.

"Let's say Carl found her diary last night," said Lloyd. "He leaves the house as usual, but he doesn't go to rehearsal—instead, he drives round thinking about what's been going on, then comes back, goes in and finds her in the altogether except for a bathrobe, having just entertained Papa. They have a row, they struggle—she cries out, and he pushes her face in a cushion or whatever to keep her quiet. If he had a hand on the back of her neck, that would produce the bruises at either side of her jawline, according to Freddie. He's angry, and he doesn't let her up for air until it's too late."

It seemed a lot to assume, but Judy didn't interrupt. It was always best to give Lloyd his head when he was theorizing. Forensics would or wouldn't back up the cushion theory.

"So now she's dead, and he has to do something. So he leaves her trussed up and gagged, shoves some presents into a bin bag, and breaks the window." His face lit up, as it always did when a little puzzle had been accounted for. "It opens inward, so he can stand inside the house but break the glass from the outside, and he used the curtain to try and deaden the noise—*that's* why there was glass in the curtain. And when he let go of the curtain, the glass would fall straight down. Once the window was closed again, it would be about two feet away. It was the *window* that was open when the glass was broken, not the curtain."

Judy hadn't the faintest idea what he was talking about, but he seemed to, so that was all right.

"He goes out, and runs down the driveway, locking the gates behind him so no one can get in, which will buy him a little time." Lloyd brought his chair forward with a thud. "Dexter runs too, triggering the security light, and the rest of it happens just as Ryan said it did. Then Carl turns up at rehearsal and tells us that Estelle has a cold, to lend credence to what will appear to have happened." He sat back. "Well? Objections?"

Her first objection was why did Carl Bignall leave the diary lying around for Marianne or anyone else to find? Surely he would have disposed of it if he'd killed Estelle as a result of what he read in it.

"He didn't mean to kill her," Lloyd said. "Perhaps he forgot that the diary *was* evidence. Perhaps he believes in hiding things in plain sight—if it was just lying there, no one would think anything of it. And he was right, wasn't he?"

"Could be." Judy moved on to her next objection. "Wouldn't a doctor know that the gag would give him away?"

"Perhaps," said Lloyd. "Perhaps not. I don't really know. But all this would have been done in a panic, and in a very few minutes. Given that the times aren't exact, I would estimate seven or eight at the most. So I don't suppose he gave a lot of thought to that."

"Which brings me to my third objection," she said. "He would have to be able to think like lightning. And he didn't look like a man who had just committed a crime of passion when he did turn up last night. He must have arrived at the theater within twenty minutes of doing all that, thinking, presumably—what with the security light going on and people coming out of their houses—that the police would practically be following him there. And he was perfectly calm."

Lloyd assumed the slightly mutinous expression he always had when she argued with his theories. "He's an actor," he said. "He pulled it off, and hoped for the best."

"And I thought Mr. Jones said the noises he heard were outside."

"He left the French window open—they were close to it."

"And why was Dexter there?" She smiled. "He doesn't exactly fit the bill as the boyfriend."

"No," Lloyd agreed. "But he did have a crush on her. Maybe he knew about the boyfriend. Maybe he was there because of the boyfriend. Envious, jealous—worried about her, even. With good reason, since he seems to have been taking advantage of her."

"Could be," said Judy, nodding. She could imagine Dexter worrying about Estelle's unsuitable liaison.

"I might have another word with Dexter—see if throwing Carl Bignall's name into the conversation produces a reaction." He smiled. "You've got more holes to pick in it, I know you have."

"Who walked the mud through the house? Not Carl, presumably, because why would he step in the mud at the bottom of his garden? He wouldn't need to get in from Watson's garden."

"Pass."

"Why did he leave her in the kitchen?"

"Pass."

"And when did he tie her hands? She struggled to free herself, didn't she?"

"Pass. But let's forget theories and look at the facts. He wasn't happily married, his wife was having an affair, his car was seen in Eliot Way *when* the window was broken, two people were heard having a row *before* the window was broken, the burglary seems to have been staged and the proceeds dumped, and this all happened when he says he was 'driving around.' I think that's more than enough grounds for bringing him in for questioning, don't you?"

Judy nodded. "Does this mean you won't be coming with me to the clinic?" she asked.

"Not necessarily," he said, immediately on the defensive, as he always was when pretending he didn't use every excuse in the book to get out of this particular duty. "When's the appointment?"

"Half past five."

Lloyd looked at his watch. "Half past five," he said, setting its alarm. "There." He patted the watch. "I'll be home by quarter past."

Oh, sure he would, thought Judy. She had handed him the excuse on a plate this time.

Carl sat in the interview room, waiting for the tape to be set up. He hadn't been surprised when he was asked to come in and answer questions. He knew that driving around was not going to impress them as an alibi, and he knew that Lloyd was already suspicious of him, and would want more detail about that drive, which he couldn't give. Because he had left the house and *had* just driven around. Anywhere. Everywhere. He had no idea where exactly.

He'd been cautioned, told that he wasn't under arrest, asked if he wanted a solicitor. He didn't. The first question startled him.

"What size shoe do you wear, Dr. Bignall?" asked Finch.

"Ten," he said.

"Thank you." Sergeant Finch put a familiar-looking book down on the desk. "Do you know what this is?" he asked.

He knew he'd seen it somewhere before, but he wasn't sure if he did know what it was. Oh, of course, yes, he did. He frowned. "Yes," he said. "It's Estelle's journal. Where did you get it?"

"It was handed in to us by Marianne Mackintosh," Lloyd said from over by the window set high in the wall, apparently anxious to catch a glimpse of something, standing practically on tiptoe in order to look out. "She found it when she went to your house this morning. She thought we ought to see it." He turned as he spoke.

Carl frowned, puzzled, and looked back at Finch. "Why didn't she just leave it where it was?"

"She thought we'd be interested in the contents," said Finch. "She was right. Have you read it?"

"No, of course not. It's private." He'd had no desire to read it. "She started keeping it when she joined the writer's group—the others suggested it. Keeping a journal helps you learn how to put things down on paper."

"I think perhaps you should read it now." Lloyd left the window and pushed the book across the table to him. "If you don't mind."

Carl picked it up and opened it where someone had thoughtfully provided a Bartonshire Constabulary bookmark. He was startled, to say the least, by what he found himself reading. He leafed back through it; the previous entries were her thoughts on current affairs, on the weather. This announcement that she had taken a lover just suddenly appeared, and then there was nothing but weekly accounts of this apparent love affair. He looked up, shaking his head. "I don't understand," he said.

"Seems clear enough to me," said Finch. "Did you find it? Read it? Decide to face her with it?"

Carl stared at him. "I've never read it," he said. "This is the first time I've ever opened it."

"Did you go back home to catch her? Have a fight with her?"

Carl felt as though he was in a play that he had failed to rehearse. None of this was making any *sense*. "I've told you—whoever had that row, it wasn't me and Estelle."

"Then what were you doing between half past seven and twenty-five to nine?" demanded Finch.

"I drove round to clear my head." He appealed to Lloyd. "I told you all this last night."

"You said something happened that you had to think about," Lloyd said. "But you wouldn't tell me what. I think you found that diary, left the house, drove round, then turned back and went home again."

But this was nonsense. Nonsense. What on earth would make them think that? They couldn't just accuse people out of the blue, could they? He had never read her diary, he didn't believe for one moment that she had a lover, he had not had an argument with her, and he had not come back for any reason at all. He had driven around, and then gone to the theater. He told them that for the umpteenth time.

"Did anyone see you driving round?"

Carl looked back at the uncompromising Finch. He doubted very much that anyone had seen him. Driving around was driving around—people didn't see you. You were doing it because you didn't want to see people. That was kind of the point of it. "No," he said. "Not as far as I'm aware."

Lloyd leaned forward. "You do see our problem, don't you, Dr. Bignall? We find your wife was having an affair—meeting her lover on the nights that you were at rehearsal. You turn up at that rehearsal thirty-five minutes late, you can't—or won't—account for your movements during the missing time, and we have reason to believe that you returned to your house last night at about ten past eight."

This wasn't happening. He hadn't been anywhere near his house at ten past eight. He had left at half past seven, and returned, with Lloyd himself, two hours later. "What reason?" he asked.

"Your car was seen parked in Eliot Way."

But that simply couldn't be true. Not for the first time, he felt as though Lloyd was lying, but surely he wouldn't do that. So who was telling him all this about quarrels and cars? It wasn't true.

"It couldn't have been seen there," he said, "because I was driving it, and I didn't go back home. And anyway, you don't understand—Estelle wasn't having an affair."

"She made it all up, did she?" said Finch, tapping the journal.

"Yes," said Carl. Of course she had. It was the only way it made sense.

"I'm sorry?"

"She probably thought her own life wasn't exciting enough for a journal. So she began making something up. That's what it is—she was in the writer's group partly so she would learn how to write. It's fiction."

"Fiction? What—some sort of project for her group?"

"Yes," said Carl. "That *must* be what it is. Look," he said, pushing the book across the table. "She only wrote in it on Mondays. She probably wrote it *at* the writer's group."

"Except that she hadn't been going to the writer's group."

"What?" Carl blinked at Finch. "What do you mean, she hadn't been going?"

"I mean she hadn't been going in the sense that the writer's group didn't see her after the first three weeks."

Carl tried to take that in. He couldn't believe she hadn't told him, but he supposed since communication between them had reached an all-time low, she probably hadn't felt obliged to. But it was strange.

"All right," he said. "All right. If you say she wasn't going there, then she wasn't. But she wasn't having an affair. She was making all that up."

"What makes you so sure about that?"

"Because she didn't know anyone but other women, for a start. Christine, Marianne. She didn't *go* anywhere else without me except to this writing group—and now you're saying she didn't even go there."

"Who's Christine?" asked Lloyd.

"Christine Jones, our neighbor," said Carl. "Her husband Geoffrey called the police last night." He nodded as he realized who had been telling them all this nonsense about overhearing some sort of argument. "He's the one who's supposed to have heard this quarrel, isn't he?"

Two poker faces looked back at him.

Carl sighed. "And I don't suppose you're going to tell me who says my car was there, are you?"

"No," said Finch.

"Oh, what does it matter? The whole *thing's* fiction. Estelle and I didn't have a fight, my car wasn't there, and this—" He waved a hand at the journal. "This is fiction too."

"If it's fiction, why does she use your name?" asked Finch. "Don't people writing stories usually make up names?"

"She did. Papa and Nicole—they're from an advertisement, in case you don't know."

"Oh, I know," said Finch. "But Carl isn't. And Carl is mentioned over and over again. Why would she do that if she was just writing a story?"

"I don't know. Except—" Carl looked up at Lloyd, who was now leafing through a booklet hanging from a pin on the wall. Perhaps he could make him understand—he didn't think Sergeant Finch would ever be able to grasp something as utterly perplexing as Estelle. "—it might not have been fiction in the sense of actually writing a story. I know she didn't have a lover, but—she might have believed she had," he said.

Lloyd looked just as skeptical as Finch. "I think you're going to have to explain that, Dr. Bignall," he said, and sat down at last.

Explain Estelle. Carl nodded, at something of a loss. An Italian friend of his had once sat down expectantly and said, "Explain me cricket," and he felt a little like he had then. "It isn't easy," he said. "I have to go back a long way if you're to understand."

"Take all the time you need."

Where to start, though? Carl steepled his fingers and tapped them against his lips, trying to formulate his opening sentence, then began at what for him had been the beginning.

"I met Estelle at the Malworth Amateur Dramatic Society. She was fifteen when I met her, and eighteen when we first went out together. We married within the year. She was lovely, and sexy, and full of personality, and I thought I'd won the jackpot. But—as I've told you, she was far from easy to live with." He caught the look on Finch's face. "I know how that must sound, but it's true." He paused. "And if you've been talking to the neighbors, I'm sure they've told you something of the sort."

"They mentioned rows," he said.

"Yes, we argued. I told you she was a hypochondriac. Sometimes I would lose my patience with her." Estelle had believed she had everything from anthrax to yellow fever, it seemed to him. He sometimes thought that was why she had married a doctor; it gave her more immediate access to the medical profession. He sighed. "And she imagined other things, besides illnesses."

"Like she was having an affair?" said the ever-doubting Finch.

"No," said Carl. "That I was having affairs, or that people were watching her, or following her—she had delusions of conspiracies against her, and deep depressions when she felt she was worthless and might as well end it all. But when she wasn't like that, she was gregarious, funny—she was full of confidence, she was great fun to be with. You never knew which way she was going to be, or how long it would last."

"Did you ever seek psychiatric help?" Lloyd asked.

"Oh, yes. She was diagnosed manic-depressive, and for a while she was on drugs that controlled it, but she wouldn't take them. She stopped going eventually. To start with it was very difficult, but things settled down a bit, thanks to Denis, mainly. He helped her a lot—the mood swings weren't so wild, or so unpredictable. She was still suspicious of everyone she didn't know, and she still wouldn't go anywhere without me or Marianne, but she was better than she had been. She got friendly with Christine Jones, as I said. She would never have done that at the beginning. Until this year, it was just about livable with her."

"Was she like that before you married her?" asked Finch.

"Well, the warning signs were there, if you knew to look for them, I suppose, but I didn't know to look for them. It wasn't until we were married that I found out she was pathologically possessive and jealous—needed constant attention, constant reassurance that I loved her."

"And did you?"

Finch got straight to the point. It was commendable, Carl supposed. A nice, direct, simple question. But he wasn't entirely sure of the answer. "I think so," he said. "I thought she was wonderful—I'm not sure if that's the same thing. And I quite enjoyed someone feeling that jealous of me, someone who needed me to prove to her how much I loved her, being the only man in the world that she wanted, the only man who could make her feel really good about herself—discovering you're that important to someone gives you an ego boost, I suppose. And of course, when you're first married you're wrapped up in one another, so I didn't really acknowledge that there was a problem at all. I couldn't wait to get home and be made to feel like a god."

"So what changed?"

"You can't live at that pace forever," Carl said. "Eventually I . . . well, it was a turn-off, to be honest. Having someone worship you might sound wonderful, but believe me, it isn't. It's exhausting, and you can't ever live up to it." He thought then, of how he had concocted reasons not to go home until later and later, hoping she would have retired for the night and be asleep by the time he got to bed. But that hadn't been the answer; that had confirmed her belief that he no longer loved her, that he had other women. "And it was when I cooled off that the paranoia and the hypochondria and everything really came out," he said. "And after a couple of years of that I was ready to walk out, but I didn't."

"Why not?" Finch again.

"We came to . . . an accommodation, I suppose. And I'd gone into partnership with Denis by then—he worked wonders with her, as I said. So Estelle and I talked things out, and held the marriage together, more or less."

Lloyd nodded, and Carl got the impression that holding a marriage together was something that Lloyd knew a little bit about. He knew that Lloyd had grown-up children from a previous marriage; perhaps Judy had been an extramarital affair. He hadn't had affairs; he had never been unfaithful to Estelle, but his fidelity had been prompted more by self-preservation than by morality, because he hadn't needed to complicate that area of his life any more than it was already complicated.

Then Lloyd asked the question Carl had been expecting ever since he'd been brought in. "Was it important to you—holding the marriage together?"

Someone had told him about Estelle's money. He had known someone would; Marianne, Christine Jones—one of the women Estelle had unburdened herself to. And it would be much more acceptable to say that he had promised to take her in sickness and in health than to tell the truth, but he wasn't going to lie about that.

"It was important to Estelle," he said. "And the unromantic, ungallant fact is that I couldn't honestly afford to leave her."

Lloyd's eyebrows rose inquiringly; Carl elaborated on that.

"I'm extravagant by nature—I've always spent more than I earn. That was partly why my first marriage failed. Estelle had an income from a trust fund, and she encouraged me from the day we married to spend the money—part of her expansiveness when she was up rather than down. I bought cars, watches, jewelry, had my clothes tailored—I still do. We gave huge parties. Everything you can spend money on, I do spend money on. You name it, I've got it, or more probably, I haven't got it anymore, because I give away things once they bore me and buy new ones." He shrugged. "Classic retail therapy, I suppose, but it didn't start out like that. It was all part of what seemed like the fun of being married to Estelle, until being married to her stopped being fun, and I realized I couldn't just leave her. It's my name on the credit cards, but it's Estelle's money that pays them each month—I could never hope to pay what I owe. So I needed her just as much as she needed me."

"That was the accommodation you came to?" asked Lloyd.

"More or less. It wasn't just as cold-blooded as that, but that was the effect. She didn't mind financing my lifestyle if it meant I stayed with her. She would beg me not to leave her even after we stopped having any relations of any sort."

"So that bit's true?" said Finch. "She says in her diary that you weren't interested in her anymore. That isn't fiction?"

Carl shook his head. "No, it's true. She got much worse when Watson moved in next door," he said. "Accusing him of taking photographs of her, saying he was spying on her." He could stop worrying about Dexter, he realized. If she had fantasized meetings with a lover, she had doubtless fantasized the story about Watson. "She started saying crazy things about him—I don't want to repeat them."

"No need," murmured Lloyd.

"She got so as she didn't want me to go out, even, and the more demanding she got, the less responsive I got. She began thinking she wasn't good enough for MADS—she wouldn't perform in any of the productions anymore, but she still came, and as long as I was there, she was all right while we were out, more or less. When we got home it was a different story."

"Why did she leave the dramatic society?"

"Denis suggested trying to make her more independent. He persuaded her to leave, and I think it was his idea to try writing as therapy."

What he was telling them barely scratched the surface; the bald facts didn't begin to convey the tears, the tantrums, the suicide threats, the sheer hell of it all, but perhaps they would understand that they couldn't take what she had written in this journal as gospel. Estelle didn't think other men existed; she had wanted him, and no one else, and surely this fiction that she had concocted proved that.

"She joined this group and began the journal, but I don't think it was supposed to be a blow-by-blow account of her day. It was supposed to be anything that came into her head, anything she wanted to write. By the time she wrote that—" He nodded toward the journal. "—she and I hadn't had any physical relations for almost a year, and very little in the way of normal conversation even. It's fiction. It made her feel better, that's all."

"It doesn't read like fiction," said Finch. "He sounds real to me. He's older than her, he's married, she knew him a long time before anything happened—pretending he's you so that it doesn't feel like she's cheating on you—there's a lot of detail in there for a fantasy."

Carl tried to make him understand. "That's just my point," he said. "It is me. I'm older than her. I was married when we met. She knew me a long time before anything happened between us. Don't you see? It *is* me. A sort of fantasy me, one that still does want to make love to her and make her feel good. As far as Estelle was concerned, there *weren't* any other men. There was only me. That's what was so impossible to live with. And that's why there is no way that she was having an affair."

Finch looked back at him, unmoved. "Except that she had sexual intercourse with someone shortly before her death," he said.

Carl sighed. So that was it. "I know she had," he said. "But it wasn't with some phantom lover, Sergeant Finch. It was with me."

❦

"Oh, Dr. Leeward!"

Denis turned to see his receptionist coming out from her desk and along the corridor toward him.

"I think there must be something in your shoe," she said. "Look—you're scratching the tiles."

He looked down to see a trail of small scratch marks, and used his receptionist's shoulder to balance himself while he examined the sole of his shoe.

"Oh, yes," he said. "It's a piece of glass." He picked at it to no effect, and smiled at her. "You don't have a Swiss Army knife on you, do you?"

She laughed. "Do you want a lift to your surgery?"

"I'll hop," he said. "Thank you."

It wasn't until he had made his way to his office, limping in order not to damage the floor surface any more than he already had, and had sat down, one leg hooked over the other in order to facilitate the removal of the offending piece of glass with the end of a pen, that he realized where he must have picked it up.

He dropped it in the wastebasket and wondered how long it would be before his luck ran out.

❦

A silence had fallen after Carl Bignall's last statement, and Lloyd could practically feel Tom's total disbelief. He had intended leaving most of the interview to him; he'd wanted to see how the smooth, playwriting doctor coped with Tom. But he hadn't anticipated Carl's complete bafflement, and he certainly hadn't anticipated his last answer.

"I thought you just said your marriage had gone down the tubes a year ago," said Tom. "Now you want us to believe you were making love to her yesterday?"

Bignall nodded. "It had," he said. "I thought it had. I was going to throw myself on the mercy of my bank manager. Spread out the credit cards, ask him to consolidate the debt and let me pay it off over a very long time. That way, I could leave Estelle."

"But?"

"But the bricks arrived." Bignall smiled sadly. "For Estelle's wall. I knew Estelle was going to lunch with Marianne and would be out most of the day, so I had arranged to take the afternoon off to supervise the delivery, but I came home to find that I couldn't get my car into my driveway because the idiot driver had come early and dumped them right inside the gates. I moved them—by the time I was finished I was all dusty and sweaty, and had to have a shower. Estelle was already in the shower, and—well, one thing led to another." He looked at Tom. "If you don't believe me, I'm happy to provide a blood sample for DNA testing."

Lloyd frowned. It had to be true. Did that mean the lover theory had gone the way of all theories? Looked like it.

"And it was great," Bignall went on. "I don't know—maybe it was because it had been so long, but it was like when we were first married. We couldn't get enough of one another. And it threw me into total confusion." He shrugged. "I was making arrangements to leave her, and there I was in bed with her, wanting never to let her go. I needed time to think—so I told her I had to go to rehearsal."

"I don't suppose that went down too well," said Tom.

Bignall shook his head. "No," he said. "It didn't. She went through her entire repertoire. I didn't love her, I was having an affair with Marianne, I found her unattractive—all the usual stuff. And I found myself reassuring her, just as I always had before. I did love her, I just didn't want to let Marianne down . . . I was telling her I loved her, for God's sake! I was supposed to be telling her I wanted a divorce. And it worked, like it had when we were first married—she was reassured. But she said she was tired and that she was going to stay in bed. I left to go to the theater, but I couldn't, not without sorting myself out. I had to try and work out what I'd done. What I was going to do."

"And did you?" asked Lloyd.

"Yes. I decided to give it another go. For her sake this time—not the way we'd done it before. I would still sort out the money side of it, so I wasn't dependent on her, but I'd stay with her, really try to make it work this time. But—" He shook his head. "—a couple of burglars had other ideas about that. I still can't quite make myself believe that."

Lloyd got up and, under the pretext of stretching his legs, sneaked a look at his watch. This interview hadn't gone at all as he'd expected; it looked, unfortunately, as though he would be able to make it to the prenatal clinic after all. He had expected a high-powered solicitor querying every question, demanding to know the source of their information, dragging the whole thing out. Not the total bafflement that he had seen from Bignall. But he still had some pertinent questions to ask; he always allowed talkers to do just that, and then he would take them over what they had said.

"You said your wife didn't know any other men." He turned to look at Bignall as he spoke. "But she did. There are men at the dramatic society, for instance. Of course she knew other men."

Bignall nodded. "Yes, yes—you're right, of course you are. But she was obsessive about me. Everything I did affected Estelle. If I looked at her the wrong way, she developed symptoms of some illness or other. Everything she did was attention-seeking, and it was my attention she sought. She simply didn't consider other men." He shook his head. "This isn't boasting," he said. "It's just a fact. That's what I meant, really. Her other significant relationships were with women."

Lloyd nodded. "You say that what she's written in her diary—her journal—is about you," he said.

"I think so."

"Did you have a relationship with Estelle while you were married to someone else?"

"No. I had been divorced about a year before Estelle and I began our relationship."

"That isn't what she says in the diary, is it?"

"No," said Bignall. "But perhaps she felt like that about me before I was divorced. Or—given that she always accused me of having affairs with other women—maybe she was fictionally having an affair with me. Being the other woman. I don't know. Who knows what went on in Estelle's head? Not me."

"Do you think she meant you to read it?"

"Quite possibly. She made no attempt to hide it—she kept it by the bed. As I said, everything was done in order to get my attention, and she had lost it entirely by then."

"But you didn't read it—was that due to morality or lack of interest?"

"Guess." He looked down, then up again. "I know I don't come out of this very well," he said. "I'm a doctor, I had a sick wife, and I hadn't the faintest idea what to do with her. So I gave up. No—I wasn't in the least interested in her diary."

"But last night everything in the garden was suddenly lovely again?" said Tom.

Bignall looked at him for a moment. "No," he said. "But I remembered why I had married her. I wanted to try again. That's all. I don't know if it could have worked, and I never will. Because she died before I could find out."

"While you were driving around," said Tom.

At last Bignall lost his cool. "Yes!" he said. "While I was driving round! I'm sorry I can't prove that to your satisfaction, Sergeant Finch, but it just didn't occur to me to get a parking ticket or let some speed camera clock me doing eighty miles an hour. I didn't conveniently park somewhere I had to pay for, I didn't happen to wave to someone I knew. To the best of my knowledge I was not driving in the sort of place that has surveillance cameras—all I can tell you is that I drove around country lanes and tried to sort my life out, only to find out that some burglar had sorted it out for me!"

"We aren't convinced about the burglar," Tom said. "There are question marks over your wife's death, and the burglary itself."

And Bignall surprised him again. Lloyd had expected the anger to increase with righteous indignation at the suggestion being made.

But Bignall was nodding. "I thought there must be," he said. "Or you wouldn't have thought I'd had anything to do with it. Besides—they hardly took anything. I couldn't see why they would have to do something like that—why wouldn't they just run away with whatever they'd managed to grab?"

"Why did you tell Marianne Mackintosh that your wife had a cold?" asked Lloyd.

"I had to give her some reason for being so late," said Bignall. "I said Estelle wasn't well, because that was something she would just accept without asking questions."

"Why a cold in the head, particularly?"

Bignall shrugged slightly. "She asked if she had flu—I just downgraded it a little."

Lloyd really couldn't see any reason to continue the interview. He took Bignall up on his offer of a blood sample; the doctor could deal with that while he was dealing with Watson. Just because she and her husband had sexual relations prior to the break-in didn't mean that she hadn't been sexually assaulted, and the Pink Panther theory hadn't been disproved yet. Perhaps some psychotic friend of Baz Martin's *had* tied her up and raped her.

Besides, he still wasn't at all sure about Bignall, but until they had something more than very circumstantial and doubtful evidence, there seemed little point in keeping him here, however much of a motive he had. And they did still have the unidentified shoe prints and fingerprints to account for.

Back in the incident room he had a few moments before his alarm told him it was time to go home. He looked at Tom, who looked as puzzled as he felt. "What do you make of it?" he asked.

"He seemed genuine enough when he got angry," said Tom. "And I don't think his car was there, guv. He looked as if he thought you were making it up."

Lloyd nodded. "I think we have to assume that Ryan was making it up," he said. "Have you had any luck with the Pink Panther?"

"No," said Tom. "It was all a bit of a shambles—and it wasn't the same people using the costumes all the time, because people got so hot in them. I don't think it's possible to trace one of them in particular." He shook his head. "It would be a waste of time, anyway, guv. I reckon he got it all out of the paper."

Lloyd was beginning to see another puzzle presenting itself. "If Ryan's lying about seeing Bignall's car *and* about being in the traffic jam, then what was he doing?"

"Burgling the Bignalls' house," said Tom.

"Then who owns the shoe and fingerprints?"

"Probably the two uniforms," Tom answered morosely.

Lloyd sincerely hoped that Tom's throwaway remark wasn't right. Perhaps they had been demanding shoes and fingerprints from half of Malworth while all the time it had been the police called to the scene who had left the ones they'd found.

On the other hand, if they had, it would solve a lot of little puzzles.

Chapter Eight

"Thanks," Eric said as he was being shown out. "For nothing."

"I am terribly sorry if we inconvenienced you," said Finch, with heavy sarcasm. "You could have avoided a trip to the station if you had just told me the truth earlier."

Inconvenience *and* expense, thought Eric, as his solicitor made his way out ahead of him, his clock still running.

"Why didn't you think the break-in was worthy of even an anonymous call to the police?"

"I told you—I didn't give a damn." Eric stood in the open doorway. "I've had nothing but aggravation from them—why should I care if their house got robbed?"

"You weren't worried for Mrs. Bignall's safety? I mean—I know you didn't get along, but even so, you were a policeman once, and you thought the intruders were still on the premises, didn't you? You thought they were still there when the uniforms arrived—one of them said you'd called him out on procedure because he let his mate go into the house alone."

Eric shrugged. "Well, I hadn't seen anyone leave after Dexter," he said. "So I didn't think he should be letting that kid go in without backup, and I told him that."

"You were worried about a rookie cop running into the intruders, but Estelle Bignall could take her chances with them?"

"I thought she was out!"

"What made you think that?"

Eric sighed. "Because I saw him drive off, and she usually left before him on Mondays. I thought the house was empty apart from the burglars."

That seemed to interest Finch a great deal. Eric shook his head as he went out into the night. Cops. He'd never been able to work them out, not even when he was one.

Judy had been startled to hear Lloyd's car horn; she'd resigned herself to yet another solitary appointment. He really was trying very hard to be a new man, and she supposed she ought to be trying a lot harder to be a new woman.

She didn't even really want him with her, not from the caring, sharing point of view. Anyone would do for checkups, if she was honest. Her mother, her next door neighbor. Tom Finch, Alan Marshall. Even Joe Miller. She just didn't want to do any of this on her own, and if someone else was with her at the clinic, they could listen to the advice too, and it wouldn't be solely her responsibility to remember what she was supposed to be doing.

But it was definitely Lloyd whom she wanted there when she was actually giving birth. She had a feeling that something just might come up at work when that time arrived, and hoped she would be too busy to care.

Everything was fine, and now she and Lloyd were making their way out of the Health Center. She smiled at him. "How tempted were you to ring and say you couldn't get away?" she asked as they walked toward the small, rapidly emptying car park.

"Not very," said Lloyd. "We're getting nowhere fast. Bignall seems totally baffled about his car being seen there. And he dismissed the diary altogether. He thinks she was fantasizing."

"Marianne doesn't," said Judy. "She thought Estelle was seeing someone before she read her diary. Her Monday nights were very important to her, apparently. Marianne was really surprised when Carl said she was skipping it, thought she really must be ill."

Lloyd's mobile rang just as they got to the car; Judy got in while he took the call, trying to remember what it was like just to get into a car and sit down without having to think about it.

Lloyd got in. "It seems Marianne was right," he said. "We thought she'd been entertaining Papa at home, but she wasn't—she was going out every Monday. She might not have been going to her writer's group, but she was going somewhere."

Lloyd couldn't drive and theorize at the same time, so they just sat there while he worked on that. "So she didn't go off to her Monday evening tryst, did she?" he said. "And there's Papa, waiting for her wherever it is they meet. So what does he do when she doesn't turn up? He waits until he knows that Carl's gone and goes to her. And what does he find? That she's resumed relations with Carl and doesn't want to know anymore now that she has the real thing back."

Judy didn't need to hear the rest of this theory. It was the scenario as before, but with Papa rather than Carl in a jealous rage. This time it did account for the footprints, at least. But the big objection remained.

"It's the same problem we had with Carl," she said. "When did he tie her hands?"

"I'm still passing on that," said Lloyd, starting the car and turning to look out of the rear window as he backed out. "Speak of the devil," he said.

Judy twisted around but she couldn't see anyone she knew, never mind someone they had just mentioned. "Which devil?" she said.

"Carl Bignall," Lloyd said. "There's his car."

Judy looked at the handful of cars left but she still couldn't see it. "Where?"

"There!" he said impatiently. "Beside the Range Rover."

"What—the Saab turbo? That's not Carl's car."

Lloyd was staring at her. "What do you mean?" he said.

"He drives a Mazda," she said. "What made you think it was his?"

There was a silence before Lloyd answered. "Because it is if you do a vehicle check," he said slowly, and shook his head. "I should have realized when Ryan told me about the car in the first place. That car's four years old—Bignall was bound to have bought a new one in that time."

"He's had two new ones since I've known him," said Judy. "The one before was a BMW."

Lloyd looked across at the Saab. "Ryan Chester saw that car in Eliot Way at eight-fifteen last night." He looked back at Judy. "So who would be driving a car registered to Bignall and parking it here?"

Judy could think of only one person, and she knew that Lloyd neither needed nor wanted an answer. There was a moment when they were both unwilling to believe what they were both thinking; it was Lloyd who finally put it into words.

"Denis Leeward fits the bill. He's someone she's known a long time. An older man. Married. And if half of what Carl Bignall says about Estelle is true, she was in no fit mental state to make a rational decision about something like that. And it is true—think about what she wrote, Judy."

Judy could see the scrawled handwriting of the first account of this affair. *He made love to me tonight. I didn't really want him to, but he said it would help me, so I let him.* She swallowed as the tears that came embarrassingly easily to her in her current state welled up in her eyes. That wasn't just some fly-by-night chancer taking advantage of Estelle's fragile mental state, her crushing loneliness; that was her doctor, her friend, her husband's partner. "How well do you know Leeward?" she asked.

"Not particularly well. Not well enough to know if he would do something like that."

"We could be jumping to conclusions."

Lloyd shook his head. "We could, but I doubt it."

The scenario was a little different, though. And even more sinister. "Do you think he murdered her?" she asked.

"It answers your objection if he did. She might have been threatening to tell her husband what had been going on. He could see himself being struck off if he didn't stop her. The threat of being banned from practicing medicine might well have been motive enough." Lloyd sighed. "You'd better take the car home," he said, giving her the keys.

She got out and walked around, sliding over no longer being an option. "Good luck," she said.

"Thanks. I'll see you when I see you. It'll probably be very late." He gave her a kiss. "Drive carefully."

She got into the car and watched him as he walked back into the building. She missed all this. She didn't like sitting at a computer, and anyway, Joe Miller was running a betting pool on exactly when they would pull the plug on LINKS, because it would cost so much. Her forecast was even more pessimistic than his. Or optimistic, of course, depending on how you looked at it. It was a good idea, but it wasn't going to happen, and as far as Judy was concerned, the sooner they released her from her transfer, the better. She wanted to get back to doing real work. Her mother said that her views on that might change when the baby was born, but she doubted it.

"Take one three times a day," Denis said, handing his last patient a prescription. "If there's no improvement, come back and see me again."

As the door closed, his phone rang, and the receptionist told him that a Chief Inspector Lloyd wanted a word with him. Denis closed his eyes briefly and wondered just what the blood-pressure kit lying on his desk would register if he were to use it now. He steadied himself with deep breaths. "Yes, of course," he said, his voice sounding surprisingly normal. The right amount of puzzlement, the right amount of confidence.

"Lloyd!" he said, as heartily as he could, when his visitor arrived. "It's been a long time—how are you?"

"Well, thanks, Doctor," said Lloyd.

"How can I help you?" It was almost easy. Maybe he should have gone in for amateur dramatics, like the Bignalls.

"I'd like to talk to you about Estelle Bignall," said Lloyd.

"Dreadful business." Now he could switch to professional mode. "Of course, I can't discuss her medical history with you unless you think it has a direct bearing on her death, and in this case I don't see how it can."

"No, nothing like that," said Lloyd.

Denis was still holding the previous patient's medical records; he realized he was fiddling with the envelope, tapping it on the desk, turning it, tapping it, turning it, tapping it. And he realized it because Lloyd had noticed, his watchful blue eyes interested in this nervous reaction to his visit. It was odd, Denis thought: he had time, somehow, to wonder whether stopping would look worse than just continuing, as though it was just a habit, like drumming your fingers or stroking your chin. But the decision had been made for him; once it became a conscious act, he wasn't sure how to do it. He put the envelope in the out tray and indicated that Lloyd should ask his questions.

"Am I right in thinking that you drive the Saab parked outside?"

"Yes."

"And that it's registered to Carl Bignall?"

"Yes. He regards it as belonging to the practice, but I have the use of it."

"And can you tell me where it was last night at about eight-fifteen?"

Suddenly and without warning, Denis's intellect deserted him. "It—It was probably outside the Horse and Halfpenny," he said. "That's a pub in the village where I live."

"We've been told that it was at the rear of the Bignalls' house at that time."

"What? No—I don't think so. I—I don't think . . ." He tailed off, his brain having virtually ceased to function, then tried again. "I was with my brother Alan last night. All evening."

"Perhaps you could let me have his address?"

But he couldn't do that to Alan. It was one thing asking him to provide an alibi if Meg asked—Alan had, albeit reluctantly, been prepared to do that; Meg had never asked. But he couldn't expect him to do it if the police asked; for one thing, it would be unfair, and for another, he wasn't at all sure that Alan would do it.

"What? No. No—I wasn't with him. I was getting mixed up." He glanced at the clock above his door. Not quite twenty-two hours.

That was how long it had taken them to get on to him. "I—I can't remember where I was."

"Were you having an affair with Estelle Bignall?"

Denis thought about that for a long time before he gave Lloyd an answer. An affair presumably meant a love affair, but he hadn't loved her, and she hadn't loved him. She had loved Carl, to the point of obsession, but Carl hadn't even wanted her; he had grown tired of her, had lost interest in her, like he lost interest in his cars and his gadgets.

Carl, the man who had everything—looks and personality and a lifestyle to match—had by his indifference reduced someone who had refused to rely on drugs, who had held herself together by sheer strength of will, to a mass of neuroses and hang-ups within the space of twelve months. Denis had to begin all over again with her. He had advised her to leave the amateur dramatic society, to find something to do that didn't involve Carl. She had found a writer's circle that met on the same night as the society's rehearsals; she had chosen writing as her new hobby because that way she would only have to endure one evening away from Carl, and it might make him more interested in her if she wrote too. It wasn't quite what Denis had meant, but it had been a start.

The craziness had begun one Monday night, when she turned up at the surgery just as he was leaving. She had said she wasn't going back to the writer's circle, that she was going to join MADS again, because at least if she and Carl were acting together they had some communication. She had really believed that if she was acting, playing someone else, he might want her again, that as herself she was so unattractive, so ugly, so repellent, that he couldn't bring himself to make love to her.

Everything else Carl grew tired of came Denis's way; his car, his computer, his golf clubs. Why not his wife? Carl had passed responsibility for her over to him, and if he didn't want her, Denis did; he had wanted her for a long time. She had desperately needed something to raise her self-esteem, and he had provided it, telling himself, telling her, that it was all right; it was just treatment, like giving a heroin addict methadone. She had said he reminded her of Papa in the car ad—

he had called her Nicole, and somehow it had seemed like two other people altogether. And she responded to the treatment in the end.

"Dr. Leeward? Could you answer the question?"

It had been crazy, he knew that now. But it hadn't been an affair.

"No," he said.

"Did you see Estelle Bignall last night?"

"No."

"Were you in the Bignalls' house last night?"

"No."

"What size shoes do you wear, Dr. Leeward?"

Denis tried hard to make his brain function. "Shoes?" he repeated.

"Shoes. What size?"

"Eleven."

"And are those the shoes you were wearing last night?"

He nodded. He considered, briefly, picking the bit of glass out of the wastepaper basket, handing it to Lloyd, telling him everything. But he didn't.

"I would like you to come to the station to answer some questions in connection with the murder of Estelle Bignall," Lloyd said. "You are not under arrest, and you do not have to say anything, but it may harm your defense if you do not mention when questioned something you later rely on in court. You are entitled to free legal advice at any time, or you may ask us to contact a specific solicitor for you."

"Not under arrest?"

"No," said Lloyd. "But if you refuse to come voluntarily, I will place you under arrest."

Not under arrest. Not under arrest. That was all he had to hang on to. He wasn't under arrest. He should get his solicitor, really. But he wasn't under arrest, so they didn't know for a fact that he'd been in the house. If he just said nothing, then maybe there would be nothing they could prove. How many times had he heard them complain about suspects who said nothing? Every word you uttered could betray you. He could get out of this without Meg or Carl or anyone ever knowing.

That was it. He didn't need a solicitor to tell him to say nothing. He could do that for himself.

Lloyd had done what Tom privately called reading Leeward his rights, but Lloyd always gave him a lecture when he said it. In Britain, he would say, it was called administering the caution.

This, of course, ought not to be confused with the other caution, the official warning given to offenders if the police thought prosecution unlikely to benefit anyone, and it seemed to Tom that using the same word to mean two entirely different things was a bit eccentric, but Lloyd said the British legal system *was* eccentric, and he liked it that way. He'd already had to learn to live with autopsies instead of postmortem examinations, not to mention witnesses taking the stand instead of entering the witness box and testifying instead of giving evidence, and he was damned if he was going to have people read their rights into the bargain.

Tom usually liked irritating him, but he'd decided to cool it with that one, even though Judy had told him that Lloyd was pulling his leg and didn't really mind at all. He'd had too many dressing downs lately as it was, from practically everyone.

He had time to reflect on all of this because Leeward had said nothing. Absolutely nothing. He hadn't even confirmed his name. He had literally not opened his mouth, to the extent that Tom was seriously wondering if he was suffering from shock or something. Lloyd had repeated the contradictory statements Leeward made to him in his surgery, repeated his denial that he'd been having an affair with Estelle Bignall, had asked if he wanted to say anything more, but Leeward said nothing.

He had shown him the glove, asked if he recognized it, and Leeward said nothing.

He had asked him again if he'd been having an affair with Estelle Bignall, and Leeward said nothing.

The shoes had been taken over to the lab before it closed in the hope that they could be examined first thing in the morning; Lloyd sent a note with them, begging them to do them the minute they got in. It was Christmas Eve tomorrow, and Lloyd was absolutely determined to get this one sewn up, at least to the extent that Estelle Bignall's murderer had been charged, before the holidays hit.

Leeward's fingerprints had been taken, and they'd know tomorrow if he'd been in that house.

In the meantime they didn't have hard evidence with which to force a response out of Leeward, and he just sat there. Saying nothing.

"Did you see Estelle Bignall last night?"

Nothing. Tom felt extraneous to this cross-examination—he and Lloyd had worked out a strategy, but his rapid questioning approach only worked when people answered you. You couldn't trip someone up if they were saying nothing at all. Dr. Leeward had not wasted his years as a forensic medical examiner.

"Did you kill Estelle Bignall?"

That produced a flicker of something; his expression changed. And Lloyd capitalized on it immediately.

"Your shoes will be forensically examined, Dr. Leeward," he said. "They will be compared with impressions taken at the scene. Whoever wore the shoes that made those impressions walked into the Bignalls' house, and his shoes took brick dust with them. That brick dust will still be detectable. So if it was you, I suggest you tell us you were in that house before we tell *you* that you were."

Leeward nodded slowly.

Tom was startled; he almost forgot to mention it for the tape's benefit. "Dr. Leeward nods his head," he said.

"Are you admitting that you were in the Bignalls' house last night?" Lloyd asked.

"Yes," said Leeward.

Lloyd picked up his pen; it was Tom's turn now. "Why did you go there?" he asked.

"She hadn't turned up. I knew something had to be wrong—it was too important to her for her just not to turn up."

"What was?"

Leeward smiled a little. "Her methadone."

Tom stared at him, feeling his face grow red with anger. Freddie had phoned less than an hour ago and said he hadn't found any evidence of drugs in her system at all. What was Leeward trying to pull? "Are you trying to tell us she was a drug addict?" he said.

Leeward shook his head. "No," he said. "I was speaking figuratively."

"Well, I'd rather you spoke English."

"*I* was her methadone. I was trying to reduce her dependency on Carl, that's all."

"How?"

"By proving to her that she was desirable."

"How?"

Leeward still smiled. "The usual way," he said.

Tom ran a hand over his cropped hair and didn't speak for a moment, because if he had, he would have been calling Leeward very unpleasant names. "Are you now saying you *were* having an affair with Estelle Bignall?" he said, when he felt able to be civil.

"Yes," Leeward said. "If you want to call it that."

"What would you call it?"

"Therapy."

"*Therapy?*"

"Yes. But—it wasn't something I set out to do. I didn't mean it to happen. It just did. I thought it would help her. She was obsessed with him, and she . . . she seemed so alone. She said he wouldn't have anything to do with her, that he hated her, that she was so unattractive that he couldn't bear to touch her. Yes. At the time, I thought it was therapy."

Tom jumped on that. "At the time?" he repeated. "What do you think it was now?"

Leeward shook his head, and thought for a moment. When he spoke, it was in a mocking tone, stressing the word "think" each time he used it.

"I think," he said, "I was allowing myself to be deceived. I think she might not have told me the truth about their marriage, because Carl is devastated now that she's dead. I think I was just jealous of Carl, and I think she knew that, used that knowledge to . . . ensnare me, I suppose. That, Sergeant Finch, is what I think."

Tom was open-mouthed. "You took advantage of a vulnerable patient, and now you're saying she seduced *you*?"

"I suppose you've been made to believe that Estelle was a raving lunatic," Leeward said.

"No," said Tom, his voice cold. "We've been told she was a manic-depressive."

Leeward smiled again. "Labels," he said. "It's very easy to put labels on people. Psychiatrists love doing it."

"Are you saying there was nothing wrong with her?"

"No. There's no doubt she had psychological problems. But I think that Carl has a tendency to blow them out of proportion. He behaved to the outside world as though there were no problems at all, and all that does is exaggerate what problems there are when you have to go home to them."

"Is this relevant?" asked Tom.

"I think so. You said I took advantage of her, but Estelle was perfectly capable of living her life without Carl—she just didn't believe that she could. She was an intelligent woman, she was popular, she had friends. But she did have low self-esteem, and the impression given to me was that this was because of how Carl saw her. I saw her differently, and at the time I believed she needed to know that."

"By having sex with her?"

"The ethics involved here don't actually concern the police," Lloyd said. "It's a criminal offense if you work in a mental institution and have sex with a patient whom you know to be mentally ill, but that doesn't apply here, as I'm sure Dr. Leeward is aware."

"You're making it sound as though I *planned* it," said Leeward. "I just saw her there, in tears, desperate for Carl, who didn't want her anymore. She thought no one wanted her. I just wanted to prove to her that she was desirable. It was . . . crazy. I know that now. I think I got it all wrong, anyway, and I don't know how I allowed it to happen."

"How you *allowed* it to happen? You *made* it happen!"

"It takes two to tango, Sergeant Finch."

Tom tried to calm down. As Lloyd had just pointed out, all this was only relevant in as much as it gave Leeward a motive. He knew that he would be no use to Lloyd if he stayed angry; two-handed interviews only worked if you were aware of what the other was doing, and Lloyd was being the friendly cop. He was the aggressive one, but the aggression wasn't supposed to be real; Lloyd needed him to be on the team. He took a deep breath and expelled it slowly. "Why did you go there last night?" he asked.

"As I said, I was worried when she didn't turn up, because it was very important to her. I waited until I knew that Carl would have gone to his rehearsal, and I went over there. The house had been broken into, and I could see her in the kitchen. She was . . . tied up. Gagged. She was *dead*."

"I don't think so," said Tom. "I think she was alive when you got there. But you found out that she didn't need your so-called therapy anymore. That's why you think she lied to you about her marriage, isn't it? Why you think she deceived you? Because she told you that she and her husband had got it together that very evening."

"No," said Leeward, his eyes widening. "No."

"Then what happened?" Tom carried on, deliberately ignoring Leeward's denial. "She threatened to tell her husband? You went for her—she tried to get away from you? Ran into the sitting room, making for the French window? You caught her as she opened it, called her names, struggled with her, decided that she had to die. That's what happened, isn't it?"

Leeward was shaking his head.

"You were heard! The people next door heard a row. Then a scuffle—that was when you tied her hands so she couldn't defend herself, wasn't it?"

"No!"

"And then there was silence," Tom said. "That was because you had suffocated her, hadn't you? Then you got to work and made it look as though someone had broken in."

"No! No, she was dead! She was dead when I got there!"

Lloyd put down his pen. Tom sat back. He had enjoyed that; it had gotten some of the anger he felt out of his system.

"All right, Doctor," Lloyd said. "Tell me exactly what happened. From the moment you arrived."

Leeward looked nervously at Tom, then took a deep breath and calmed himself down. "I parked at the rear, but I couldn't get in that way, because the gates were locked. I was going to go round to the front, but as I walked past the house next door I realized I could get into their garden through that one. So that's what I did, and when I got to the house, I could see that the French window was broken. I opened it and saw there had been a burglary. And then I saw Estelle. I went to her, and felt her pulse, but she was dead. I didn't know what to do."

Lloyd frowned. "You had found a house that had been burgled and a woman dead, and you didn't know what to do? I can't really believe that, Dr. Leeward."

Leeward shook his head. "I had no reason for being there," he said. "I couldn't tell how long she'd been dead—I couldn't say she'd called me out, because for all I knew she might not have been able to. I had known Carl would be out, so I couldn't have been calling on him. Don't you see? If I'd called the police, it would all have come out. I'd lose my job, my marriage—everything. Everything. And she was dead—there was nothing anyone could do for her. It would have helped no one, and done a great deal of harm."

He pulled a handkerchief from his pocket, blew his nose. "Maybe if I'd taken just a moment to think I would have come to my senses. But I ran. I ran back out, and over the wall, but it was dark, and there were bricks piled up—I fell and hurt my ribs." He paused in his account to pull his shirt out and show them his bruised ribs, as though that proved something. "I picked myself up, got over the wall, and suddenly a light came on. I almost died of fright, and I just kept going until I got to the car. It wasn't until I was driving away that I realized I was only wearing one glove. I'd taken the other one off to feel for a pulse."

Lloyd shook his head. "Dr. Leeward, I'm sorry, but your story doesn't add up."

Leeward stared at him. "What?"

"What time did you get there?"

"I don't know for certain."

"Where had you arranged to meet Mrs. Bignall?"

"We met at the surgery."

"What time did you leave the surgery?"

"Quarter to eight—I wanted to be certain Carl was gone by the time I got there."

"And the journey takes how long?"

"I don't know . . . fifteen, twenty minutes. I got there just after eight, I think. A few minutes after eight."

"At a few minutes after eight the next door neighbors heard an altercation between a man and a woman. Then silence. Then a few minutes after that they heard a window breaking. Four people heard the window breaking, and one heard the bricks being dislodged. They all saw the security light. And you triggered it when you ran away. I think you broke that window. I think you killed Estelle Bignall and faked a burglary."

"No, no. No!"

Tom supposed that anyone who could convince himself that it was okay to screw your psychologically disturbed patients could convince himself that he hadn't done away with them, because Leeward truly seemed to believe that they had the wrong man. But five witnesses, even if one of them was Ryan Chester, was a bit difficult to get around.

"I—I saw the man who did it!" Leeward shouted. "He was trying to steal my car! He ran away."

That clinched it. Tom had never felt kindly disposed toward Ryan Chester, unlike Judy Hill. But he did now. Because he was going to put Leeward where he belonged.

Lloyd sighed. "Denis Leeward, I am arresting you on suspicion of murder. You do not . . ."

There was no reaction as Lloyd went through it all again, making certain the procedure was followed to the letter, because Leeward obviously knew something about all of this, and one slip-up could cause trouble if you weren't careful. Leeward was sitting there, his eyes wide, but they weren't seeing Lloyd, Tom was sure.

"You have the right to have someone informed of your arrest, and you can make a telephone call if you wish," Lloyd concluded.

"I think," Leeward said slowly, "that it was when I found the glass in the sole of my shoe that I knew I couldn't hope to get away with it."

"With what?" said Tom. "Murdering Estelle Bignall?"

His eyes seemed to focus for the first time since Lloyd had arrested him. "No," he said. "And I don't want to answer any more questions."

"Very well," said Lloyd. "Interview terminated, 7:05 P.M. We'll see how you feel in the morning, Dr. Leeward. I would advise you to think very carefully about legal representation. Take Dr. Leeward to the custody suite, Sergeant Finch."

Tom got wearily to his feet and took Leeward's arm.

"Can I phone my wife?" he asked.

"What's going on, Dex?"

Dexter looked at Ryan, his eyes wide with would-be innocence. "What do you mean?" he asked.

"I mean why were you anywhere near the Bignalls' house last night?"

"I went for a walk."

"Come on, Dex—don't give me that! What were you doing there? Who did that to you?" He shook his head. "And why did you lie about me?"

Dexter frowned. "I didn't," he said.

"You told them I wasn't there! You said you hadn't seen a car there!"

Dexter was shaking his head. "I didn't," he said.

Ryan leapt to his feet. "Were they lying to me? They've no right to do that. If they were lying, I'll—"

"No," Dex said, agitated. "No, Ryan—listen! I didn't mean I hadn't said that. I meant I *didn't* see you. Or a car."

"But you must have!"

"I didn't," said Dex. "There was no one there. The road was empty."

Ryan sat down again. What the hell was going on? He hadn't imagined the bloody car. So if Dexter really hadn't seen him, then it was Dexter who wasn't there. He looked at him. "Where were you?" he asked.

"Eliot Way."

"Before you were in Eliot Way."

"Nowhere." He looked scared.

"Dexter, tell me where you were!"

"I wasn't anywhere!"

And with that, he ran upstairs. Ryan heard his bedroom door slam, heard him crying. He thought about going after him, then thought better of it. He'd get nowhere. Better to leave him alone, let him calm down.

Whoever had done that to him had scared him. Scared him into lying about everything he'd done, everything he'd seen. And Dex *had* been a bit funny for a long time now, now that he came to think of it. His mother had noticed long before it got to this stage, and as usual had ignored it for as long as she could. But he had to have it rammed down his throat, hadn't noticed until the poor kid was beaten up and was upstairs crying his eyes out because he was too scared to tell even him the truth about what had gone on in Windermere Terrace last night.

Neither of them had been much help to Dex, whatever it was that he'd gotten himself mixed up in.

"He's been *arrested*?" Carl wouldn't have believed that things could become more incomprehensible, but they just had.

"He's at the Stansfield police station. I wanted to go, but he said they were locking him up for the night and I wouldn't be allowed to see him anyway."

Carl sat down with her on the sofa. Perhaps he was jumping to conclusions. "But what's he been arrested for?" he asked. "Drunk driving or something?"

She shook her head. "It—It's about Estelle, Carl," she said, her voice a whisper. "He says they've arrested him on suspicion of murder. It's ridiculous—I don't understand what's going on. It's obviously all some dreadful mistake. I don't understand why he hasn't told them that he was with his—"

"But—why?" Carl spoke through whatever she was saying. His head was spinning. "What's Denis got to do with what happened to Estelle? Why on earth would they—" And then, in the world's slowest double take, he realized why the police had been so certain his car had been outside his house last night.

Denis had been there. He put his hand to his mouth and closed his eyes, unwilling to think beyond that point.

"Carl?" she said, her voice fearful. "What is it?"

What in God's name had been happening in his house last night? He didn't know the answer to that, but he did know what had been happening with Estelle and Denis for the last two months. It hadn't been a fantasy. It hadn't been a writing project. It had been the truth.

He saw Meg's anxious face looking into his. "I—I think Denis was at my house last night," he said. "I think someone saw his car."

She looked puzzled. "No," she said. "He was with his brother. They've been going out for a drink on Monday nights for weeks. That's what I was going to tell you. It's all some mix-up, it must be. I don't know why he hasn't told them where he was, but Alan will clear it all up."

Carl shook his head. "I don't think so," he said. "I don't think he does go out with Alan on Mondays." His mind was racing through all the possibilities, rejecting all but one of them. His voice was far away, as if someone else was speaking. "I thought Estelle went to a writer's group, but she didn't."

"Carl, what are you saying?"

Carl closed his eyes, shook his head. "I think they were having an affair," he said. "She wrote about it in her journal. I thought she'd made it all up."

"Denis and Estelle?" she said, her lip trembling. "But he was—she . . . she was his patient! He wouldn't do that. She wasn't . . ." She tailed off, then swallowed. "She wasn't *well.*"

Carl half laughed, half sobbed. "Tell me about it," he said.

She hadn't been making it up about having an affair, he thought, and maybe she hadn't been making it up about Watson. He had to tell the police. Now. Dexter could be in danger.

"I—I've got to go, Meg," he said.

"Where?"

He didn't answer. "I'll be back as soon as I can."

Lloyd was busy when Carl got to the Stansfield police station, but he said he'd wait. He didn't want to talk to anyone else. He waited in the small anteroom at the entrance to the station, not exactly happy about what he was about to tell Chief Inspector Lloyd, but if he was right, Dexter had to be gotten out of the situation he had found himself in.

"Dr. Bignall," Lloyd said as he came in. "Have you remembered something that might be of use to us?"

"Not exactly," said Carl. "But I understand that Dexter Gibson was seen running away last night, and that you think he was running away from my house."

"I'm sorry," said Lloyd. "I'm afraid I can't discuss that with you."

"I realize you can't confirm it, but Janet herself told me. The thing is—I think I might know why Dexter was there."

"Oh?"

"I . . ." Carl took a moment. This was not going to show him in a good light, but he hadn't thought there was a scrap of truth in it. "I told you that Estelle got much worse when Watson moved in next door," he said.

"Yes," said Lloyd.

"She would say things about him. They sounded ridiculous. That she saw people going in there but she could never see them in the house, that he must have some secret room where he took them—all that sort of paranoid stuff."

Lloyd frowned. "Had she ever said that sort of thing about anyone else?"

"Not like that," said Carl. "And it sounded ludicrous. I asked her if she saw them come out again, because I thought she was accusing him of being a serial killer or something. And she said of course they came out again—it was what they were doing while they were in there that bothered her. And who they were doing it to. It really did sound crazy."

He saw Lloyd sneak a look at his watch. "Sorry," Carl said. "You've had a very long day—I realize that. And I am getting to the point. It's—It's just important to me that you understand the kind of climate we lived in."

"Oh, that's all right," said Lloyd. "Take all the time you need."

"The thing is, she went on like that about people all the time—well, not like that, exactly, but she was always thinking people were out to get her, up to something, conspiring against her. I really didn't think anything much about it."

"And now you think there was something to it?"

Lloyd clearly thought it was time he stopped trying to justify his lack of interest, though he honestly did feel it had been justified. Estelle's misgivings about everyone and everything had been constant, her capacity for invention staggering at times. He'd grown used to ignoring her.

"I don't know if there was something to it," he said. "But in the summer she told me she'd seen Dexter Gibson leaving Watson's house, that she believed Watson was sexually exploiting him, that the other people she saw going in there were abusing him and Watson was photographing it all in this secret room. That was too much—I told her to get help from someone more qualified in that area than Denis." He felt his face burn. "I know how that sounds. But—But I had to live with that sort of thing day in, day out. I'd long ago exhausted my supply of understanding."

Lloyd didn't speak. Carl had no idea what he was thinking.

"And then she told me that when she was thirteen she desperately wanted to be a model or an actress—you know, like little girls do. She was in a school play, and Eric Watson came to take photographs for the program. He told her that if she wanted to be a model, she had to have photographs to show the agencies, and he would take them for her, that she wouldn't have to pay him, just help him out with some odd jobs."

"I expect I can guess the rest," said Lloyd.

Carl nodded. "She found that the 'odd jobs' meant taking her clothes off and modeling in provocative poses for him. He told her that models and actresses had to get used to that sort of thing, so she did it. And then he said he would like her to pose with other people, and he would pay her to do it. She agreed to that as well, and found she couldn't get out of it—whenever she said she didn't want to do something, he would threaten to send the photographs to her grandfather. So she found herself performing all manner of sexual acts with all manner of people in all manner of places until she was too old to be of interest to him."

"And you didn't believe her when she told you this?"

He sighed. He knew what it sounded like, but she'd been dramatizing herself and her life for years. "No," he said. "I thought she was just trying to draw attention to herself, as usual. I told her that she would find herself in court if she continued saying things like that."

"Did she say that Watson himself had abused her?"

"No." Carl frowned, thinking about that. If he hadn't dismissed it as he had, perhaps that would have struck him, but it hadn't. "I should probably have taken more notice of that, shouldn't I? It's not the sort of detail you'd expect in a fantasy."

He was reminded then of Finch, who had said almost exactly that about Estelle's journal. He obviously wasn't very good at spotting the truth when he saw or heard it.

"She told me that he just took the photographs," he said. "That he called the people who bought them pervs."

"If she thought he was doing that to Dexter, did she try to do anything about it? Did she speak to Watson about it?"

Carl shook his head. "I don't know."

"And she didn't contact us, I presume."

"No. I tried to call her bluff, told her to tell the police, but she said if it went to court, she couldn't bring herself to give evidence, which I said was very convenient." He shook his head. "I know I sound like a brute, but I'd had years and years of her paranoia—I thought this was just a new twist."

"What's changed your mind?"

Carl shook his head. "I have no more proof now than I had then. But I know you've arrested Denis Leeward." He shook his head. "I don't think for a minute that Denis had anything to do with Estelle's death, but I am assuming it was his car that was seen, and that he is the lover Estelle was writing about."

Lloyd didn't confirm that, of course, but if he'd been wrong, Carl was sure that Lloyd would have put him right.

"If she was telling the truth about that, then I have no reason to suppose she wasn't telling the truth about Watson. And what I do know is that Watson has a studio in Welchester—which is where Estelle lived until she was fifteen—and that he met Dexter during the school holidays, when Dexter came to my house with his mother one day, and now I know that he does a Saturday job for Watson. And the more I thought about it, the more I realized it could explain an awful lot about Estelle and the way she was, couldn't it? It would certainly explain how she was about Watson."

"It would," said Lloyd.

"And Estelle said she saw Dexter coming out of Watson's house, so if he was seen running out of Watson's garden last night, it seems possible he was in Watson's house rather than mine."

Lloyd nodded seriously and stood up, holding open the door much as Carl himself had held the door open for Marianne, no doubt with just as much relief that his visitor was going.

Carl got to the door. "If that story about Watson is all just a sick fantasy of Estelle's, I'm sorry. And I didn't mean to take up so much of your time, but I wanted you to understand why I didn't react the way another husband might have reacted to his wife telling him something like that. If I'd thought for a minute it was true, I'd have tried to get Dexter out of it."

"Thank you, Dr. Bignall. I will look into it."

Carl paused. "I hope it *was* a sick fantasy," he said. "Or if it wasn't, I hope that Dexter is better able to cope with it than Estelle was."

He left the police station feeling a little bit better now that he'd told them what he feared about Dexter, and a little less confused. At least he knew who one of the people was who had been in his house last night. But the police had said there were two sets of unidentified fingerprints, and that was what worried him. Was the other person just a burglar? Or was that also someone he knew?

❦

At nine-fifteen Lloyd left the busy Riverside Family Center, having spoken to Mrs. Gibson, who was going to bring Dexter to see him at the Malworth police station, preferring that to having him visit Dexter at home. He was taking Estelle a great deal more seriously than her husband had done, and not just because he felt heart sorry for this woman who had found herself being exploited all her life by every man she had ever met, but because what had come across very clearly from his interviews with Mrs. Gibson's sons was that Ryan was very fond of Dexter, and that Dexter was not at all afraid of him. But Dexter was afraid of someone, and that someone was looking ever more like Eric Watson.

Lloyd had done some checking up with people whose local knowledge was more extensive than his; twelve years ago, when Estelle would have been thirteen years old, the West End Studio had been in a backstreet in Welchester, part of an old tenement building divided into small units, and it still was. It was by no stretch of the imagination successful, and yet Watson had bought a house in a very expensive area of Malworth, had one full-time employee in the studio, and usually employed at least one youngster after school or on Saturdays, paying them well. So where had he gotten the money? Tom had rightly been suspicious of his affluence all along.

His interview with Mrs. Gibson had gone better than he could possibly have hoped, given the very disturbing idea that he was presenting to her. Once she got over the initial shock, she pulled herself together, and he felt that she wouldn't go to pieces on him if they found out that the same thing had been happening to Dexter as had happened to Estelle. Most important of all—she understood that her presence might inhibit Dexter, and agreed to a social worker being present instead if that proved to be the case.

At half past nine they came in to see him, and Lloyd got straight to the point as soon as the interview began; if there was nothing in it, they would soon know. "What sort of work do you do for Eric Watson, Dexter?"

And he saw it; the instant evasion, the dropping of those expressive eyes, the shrug. "Go out with him on jobs," he said.

"What sort of jobs?"

"Photo shoots. For catalogues and calendars and things." Dexter still wouldn't look at him.

"What sort of catalogues and calendars?"

A shrug. "Clothes and that. Scenery."

"And what do you do on these photo shoots?"

"Just make sure he's got film in all his cameras, and fetch things when he needs them."

"And where do these photo shoots take place?"

"All over."

"Has he ever asked you to model for him?"

He shook his head.

"Have you ever been in Mr. Watson's house?"

He shook his head more vehemently, but he didn't speak.

"I think you have, Dexter. Mrs. Bignall saw you there once, didn't she?"

His head still shook, his lips tightly closed, his eyes cast down.

"And I think you were in his house again last night."

Still just the constant shaking of his head.

"Did he give you that beating?" asked Lloyd.

Dexter's head stopped shaking, but he didn't answer.

"Okay," said Lloyd. "Tell me more about the photo shoots. Tell me exactly what you do."

Nothing. Not even a shrug.

Paradoxically, Lloyd knew that this lapse into total noncommunication meant that he was getting there at last, and so did Mrs. Gibson, who put her hand on her son's back, gently patting him.

"Dexter," she said. "Tell Mr. Lloyd. You're not in trouble. Not with the police, and not with me. Just tell him what goes on."

Dexter's eyes slid around to look sideways at her.

"Do you want me to go?" said Mrs. Gibson.

He nodded, and Mrs. Gibson left, to be replaced by the social worker, who breezily informed Dexter that nothing he said could possibly shock him. He had seen it all, heard it all, and these things had been going on since time began. And from there, slowly at first, the story came out. No prompting, no suggesting. Dexter wanted to talk, and now that he knew they knew, he had no reason to stay silent.

His story was the same, in all essentials, to the one Estelle had told Carl Bignall. Watson had talked to Dexter the day he'd gone with his mother to the Bignalls' house, had found out that Dexter desperately wanted to act, and told him that he made movies. He said that actors needed publicity photographs, offered to do some for him if he would help him out in his studio in return, and maybe one day he could act in one of his films.

The publicity photographs had been done, as promised, and then the payoff—nude modeling. The subsequent photographic sessions had been held all over, as Dexter had said. Abandoned warehouses, secluded woodland, the back rooms of clubs, occasionally in the Welchester studio itself. Watson would pick him up and take him to wherever he had chosen for that day's shoot.

But Watson had moved on in twelve years, and one day Dexter was taken to Watson's house. Watson had driven into the garage, let Dexter in by the kitchen, and they went upstairs, then up again into the windowless roof space that Watson had converted into a film studio. Dexter had been very impressed by the secret loft hatch.

Dexter confirmed that Mrs. Bignall had seen him at Watson's house once and asked him what he was doing there. But he hadn't told her. He confirmed that he had never, until last night, been injured by Watson in any way, that Watson himself had never taken part in the films, just directed other people. It was only for a few hours a week, and he got paid for it, so he didn't mind it all that much.

Indeed, Dexter seemed to have taken it all in stride. But who knew how Estelle had felt about it at the time? Perhaps it was only later, when she tried to form real sexual relationships, that her problems had begun. Or perhaps her problems had begun long before that, when her parents died. Perhaps that was why everyone could, and did, exploit her. Dexter was different; he had his mother and his brother, and whatever their shortcomings, their love was unconditional.

His mother blamed herself for not finding out what had been troubling Dexter, but Lloyd didn't blame her. With a hell-raiser like Ryan to keep an eye on, she would relax her vigilance with the apparently trouble-free Dexter, put any moodiness and secretiveness down to his age. He suspected that with one son constantly breaking the law and the other exposed to child porn, she wouldn't get the social services people out of her hair for some time to come, but he still felt that as a family, they could make it.

What seemed clear was that Eric Watson didn't want to use overwise street kids; he wanted innocence, and got youngsters into his clutches on a pretext, offered financial inducements, introduced them to what he required of them bit by bit, and then used blackmail to ensnare them if they showed signs of wanting out.

He doubtless only approached the ones he recognized as vulnerable to his initial offer, and had homed in on Dexter's desire to act, just as he'd homed in on Estelle's wish to be a model. And Lloyd didn't suppose it was an accident that they were both children who lacked the traditional complement of parents, though he could already hear Judy giving him an argument about that. She believed that one-parent families were just as viable as any other, that values were instilled by example, and one parent could set an example just as easily—perhaps more easily—than two.

He wondered where she would stand intellectually on the responsibilities of parenthood now; would she hold Mrs. Gibson entirely responsible for failing her sons, or would their own impending responsibility temper her judgment? Would she be a little more sympathetic to the traditional setup once she knew what an enormous undertaking it really was?

When Dexter had finished his statement with regard to Watson's usual activities, Lloyd turned to the assault.

"What happened yesterday, Dexter?" he asked.

"He came to see me after my mum had gone to work," said Dexter.

"What time was that?"

"About half four. He said I had to go with him to his house. I said it was supposed to be just Saturday mornings, but he said Saturday was part of the Christmas holiday and I wouldn't be needed then. He said I had to go because he'd paid for three other people to be there."

"And what did you say?"

"I said I couldn't because I had a rehearsal for the pantomime, but he said I'd better get out of it. So I called Marianne and told her I wasn't well."

Lloyd nodded. "What happened when you got to his house?"

"We went up to the studio, but someone came knocking on the door and wouldn't go away. He went down, and I could hear Estelle and him arguing. She said she knew what he was doing and she was going to go to the police about it."

Lloyd could see the tears not far away; he let Dexter gather himself without hurrying him.

"Then he came back up and we worked for about three hours. Then at eight o'clock I said I had to go home because it would take me an hour to walk it and my mum comes home at ten past nine. He said the others could have a break, and went down into the house. I got dressed, and when I went down he was waiting for me in the kitchen, and he just went ballistic at me. He said I'd been talking to Estelle about him. I said I hadn't told her anything, but he didn't believe me. He said he couldn't use me anymore because she knew about me. It was ten past eight, and I said I had to go, but he swore and came at me, so I ran out through the garage. I thought it would be dark and I would be able to hide from him, but the security light was on so I just ran out, but he caught me at the door and dragged me back in."

Lloyd made a mental note to come back to that. "And what did Watson do then?"

"He said I'd be sorry I'd talked to Estelle."

"Did he call her 'Estelle' when he said that?" asked Lloyd.

"No," said Dexter, and told Lloyd what Watson had called her.

Lloyd had the exceedingly small satisfaction of knowing he'd been right in the first place about the "woman" Jones had heard being assaulted.

"And then he hit me. He said if anyone asked, I had fallen down some steps, and if I said anything different, I'd get worse the next time. He went back into the house after that."

"And what did you do?"

"I stayed there. My nose was bleeding and I felt sick. I didn't want to go home. I didn't know what I was going to tell my mum and Ryan—I knew Ryan wouldn't believe me if I said I fell. I stayed there until I heard the window break. I was scared he'd think I'd done it, so I ran. I heard him yelling at me to come back, but I just kept running as fast as I could."

Lloyd sat back and looked at Dexter. "Do you think you could say all this in court, Dexter?" he asked.

"Will my mum be there?"

"Probably," said Lloyd. "But I think she'll have a good idea what's been going on anyway."

Dexter looked resigned, and nodded.

"Now—could I just go back over your statement and ask you some more questions?"

Dexter nodded.

Lloyd cleared up a few details and then moved on to the ones that interested him in regard to Mrs. Bignall's death and the supposed burglary.

"You ran into the garage at ten past eight, is that right?"

"Yes."

"And the security light was on? Had someone else arrived by the back way after you?"

"No. They were all there when I got there. And Estelle came to the front door."

"Can you remember when the light went off again?" Lloyd asked.

"It went off just as he caught hold of me."

"So that would still be at about ten past eight? And did it come on again while you were in the garage?"

"No. It was dark all the time until I ran away. It came on then."

"Good lad. Now, we'd like to take photographs of these bruises, and get your statement typed up for you to sign. Your mum's waiting for you—she'll go with you."

Then he remembered that Dexter was a witness, of sorts. "When you ran away from Watson's house, did you see Ryan?"

"No."

Lloyd smiled. That was always going to be the answer as long as he thought that saying he had seen Ryan would mean getting his brother into trouble. And perhaps Ryan hadn't arrived when Dexter emerged from Watson's garden. The next question was a little more important.

"Did you see a car?"

"No."

"Is that the truth, Dexter?"

"Yes."

Lloyd went back to Stansfield and arranged for another dawn raid to take place. He'd be heading this one himself, which wasn't something he would choose to do, but he'd sent Tom Finch home after they handed Leeward over to the custody sergeant, because Tom had been practically asleep on his feet. Lloyd didn't hold out much hope for the raid; Watson had had a great deal of police interest, and Lloyd doubted that anything worth seizing would be left in his studio.

But there was a fax on the machine that told him the fingerprints on the window frame and the shoe prints on the patio were none other than Eric Watson's, and at first Lloyd felt excited about that, until he realized that it meant very little. Forensics had found nothing to suggest that the person on the patio had gone inside.

Which was a pity, because he wasn't convinced that Denis Leeward had killed Estelle. Watson had seemed a good bet, if just for a moment.

Chapter Nine

Judy opened her eyes as Lloyd slipped into bed beside her, and shifted herself into a more comfortable position.

"Sorry," he said. "Go back to sleep."

"I can't." She knew that already. Sleeping had never presented a problem to her; she'd always been able to sleep, no matter what, and waking up in the middle of the night had once been unheard of, but Lloyd's habit of watching old movies until two in the morning had gotten her used to it, and she would just go back to sleep, unless they could think of something more interesting to do. But at the moment going back to sleep was difficult, and the diversion simply too awkward. "Are you sleepy?" she asked.

"No," he said, turning on the light. He grinned at her. "We could play cards, I suppose."

"You can bring me up to date." Judy rearranged her pillows and sat up. "How did the interview with Leeward go?"

If all police officers were like Lloyd, she thought, there would be no need to tape interviews. Unlike her, he remembered every word uttered. She had to write things down, but with Lloyd it was as good as being there. It was the same with films, or TV programs—she often thought she'd actually seen something that she had been told about by Lloyd.

He didn't say so, but she could tell Lloyd wasn't convinced that Leeward had murdered Estelle, and there was something in his account of the interview that had seemed wrong. She couldn't quite pin it down, but she would. She glanced at the clock, frowning when she saw the time. She assumed it would be the middle of the night, and it was just after midnight—early evening as far as Lloyd was concerned. "Why are you in bed so early?" she asked.

"I have to be up at half past five."

She felt even sadder about Estelle Bignall when Lloyd told her about Watson. He didn't hold out much hope for the raid.

"I'm not even certain we can get him for assaulting Dexter," he said. "One witness who saw nothing and couldn't identify the voices—it isn't good. If he denies it . . ." He shrugged. "With no Estelle to back up what Dexter's told me, I'm not sure we're going to get anywhere."

"But you know he was at the scene of crime and has denied being there," Judy said. "That's something to go on, isn't it?"

"Yes," said Lloyd. "But he couldn't have done it. The only time he could have, we know where he was, because Dexter's told us."

"*I* know that," said Judy. "And *you* know that. But would the Crown Prosecution Service know that? Would a jury know that?"

Lloyd smiled. "You seem to be suggesting framing him," he said. "I presume it's your hormones again."

She hit him. "No," she said. "I'm merely suggesting that if you discount what Dexter's told you—which he will be urging you to do—then you could build up a case against Watson. I shouldn't have thought letting a little thing like knowing he didn't do it put you off—you *don't* know he didn't do it. You don't *know* Dexter's telling the truth."

Lloyd's eyes widened as he understood what she was suggesting. "Brilliant," he said, and kissed her. "I think I'd better try to get some sleep—do you want me to leave the light on?"

"No," she said, adjusting her pillows once more, and maneuvering herself into her sleeping position.

When the light was out, and she was awake, thinking about what Lloyd had said, she knew what had been bothering her about Leeward. "Lloyd?" she said into the darkness.

"Here."

"How did Leeward get glass in his shoe?"

⸙

They'd been all over the house like a plague of bloody locusts, taking away all the equipment, all the props, everything they could lay their hands on. Nearly twenty years he'd been doing this, and had virtually no trouble at all, certainly not since he'd been doing it full time. No cops had ever so much as crossed the threshold except for that raid that left them with egg on their faces. Not even though he worked out of a backstreet studio so sleazy it might as well have had a sign outside saying CHILD PORN AVAILABLE HERE.

Because he'd been careful. Never went so far that the kids would go running to the police despite the consequences. Just got them to do enough to keep the pervs happy, and paid them enough to keep quiet about what they were doing. And in all that time, he had only once made the initial approach to someone who told his parents, and he'd smoothed that over. Just a misunderstanding. Only two of his employees had needed a reminder to keep their mouths shut, and Dexter was the first one of the kids to cause a problem. Dexter was why he was sitting here now, but Dexter wasn't the original cause of his problems.

Since he'd moved to Malworth, he'd had cops in the house five times, thanks to that madwoman next door. She was the one who got to Dexter, and despite his advice to the boy, Dexter had told the cops everything; obviously, because they'd shown him the search warrant, gone straight upstairs to the landing and released the ceiling molding to get into the loft. But they found nothing worth finding, because he had made sure of that. They'd raided the Welchester studio too, but they wouldn't find anything there either.

So all they had was Dexter Gibson's word against his about everything, including the assault. He'd be walking out of here in no time, and he had decided to let his expensive solicitor stay in bed this morning. It was Christmas Eve, after all, and he could handle this himself.

He denied everything that Dexter had said about the photographs and the films, and now Lloyd was moving on to the assault.

"It's been alleged that you assaulted Dexter Gibson in the garage of your home between eight and eight-fifteen on Monday night," Lloyd said. "Have you anything to say about that?"

"I didn't assault anyone."

"Was Dexter Gibson in your house that night?"

"No. I heard a window break, came out, and saw him running away, that's all." He smiled. "And you can't prove any different."

"We now have reason to believe that your next door neighbor, Mrs. Bignall, knew of your activities and threatened to go to the police," said Lloyd. "You held Dexter responsible for this, which is why you assaulted him."

God, that was the oldest trick in the book. Lloyd was trying to get him to say that Dexter was lying about what the mad cow had said, thus proving that Dexter was in his house. He'd have to sharpen up his act a bit if that was the best he could do.

"That's rubbish," said Eric. "What activities? The woman was a nutcase. I keep telling you. She accused me of everything under the sun."

"How long had you known her, Mr. Watson?"

Eric frowned. "What's that got to do with the price of fish?" he said. He couldn't understand why he was being asked, but he couldn't see how answering it could hurt. "I didn't know her at all. I moved in next door to her in February. I saw her from time to time, that's all."

"Did you ever take photographs of her?"

"For the umpteenth time, no. I didn't spy on her, and I didn't take any photographs of her."

"Never?"

"No, never!"

"Are you sure about that?"

"Of course I'm sure! What the hell are you bringing all this up again for? I told you yesterday I'd never taken any photographs of her. And I told that WPC at the time—I was photographing blue tits feeding. I'm sorry it was something with suggestive connotations, but that's what I was doing! And it's *all* I was doing! Why the hell would I want to photograph her?"

"Cast your mind back," said Lloyd.

Eric frowned. "To when?"

"To a thirteen-year-old girl to whom you offered a Saturday job," said Lloyd. "You keep excellent business records, Mr. Watson. Everything by the book. But then, you didn't want to get caught in the same way as Al Capone, did you?"

"What?"

"You didn't want bureaucracy to get in your way. You pay your taxes, and you charge VAT, and children must be thirteen years old before they do any work in your studio or accompany you on your photo shoots, mustn't they? All in accordance with the Children and Young Persons Act. Very commendable."

The Saturday job was a great cover—he wouldn't risk being found out by having officialdom sniffing round. He didn't want to use little kids anyway. You could get away with a lot more once they were thirteen, fourteen, and the sentences weren't as daunting if you got caught, providing you'd been careful. So he used them when they were prepubescent—the pervs liked them like that. Almost, but not quite, adults.

And they always did it voluntarily, at least to start with—if they said no to the nudie pics, he didn't take it any further. If they said yes, then he knew he'd got them, and he'd hang on to them until postpubescence. Once the down had turned into hair and their voices had broken, they were no use to him, so he had to make the most of them while he had them.

"Estelle Greaves," said Lloyd. "Remember her? She was your first Saturday employee."

Estelle. Sure, he remembered Estelle. He didn't use many girls; they matured too early. By the time they were thirteen, some of them were having babies; they might be kids in the eyes of the law, but they weren't what his pervs wanted. Estelle had been a late developer; at thirteen she was just right. Good little body. Just the right waiflike proportions, but with a hint of adolescence. The photographs were doing good business on the net even now.

He couldn't see what she had to do with anything. "What about her?"

"She became Mrs. Estelle Bignall," said Lloyd.

Eric stared at him in sheer disbelief.

"You didn't know?"

Jesus. He had had no idea. He'd never heard Mrs. Bignall's first name, or he might have made the connection. But Christ Almighty, the woman had worked for him. No wonder she knew why Dexter was there. But she was dead. It was still just Dexter's word against his.

"Well?"

He gathered his thoughts. "Yes, I remember her. I did take photographs of her—I did a modeling portfolio for her. She worked for me for a couple of years, I think."

"I think you did rather more than a modeling portfolio in the way of photographs."

Eric shook his head, smiling again. "No," he said. "And there's no way she can give you a statement lying in the morgue."

"Quite," said Lloyd. "I think you had good reason to want Mrs. Bignall out of the way."

Too true, he had; the crazy bitch had given him nothing but grief since he'd moved in. Then Eric realized what Lloyd was saying and his mouth dropped open. "Now, wait a minute," he said. "I didn't kill her. And you can't go saying I did."

"Can't I?" said Lloyd. "Your fingerprints have been found on the frame of the Bignalls' French window, and your shoe prints on the patio. Can you account for that?"

Oh, Jesus. He must have stepped in wet earth when he went over the wall. He hadn't known the woman had been killed, for God's sake. He simply hadn't thought about it. He hadn't been taking precautions—why would he? He thought whatever shoe prints they'd found belonged to burglars, not him. And the fingerprints hadn't even occurred to him; he hadn't realized he touched anything, but he wasn't trying not to. He had actually forgotten they would have his fingerprints on file. "I did go and have a look," he said. "But that's all."

"Then why didn't you tell us that in the first place?"

Eric sighed. Because the last thing he had wanted was to be involved in a police investigation into a break-in from which Dexter Gibson was seen running away. Well, no, the *last* thing he'd wanted was to be blown up in a gas explosion; that was why he'd gone there in the first place.

"As I was walking back from the greenhouse I could hear this hissing noise," he said. "I thought it was rain—you know, the way you do. It wasn't until I got back in that I realized it had stopped raining. And then I thought—well, I'd been assuming that Dexter had broken the window for some reason, but for all I knew it was some sort of gas buildup that had blown the window out. So, I went over and had a look."

"And?"

"And I saw they'd been burgled. But the noise had stopped, there wasn't a smell of gas, so I just went back in the house."

"A hissing noise?" said Lloyd, his face amused. "Gas? Am I being invited to believe that, by any chance?"

"Yes," said Eric, beginning to feel panicky. The truth always sounded worse than lies. "Am I being accused of murder here?"

"You admitted being on the Bignalls' premises only after repeated denials, and only when forensic evidence had been produced which proved that you had. Estelle Bignall lodged a complaint about you with the council alleging that you were intimidating her. You had a visit from her at about five o'clock on the day of her death, threatening to make your activities known to the police, a visit which was witnessed by Dexter Gibson. She worked for you when she was a child, and you have in this very interview indicated how her death has benefited you in that regard. You are undoubtedly a suspect."

"I had nothing to do with what went on in that house!" said Eric. "And there's no way you've found anything on me inside the house, so you've got no case against me."

"No? You told us you saw Carl Bignall leave at half past seven. Is that correct?"

"Yes." Eric wished it wasn't, but it was. Whoever had killed her had done Bignall a favor. But it hadn't been Bignall himself, because he hadn't been there.

"So to your certain knowledge, from half past seven onward, Estelle Bignall was alone in the house. And during that time someone murdered her. Someone who had no need to leave fingerprints or shoe prints—someone who was quite possibly admitted by the front door. Somebody she knew. That someone could undoubtedly have been you, Mr. Watson."

Bloody hell. It could.

"Later, you produce circumstances in which Dexter Gibson will be seen to be running away from the scene by the simple expedient of preventing him from leaving when he intended to, beating him up and then five minutes later stepping over the wall into the Bignalls' house and breaking their window, knowing he would run from any more trouble."

Eric swallowed.

"So I would like to know what you were doing between seven-thirty and eight-fifteen last night, Mr. Watson." He sat back and tipped his chair onto its rear legs, swinging very gently back and forth. "If you have an alibi, then I'm happy to listen to it."

Eric stared at him.

Lloyd smiled. "The words rock and hard place come to mind."

Eric asked for his solicitor and was taken to the cells. He sank down on the bench as the door banged behind him, and wished with all his heart that he *had* murdered the cow.

Denis found himself awake very early; the unusual noises, the necessary loudness of keys in locks, of metal doors opening and closing as they put someone in the cells, were bound to bring anyone to consciousness.

He didn't have his watch, but he could tell by the feel of the place that it was early morning. They took his belongings last night, listed them, got him to sign for them, and asked if he wanted any of them back. He hadn't wanted them back; having no belongings added to the paradoxical freedom that he had felt the moment he was arrested.

He could see that police cells might frighten the uninitiated, but the racket kicked up by the victims of Christmas excess was one that he was used to, and once all the banging and shouting had died down, and his fellow detainees were released or finally succumbed to sleep, it had become strangely calming to be locked in a little room with a bunk and a toilet and nothing else.

Because in here, under arrest, nothing at all was his responsibility. The people outside the room, whose footsteps he had heard as they checked on the drunks, had decisions to make, duties to attend to, orders to give and carry out. He didn't. All he had to do was wait until they decided it was time to feed him. And in the meantime, sleep had come relatively easily.

Now that he was awake, he still felt safe. For the first time he understood the monks who entered closed orders, the ones who took a vow of silence, whose only obligation was to their God. No one could reach him in here; no one could expect anything of him.

Life imprisonment might not be such a dreadful option after all.

Not nine o'clock yet, and Lloyd felt as though he had actually achieved something. And now that the rest of the world was waking up, the incident room was awash with e-mails and faxes as the lab pulled out all the stops, also eager to get this one put to bed before Christmas.

Lloyd perched on the corner of Tom Finch's desk as he read them. The prints on the door between the dining room and the kitchen were Denis Leeward's, as they had presumed. Lloyd was sincerely thankful that they didn't have yet another set of prints to account for, but Leeward was bothering him all the same, especially after what Judy had said.

The cushions and pillows had proved innocent of anyone's saliva, except one, and that, he was assured by the lab, had been only the small amount produced by someone sleeping with his or her mouth open and did not in any way indicate that the pillow had been used to smother someone.

Tom came in, and was duly impressed by the way Lloyd had backed Watson into a corner. Lloyd did credit Judy with the idea, but the Judy-proof theory had been his, and he was proud of it.

"A gas leak?" said Tom, grinning.

Lloyd nodded. "I couldn't believe my luck when he said that. What jury in the world would believe him?"

"So he's looking at a trial for murder or a full confession about his filming activities? Nice one, guv."

The report on Leeward's shoes came in, and Tom removed it from the fax, sitting down and reading it while Lloyd looked over the notes he'd taken while Dexter had given him his statement. Dexter went into the garage and the security light was on. It went out almost immediately, and didn't come on again until he, Dexter, caused it to come on by running away when the window broke.

"Are we charging Leeward, guv?" asked Tom. "Or did you want to get more detail?"

Lloyd looked up from his notes. "I don't think he did it, Tom. What he said last night rang true. Taking off his glove to feel for a pulse—that makes sense."

"What? We've got five witnesses, guv—you said so yourself."

"I know," said Lloyd. "But I think we've got four witnesses to one thing, and just one witness to the other."

Tom looked baffled.

"He told us he found glass in the sole of his shoe," Lloyd said.

"Yeah," said Tom uncomprehendingly, and held out the report. "The lab found glass too. Traces of glass and brick dust in the soles of both shoes. Just the same as was walked into the carpet. What's wrong with that?"

"Judy wants to know how he got it," said Lloyd. "And so do I. Why would he have glass in the soles of his shoes? If he did what we assumed he did, he would have killed Estelle, tied her up, gagged her, taken the bin bag from the roll, shoved the Christmas presents and a couple of other things in it, and left, pausing only to pick up a brick and break the window. With him on one side and the glass on the other."

Tom scratched his crew cut. "Guv—you're getting as bad as the forensic guys. We don't know *what* he did—it probably wasn't all as neat and efficient as that. Maybe he had to go back in for something, picked up the glass then."

Lloyd nodded. "Maybe," he said, and went back to Dexter's statement.

"The lab say they found nothing on the stereo, guv—they're sending it and the pillows and things back this morning. They're not needed as evidence anymore—should I tell Dr. Bignall he can come and pick them up?"

"Mm," said Lloyd absently. The security light, he thought. The security light was trying to tell him something.

"Telephone for you, Carl."

Meg looked very pale. Carl had heard her moving about her bedroom all morning, and it didn't take a genius to deduce that she had been packing. Finally, she'd accepted that the only possible explanation for Denis not telling the police he had been with his brother was that he had *not* been with his brother. She'd rung Alan, and after a tense, difficult conversation, he told her the truth.

Carl wasn't sure how he felt about Denis's activities. As a doctor, he strongly disapproved. He didn't actually believe that all patient-doctor affairs were to be condemned; adult people were adult people. But Estelle had been a very vulnerable patient, and just a glance at her journal was all anyone needed to know that Denis had played on that vulnerability.

And yet, as Estelle's husband, he couldn't find it in his heart to blame Denis; he knew Estelle, knew only too well what that very vulnerability had brought out in him, and it was too easy to say that in his case it had been a desire to make her happy and in Denis's it had been exploitation. It had been a little bit of both for him, and he suspected it had been a little bit of both for Denis.

He picked up the phone, and Sergeant Finch told him he could collect the items that the police had removed from the house on Monday night, as it was no longer necessary for the police to hold onto them. That was the first bit of good news he'd had since this whole thing began. He arranged to call at the Stansfield police station at eleven-thirty, and then, surely, he could begin to put all this behind him.

Tom put down the phone, and Lloyd pushed whatever it was he'd been studying so closely over the desk to him. "Read that," he said.

Tom picked it up and saw that it was a list of when Watson's security light had gone on and off, with rough timings. He looked up at Lloyd, still sitting on the corner of his desk.

"Dexter says that the light was on when he went into the garage," Lloyd said, "then went out, and didn't come on again until he ran away. And he swears he did not see a car."

Tom looked at the notes as he spoke, and that was what they said. The light was on at approximately ten past eight, and went out almost immediately, coming on again when Dexter ran away, at approximately eight-fifteen. He frowned, not sure what he was supposed to be gathering from that.

"So when did Leeward leave?" asked Lloyd. "Before or after Dexter?"

"After," said Tom. "Because if Leeward had left before Dexter, the light would have come on while Dexter was in the garage, and it didn't."

"So if he didn't leave until after Dexter, why didn't Dexter see his car?" He tapped the piece of paper in Tom's hands. "Leeward got there *after* Dexter had run away, Tom. He found the house and Estelle Bignall just as he says he did."

"Well . . ." said Tom.

"Think about it," said Lloyd. "Dexter says the light was on when he ran into the garage. Why? Leeward didn't trigger it getting in—it took him by surprise when it came on as he left."

Tom frowned. It had.

"So it was triggered by someone else, wasn't it? At about seven minutes past eight someone crossed Watson's garden in order to gain entry to the Bignalls' garden, and it wasn't Denis Leeward, because his car wasn't there until after that, or Dexter would have seen it."

Tom didn't want to believe it, but Lloyd was right. He nodded, then realized that if they were crossing Leeward off, they had nowhere to go. "But who was it?" he said. "We've got no more evidence, guv." He stared at Lloyd's notes as though they would send him some sort of sign.

"Oh, I think Leeward was right. I think *you* were right, all along."

Tom looked up at him. "Ryan Chester?"

"He and Baz were there with the van, weren't they? They've both admitted that."

"Yes," said Tom.

"Ryan and Baz were going to burgle the Bignalls' house, which they thought would be empty. Baz was parked by the bus stop, and Ryan was going to go in, gather up everything he wanted to steal, then phone Baz to bring the van and back it up to the house. But he hit problems."

Tom was listening, his face thoughtful, as Lloyd worked his way through what had happened.

"Problem number one, the back gates were locked. No matter, he can still get the stuff ready, get Baz to park the van in Eliot Way, and just do a few trips through Watson's garden. He goes in that way, but he doesn't stick to the back wall, so he meets problem number two."

"The security light comes on," said Tom.

"He hides until it goes out again. He hears what's going on in the garage, but he doesn't know it's Dexter. He waits until it goes quiet, and he's certain no one's about, and he breaks in. The light comes on again—there's a bit of a commotion, but that comes to nothing, and he's about to go to work and relieve the Bignalls of their property, when problem number three enters."

"Estelle Bignall."

"Estelle Bignall," said Lloyd. "By this time he's determined nothing's going to stop him. He grabs her, keeps her quiet with his hand over her mouth, looks round for something, finds the tie and handkerchief set, and tells her that if she doesn't make a fuss, she won't get hurt. He gags her and ties her hands with the belt of her bathrobe. What happened then?"

Tom thought about it for a moment. "Watson got curious and went and had a look," he said. "Ryan hears Watson coming, so he pushes her into the kitchen and waits until Watson's gone. *That's* why she was in the kitchen."

Lloyd nodded. "She's fighting for breath, desperately trying to get her hands free so she can pull off the gag. He sees the tape, tapes up her ankles so she can't run for help, and then realizes she isn't struggling anymore. He grabs a bag from the roll, sweeps up whatever he can from the dining room, and leaves, this time keeping as far away from Watson's security light as he can. He gets out onto the road, gets on his mobile to Baz, and finds problem number five."

"Baz doesn't answer."

"Then problem number six. A car is coming. He hides, and he sees Leeward get out, watches him as he goes through Watson's garden to the house."

Tom was nodding. "So he knows the break-in's just about to be discovered, and he tries to steal the car to get as far away as possible. But Leeward comes back almost immediately, so he takes off through the woods, and steals Hutchinson's car instead, and tells Baz just to go home." He shook his head, almost admiringly. "He told us most of that himself, crafty bugger."

"Then he realizes that Leeward is the perfect fall guy, because he obviously didn't report what he found in the Bignalls' house," said Lloyd. "And so he tells us about the Saab. Then he retracts that and makes up this business about being in the traffic jam. But Leeward saw him, so we can place him at the scene, whatever he's saying now. And he's admitted storing and selling the proceeds, and stealing the getaway car."

Tom looked at his watch. "I think I'll just take a little run into Malworth," he said. "Pop into the magistrates' court."

Lloyd frowned. "Why?"

"Because Baz Martin's up this morning," said Tom. "He might get sent down—and if I know my man, Ryan'll be there to support him."

Ryan had lent Baz a tie; he always wore one when he was in court. It was amazing what a difference looking smart made. Wearing a tie in the dock could knock hundreds of quid off a fine, and a couple of months off a prison sentence, in Ryan's opinion. That, and standing up straight, looking the chairman of the bench in the eye, and speaking clearly. They liked that sort of thing.

Christmas Eve. That might not be a bad thing—some magistrates didn't like sending people down on Christmas Eve. But Baz had packed a bag—Stan wasn't convinced he'd get away with a fine this time.

It had been a while since Ryan had been in the court at all; Baz gave his name to the desk usher, who was new, so she didn't already know it. Most of them did, like they knew Ryan's. He sat down with Baz and nodded to a familiar face.

He had been coming here since he was fourteen. At first it had been the youth court and the public wasn't allowed in; his mates would have to wait out here to see how he fared. But once he graduated to adult court, they could come in and watch. He had gotten better at evading the police, and obviously he wouldn't choose to get caught, but there had been a sort of clublike atmosphere in those days that he almost missed.

Baz went off with Stan, and Ryan was reading a paper someone had left on a chair when he saw Sergeant Finch come in. He nodded to him too.

Finch came over to him and spoke quietly. "Ryan Chester, I'm arresting you on suspicion of the manslaughter of Estelle Bignall," he said. "You do not have to say anything . . ."

Stan was right. They had run out of suspects and were determined to get anyone at all so the papers couldn't moan about them. He couldn't prove he'd been in that traffic jam, his mother worked at the Bignalls' house, his brother knew the house was empty on Monday nights, he had sold the proceeds of the burglary, and nicked the car that a stolen item had been found in. He didn't stand a chance.

Finch had just finished cautioning him when an usher Ryan did know came out of one of the courts and smiled at him in the way people did when they had decided you were a hopeless case but they quite liked you anyway.

"Hello, Ryan. I didn't expect to see you again this soon."

She had the sweetest voice he had ever heard. She was someone he knew. She was someone who had said his name many, many times, calling him into court. She was his guardian angel and his fairy godmother and Mother Christmas rolled into one.

But better—much, much better than all of that—she was the Pink Panther.

Chapter Ten

It was mid-morning now, and still no decisions had needed to be made; they'd brought him food, they allowed him exercise, and they put him back in his little room. When the hatch was opened and the key turned in his lock, it felt like an intrusion.

"You're free to go," said the custody sergeant.

Denis frowned. What did he mean? No one had interviewed him again. Lloyd had said they would be speaking to him again—advised him to get his solicitor. But that would have meant making a decision, so he hadn't even thought about it. What did the man mean, he was free to go?

"Unless you'd rather stay," he said.

Well, given that being free to go meant he was free to go home and face his wife and Carl Bignall, that he was free to appear before a disciplinary committee that would strike him off the medical register and end his career, that he was free to watch his life crumble into tiny, irretrievable pieces, yes. He would rather stay.

"Come into the office," said Hutchinson, when the less than happy Tom arrived on his doorstep. "I can explain."

The Pink Panther had corroborated every word Ryan had told them. He had indeed been stuck in the traffic jam for almost ten minutes. In Hutchinson's car. Rarely had one of his boss's theories met with such a spectacular end, and Tom had driven to Malworth, his mood growing blacker by the minute. He'd known that Hutchinson was iffy; he'd known he was worried about something. And he'd swallowed all that stuff about his looking like a heavy for a loan company, and that was why Hutchinson didn't want him checking up on him.

Hutchinson closed the door. "Look," he said, "you're a man of the world, I'm sure. It's like this. As a rule, my calls take next to no time. No one wants to chat to a debt collector. Either they've got the money or they haven't. If they've got it, they open the door and give it to me. If they haven't, they don't open the door."

"So?"

"So, the lady in London Road was the exception to the rule. She didn't have the money, but she did open her door. And we got to talking. She suggested we could come to an arrangement, if you know what I mean?"

Tom imagined he knew what he meant.

"So every week I put down in my log that I've stayed a couple of minutes here and three minutes there, and by the time I get to her, my log says it's half eight, but it isn't. It's only eight o'clock. That way, I can . . . you know . . . spend some time with her without my boss or my wife finding out, and I tide her over the weeks she's short, until she can pay me back. That keeps people who look a bit like you off her back, and everyone's happy."

"Except me," said Tom. "I'm not happy, Mr. Hutchinson. A man very nearly got charged with manslaughter because of you."

Hutchinson blinked. "How can being a little . . . off . . . with the time a car was nicked mean that someone gets charged with manslaughter? I can't believe that."

"Believe it."

"All right, all right," said Hutchinson. "I'm very sorry." He looked apprehensive. "Is it against the law to say your car was stolen at half eight when it could have been any time between eight and half past?"

"Yes. It's known as wasting police time. Unless of course it was part of a conspiracy to pervert the course of justice."

Hutchinson backed off. "Now, look—the only conspiracy here was between me and the lady in London Road. And—well, you wouldn't do me for wasting police time, would you? I didn't *mean* to waste your time. Only—you know. If you do, the wife . . ."

Oh, what the hell. It was Christmas. Goodwill to all men and all that.

Tom drove back to Stansfield wondering where you went from here. If every single one of your suspects turned out to have been doing something else altogether, what were you supposed to do? Start again, he supposed. So much for Christmas Day. His wife would go spare.

Judy Hill was in the incident room when he got back. She'd come to invite him and Lloyd to Christmas lunch, apparently. Well, that was better than a slap in the face with a wet haddock, but Tom didn't really feel like celebrating.

"I've just been hearing about the Pink Panther," she said with a smile.

"I really thought he had it figured out," said Tom. "It made sense."

Judy nodded. "Yes," she said. "I don't think I could have picked that many holes in it myself."

Tom grunted. "Is that supposed to make me feel better?" he said.

"No. But growing your hair might. Do you know you've been in a bad mood since you had it cut? I'll bet you and your wife keep having rows."

He stared at her. "We do," he said, sitting down at his desk.

"Well, there you are. Grow it back, Tom. It really, really doesn't suit you."

Lloyd came in then; predictably, everyone started up with the da-dum, da-dum Pink Panther theme.

"All right, all right," Lloyd said. "It's bad enough having to face the music without knowing exactly what music you have to face. It's not my fault if even people who get their cars stolen lie to us, is it?" He noticed Judy then, and smiled, coming over to her. "What brings you here? Come to laugh at me?"

"Yes," she said. "And to invite you and Tom to lunch at this really good restaurant in Chandler Square," she said, and looked apologetic. "I did think that this might all be wrapped up," she said. "It was to be a celebration."

"Well, at least it's something to look forward to," said Lloyd. "There isn't much of that round here at the moment."

Lloyd's notes on the security light were still sitting on Tom's desk, and Judy glanced down at them, frowning. Then she picked up his pen and started making little ticks against the times Lloyd had written down. She looked up. "You do know what the Pink Panther business means," she said. "Don't you?"

Tom looked at Lloyd, and could see that whatever it meant, Lloyd knew no more about it than he did. But he nodded, smiling broadly. "She's looking like a gun dog, Tom," he said. "We might get to enjoy our lunch after all."

"It means that Ryan and Leeward were both telling the truth," she said.

Lloyd smiled. "Well, I expect that qualifies them for the *Guinness Book of World Records*," he said, "but—"

Tom looked up at him when he stopped speaking. He seemed transfixed by something. "Are you all right, guv?" he asked.

"Yes," he said distantly. "Of course. Of course—it's a logic problem, isn't it? Leeward and Ryan are both telling the truth. Leeward saw Ryan trying to break into his car, and Ryan saw Leeward driving away. And Ryan *was* in the traffic jam, therefore . . ." He looked at Judy.

"Therefore neither he nor Leeward could possibly have been in Eliot Way at quarter past eight," said Judy. "Ryan must have been in London Road by—what—just after quarter past eight? It would take him two or three minutes to get into the center of Malworth plus ten minutes or so in the traffic jam. . . ."

"And he said he was there about ten minutes after he tried to break into the Saab," said Lloyd.

"Which means he was in Eliot Way at around five past," said Judy. "And if you look at your notes about the security light . . ."

Lloyd nodded slowly. "The light that was on when Dexter ran into the garage wasn't triggered by anyone getting *in* to the Bignalls' garden through his," he said, "it was triggered when Leeward *left*."

"At seven minutes past eight," said Judy.

Lloyd nodded. "So Ryan found a sack full of the proceeds of a burglary that had yet to be committed, and Leeward found the window broken, the house burgled, and Estelle Bignall dead eight minutes before anyone ever heard the window breaking."

Tom nodded, but he was puzzled. "Then who broke it?" he said.

"Carl Bignall," said Judy. "And, if I don't miss my guess, he broke it at teatime."

"Why teatime, particularly?" asked Lloyd.

"Tom knows. He reported to LINKS that kids from London Road were making a nuisance of themselves."

Tom knew, but its significance had entirely escaped him. Watson had said that at about teatime he'd heard kids breaking bottles or something; Tom had thought he'd said it to put them off Dexter's scent, but he had simply been telling the truth.

"Bignall probably broke the window while Estelle was in the shower," said Judy. "That way she wouldn't hear it. He did try to muffle the sound with the curtain, Lloyd. Close the door, close the curtains—no one would notice the broken pane from outside, not in the dark, and Estelle was never going to see the broken glass, because he was going to kill her before she ever came downstairs."

"So what did everyone hear at quarter past eight?" Tom asked.

"Sound effects," said Lloyd, and looked at Judy, shaking his head. "The very first time I met the man he was handing you a tape of sound effects." His eyes widened. "The portable stereo," he said. "The hissing noise. Watson told the truth about that too. What he heard was the blank tape running with the sound up full."

"That's why he thought it might be his greenhouse," said Tom. "I didn't believe him about that, because I didn't see how a little window like that could make that much noise. But it could make as much noise as Carl Bignall wanted it to." And that tape must still be on the portable stereo that was even now on its way back from the lab. "We've got him, guv."

"I'd sooner have more than just that to offer the CPS," Lloyd said. "Do we have anything more tangible to go on?"

"There's the bricks," Tom said.

"The bricks?"

"Watson says people don't park on the service road. But Bignall had to, because he had to leave by the back door with his sack full of goodies so he could dump it in the wood, and he wouldn't dare do that without the excuse of going to his car, because people would have wondered what he was doing. Trouble was, his car itself would have been remarked on if he had just parked there for no reason. But he did have a reason, didn't he? He *had* to park there because he couldn't get into his driveway for the bricks."

Judy smiled. "You said December was a bit late for someone who wanted a wall in the summer."

Lloyd nodded. "So I did. Get on to it, Tom."

Tom rang round local builders until he found the one that had supplied the bricks, and everyone fell quiet while he spoke.

"Do you have the driver's instructions?" he asked.

"They should be on the manifest. Do you want me to have a look?"

"Yes, if you would." He covered the receiver with his hand. "Keep your fingers crossed."

"Hello?"

"Yes," said Tom. "Have you got it?"

"Yeah. It just says the bricks have to be left on the hard standing inside the gates."

"The hard standing," repeated Tom. "His driveway, would that be?" He gave the room a thumbs-up. "Can you tell me when he ordered them?"

"Oh, let's see now . . . yeah, here it is. They were ordered a month ago, for delivery on the twenty-second of December between twelve and one."

"Thanks, mate," Tom said. "Someone will be round to pick that up from you, so don't lose it." He hung up. "We've got him," he said. "He arranged for the bricks to be delivered when he knew Estelle would be having lunch with Marianne, and wouldn't get the driver to put them somewhere more sensible."

Lloyd shook his head. "It was all planned," he said. "All of it. A totally cold-blooded murder to get his hands on her money."

"And he wasn't doing it all in a panic," said Judy. "That explains why he could be so calm when he turned up for rehearsal." She frowned. "He was lucky that Gary Sims removed the gag—you said Freddie thought he could have proved murder if he hadn't."

"No," said Lloyd. "He wasn't lucky. Carl Bignall didn't have good luck—he had bad luck. As it happened, the gag was removed by Sims, but just supposing Geoffrey Jones hadn't called the police. If he hadn't heard someone being assaulted, hadn't seen Dexter running away, hadn't seen the door standing open, he might not have done anything at all."

"Carl Bignall left the door shut," Tom said. "Leeward said he had to open it when he got there. And then he ran back out again, and left it open."

"Quite. It was two unrelated incidents that caused the police to be called. If they hadn't been, Carl Bignall would have come home and found his wife dead. And he, naturally, would have done exactly what Sims did—no one would have questioned it for a moment. So the gag would have been removed anyway. As would the portable stereo. No wonder he went pale when he saw it was gone."

"And it was another unrelated incident that got him caught," said Tom. "Ryan Chester doing what Ryan Chester does. Trying to steal a car." He grinned. "*You* were right all along, guv," he said. "Not me."

"Well, Bignall had the best motive," said Lloyd. "And I didn't like that artistic burglary." He sighed. "I just wish I knew how he'd killed her. I got everything that you could possibly bury someone's face in out of that house, and the lab found nothing on any of them."

"How else can you suffocate someone?" asked Judy.

"There would be bruising if someone tried to stop her breathing by holding her mouth and nose shut," said Lloyd, "so that's no good."

"It'd be a plastic bag," said Tom. "He probably threw it away."

It had seemed to him to be a less than inspiring thought, but Lloyd was beaming at him, then the next thing Tom knew he was phoning the lab and sweet-talking the young woman who tested for such things into doing just one more thing for him before she went to the staff Christmas party.

Carl Bignall went into the station and spoke to the young woman at the desk, who asked him to wait. He couldn't believe it was all over, but it was. He was getting the stereo back, and once he had that, this nightmare would be finished.

"Dr. Bignall," said Lloyd.

Carl had thought they would just give him the stuff. He hadn't thought it would involve Chief Inspector Lloyd. He got up.

"Carl Bignall, I'm arresting you for the murder of your wife Estelle Bignall. You do not have to say anything, but anything . . ."

Carl found himself in an interview room, hardly able to remember the previous few minutes, or how he had gotten there, even. But gradually it came back to him, and less gradually it was dawning on him that the game was up. He had been told that he didn't have to say anything, and he didn't.

Lloyd had proof that he'd arranged for the bricks being left when and where they had been, he had the tape with the breaking glass on it, and he had two witnesses to the fact that the apparent burglary had already taken place before the window was heard to break. He even had a witness to when he had actually broken the window. They were a soon-to-be struck-off doctor, a car thief, and a pornographer, but their stories meshed, and that was all that mattered.

"You broke the glass while your wife was in the shower," he said. "And then you went up and joined her. You knew what would happen. She was desperate for some attention from you."

He was desperate. He had lived with her for seven years—that would make a saint desperate. He couldn't afford to divorce her.

"You had to keep her from going out, so that was the best way to do it. Besides, you needed her to be in bed, didn't you? You were going to leave the house with a dead woman in it who was supposed to be alive. There had to be a good reason for people to be unable to get a reply if they knocked at the door or telephoned. It's Christmas; anyone might come calling."

Yes. That had been very important.

"So you made love to her." He shook his head. "I don't know how you could have done that."

That bit wasn't difficult. It had been good—not perhaps the life-changing experience he had led Lloyd to believe, but she had enjoyed it. He'd managed to make her happy right at the end, just as he'd made her happy at the beginning. But he couldn't keep on making her happy, because nothing he did was ever going to be enough. He wasn't a god; he had never asked to be worshiped. It wasn't possible to be the man Estelle imagined he was. That man didn't exist.

"And then a mildly kinky sex game perhaps?"

Spot on. He tied her hands, told her she should kneel in front of him, facing away from him, and then . . .

"A plastic bag," said Lloyd. "You put a plastic bag over her head, and you pushed her down into the pillow and held her there until she died." He reached down and produced one plastic bag containing another. A black plastic bag. *The* black plastic bag. He had been worried when they asked him about the roll of bags—he'd realized they were going to subject it to forensic examination. But he'd thought they wouldn't think of checking it as a murder weapon.

"This bag," Lloyd said. "The bag you put the presents and the ornaments in. The bag you dumped in the woods. It has traces of saliva in it, which will be sent for DNA analysis after Christmas. I have little doubt it will prove to be your wife's."

It had been like drowning kittens in a sack. Not pleasant, but reasonably painless, and reasonably quick. Not as quick and painless as a fatal injection, but he had sworn an oath to administer no deadly medicine, and he hadn't broken it. That wasn't why he hadn't, of course. Just that they'd have known right away that he had done it. He had rejected that out of hand.

"And then you carried her down to the kitchen," said Lloyd. "I kept asking myself, why the kitchen? But then, I thought she'd died at eight-fifteen, whereas she died at least an hour earlier than that, which was why she was in the kitchen."

He had tried to cover every angle, but other people had somehow gotten in on the act, and that had been so confusing.

"From half past seven," Lloyd went on, "you would have no control over what was happening. You had a hole in your window—the rain might give you away if her body was wet when it should have been dry, or if the carpet beneath her body was dry when it should have been wet. You couldn't risk that; you had no idea what the rain was going to do. And anyway, the warmer you kept her body, the better. She wouldn't stay too warm in a room with a broken window. So the kitchen it was."

Carl sighed. It had all started going wrong almost straight away. He'd had no reason to suppose that two police officers would unaccountably be playing the leads in the rehearsal when he got there. And when Lloyd told him that Estelle had been found, he'd almost passed out. That wasn't supposed to happen. And he definitely wasn't supposed to be driven home by a Detective Chief Inspector. And then when he'd gotten there and seen those footprints, found the stereo missing, been told that someone had left a glove behind, he thought he was going mad. It looked for all the world as though someone had broken in and burgled the house.

He had been totally convinced yesterday morning that he would be caught; everyone had taken it for grief, which had been the only good thing about it. And then there was the complication of Dexter. He'd had no idea who was in his house; it could have been Ryan and Dexter, and he half expected a blackmail note or something from Ryan. And then, when he realized why Dexter was there, he had felt so bad about it. He could have gotten him out of that situation almost as soon as he'd gotten into it if he'd paid more attention to Estelle.

Was it Watson who had made Estelle the way she was? Or was she just a victim from the moment she was born? He hadn't meant her to be his victim, not until it all became too much to bear. She had threatened suicide over and over again; he found himself hoping that she carried out her threat, and somehow the plan to murder her had evolved from there.

Then the bombshell about Denis. He had *been* there. Carl had been certain that his luck had run out right there, but once again, it hadn't. He'd come so tantalizingly close to pulling it off; he had weathered all these totally baffling complications, and sitting waiting for his stereo, he allowed himself to believe for the very first time that he would soon have the incriminating tape back, that he was home free.

"Do you have *anything* to say, Dr. Bignall?"

Carl looked at Lloyd, who had suspected him from the very first moment, as he had known he would, but who had grimly stuck to that suspicion in a way that he'd hoped he wouldn't, and he smiled. "I'm not denying it," he said. "I did murder my wife. But . . ." He sighed.

"But?" said Lloyd.

"But I think, in my defense, that she quite literally drove me mad."

Tom and Lloyd *were* enjoying their super-expensive Christmas lunch, Judy was pleased to note. No one had gone for the Christmas menu, being all too aware of the turkey-eating days stretching ahead of them. She had given up halfway through the main course, but they were on to the puddings.

She had assumed that even a place as expensive as this would be booked up for Christmas Eve, but she thought it was worth a try, and they'd had one table for three left. Her original plan had been to treat Lloyd to lunch, but since the table could accommodate three, she thought it might be nice to bring Tom along; she missed working with them both.

She had almost felt like explaining to the manager that one of the party did look as though he was on his way to a neo-Nazi rally but was really a very nice man. Her omniscience had impressed Tom; Lloyd had told her, of course, that Tom and his wife were in a semi-permanent state of hostility, but Judy felt that she was probably right about the cause.

Tom caught her looking at him and smiled. "This is great," he said. "Thanks for inviting me."

"You're very welcome. I like having you around—you're a good antidote to certain Welshmen of my acquaintance. I don't suppose I could book you for the delivery room, could I? I suspect the father of my child might go AWOL."

Tom looked at Lloyd. "Weren't you present when your other kids were born?" he asked.

"No," said Lloyd.

"Seriously? You really didn't—"

"No. Can we change the subject?"

Tom grinned. "Are you scared?"

"Too true."

"Oh, it's wonderful. It's the most amazing thing I've ever seen. You're standing there one minute with—"

Lloyd put down his spoon. "If you say one more word, I'll ask the manager to throw you out," he said.

Tom went back to his dessert, then looked up at Lloyd again. "How do you feel about me discussing work?" he asked.

"Oh, that's all right. I discuss work at all times of the day and night."

"Right," said Tom. "You know in TV series where the thick sergeant says, 'There's one thing I don't understand,' and the clever inspector explains it? Well, there's one thing I don't understand. Why did Carl Bignall rig up the sound effect to go off for a time when he didn't have an alibi anyway?"

"Oh, that was the bit that worked," said Lloyd. "He didn't fool Freddie with the gag, and he didn't fool me with the burglary, but he fooled everyone with that." He put the spoon on his empty plate and sat back. "You are very unhappily married to a very unstable woman who is worth a small fortune once she's dead," he said. "If she dies an unnatural death during a burglary at a time for which you have an apparent alibi, what am I, as the clever inspector, going to do if I suspect for even a moment that the burglary was faked? I'm going to wonder about that alibi. I'm going to wonder when she *really* died."

"Whereas . . ." said Judy, who had also been the thick sergeant, but hadn't wanted to admit it, and was now beginning to understand. "Whereas if, on the other hand, you have no alibi at all, and I suspect the burglary was faked, then I am going to run myself into the ground trying to find out where you were at that *particular* time. And since you were nowhere near the scene of the crime, I am going to prove nothing. And I am going to overlook all the time you had before you ever left the house in which to dispose of your wife and fake the burglary."

"He'd have walked away from it if it hadn't been for Watson and Leeward getting themselves involved," said Tom.

"He might," said Lloyd.

"It's poetic justice, when you think of it," Judy said. "Watson and Leeward haven't come out of it much better than Carl Bignall. She's got her own back on all of them."

"And you know," Lloyd said, "Bignall didn't believe her about either Watson or Leeward. Perhaps if he'd known her better, he could have murdered her more successfully."

Judy drove them back to Stansfield, and Lloyd went off to see what Watson and his solicitor had come up with.

"It might take a long time," he told Judy. "I shouldn't wait, if I were you." He smiled. "And I hereby declare this incident room officially closed. Have a nice Christmas, everyone."

His good wishes were returned as people thankfully packed up the incident room in the knowledge that their Christmas holiday stood a reasonable chance of being uninterrupted by work.

Tom picked up his coat and grinned at Judy. "I know there's a lot of paperwork to do, guv, but it's Christmas Eve, and I think I'd better go home now and start growing my hair."

¿

The Pink Panther had come through for him, and Ryan was a free man once more. As was Baz; since Ryan had been otherwise engaged while the trial had been going on, he had no way of knowing if it had been Stan's eloquence, the tie, seasonal goodwill, or a combination of all three that had gotten Baz off with a fine, but lunchtime found them celebrating over a pie and a pint amidst all the office Christmas parties.

Now, as late afternoon descended and the December skies grew dark, they were sitting in Baz's van, and Ryan was sorting out their immediate future. Someone had to come up with the money to pay Baz's fine; Baz had asked for time to pay, and was technically supposed to produce the money every week from his Social Security check but that wasn't going to happen; Baz and his money were inevitably soon parted. And Ryan would soon be in the same boat.

In the old days, he hadn't bothered paying fines, but that was a mug's game; fines should be treated like a business expense, paid as promptly as was necessary in order not to get into worse trouble. So the money had to be gotten from somewhere.

And now that Ryan knew exactly what had been happening to Dex, and who had been responsible, he had an idea where that money might be coming from.

"Come on," he said to Baz. "Let's go."

"Where to?"

"Windermere Terrace," said Ryan.

"Isn't that where that woman died?"

Ryan nodded.

"Why do you want to go there, Ry?"

"You'll find out when we get there," Ryan said.

Baz was used to being given enigmatic instructions; he put the van in gear and set off for Windermere Terrace.

ǫ

Eric had talked it over with his brief; if he continued to deny the assault and his filmmaking activities, they could make a not entirely circumstantial case against him for murder, and it might succeed, because they would dig and dig until they found the people who had worked with Estelle. They would have Dexter's evidence that she'd been there, threatening him, and he could end up being tried not just for what he had done, but for what he had not done.

Thus he had made a full and frank statement about what he had really been doing between half past seven and eight-fifteen, and it had taken hours. They couldn't charge him straight away; the papers had to be sent to the Director of Public Prosecutions to see what exactly they could charge him with, and he was given bail.

He came out of the police station and looked at the queue for cabs with a groan. Christmas Eve, and he'd be standing there till Boxing Day before he got one. His solicitor took pity on him and gave him a lift home, which was something, he supposed. Bloody well should, he thought, considering the bill he's going to send when this is finished.

He let himself into the house, and stopped dead.

⁂

It was very late by the time Lloyd got home; he had felt obliged to call in at the Malworth station and discuss the latest burglary, which had taken place while the resident was being held in custody at the Stansfield police station.

"With the house next door being empty, no one saw or heard a thing," said Inspector Saunders. "TV, video, hi-fi—you name it. It's gone."

"Had he put ID marks on them, by any chance?"

"No," said Saunders. "Well—people just don't think, do they? Never think it'll happen to them." He shook his head. "I shouldn't think we'll trace them."

"No," said Lloyd. "But he'll be insured?"

"Oh, yes." He grinned. "Christmas'll be a bit bleak, though. They even took his turkey. Seems he was expecting some guests."

Lloyd was still chuckling about that as he drove to the flat. He could hazard a guess as to who had relieved Eric Watson of his consumer durables and his turkey, but he'd done enough of that for one week, and nonaggravated burglary wasn't in Stansfield's purview. So any help that he could have given Malworth wouldn't have been appreciated.

He and Judy sat on the sofa and watched his video of *It's a Wonderful Life* in a room lit only by the Christmas tree lights. Judy, in her pregnant mode, had to wipe away tears at the end, and tried to pretend that wasn't what she was doing at all.

"It's Christmas Day," he said, kissing her, and turned on the table lamp so she could see. "Will you marry me, Judy?"

She frowned. "I've already said I'll marry you."

"I know," he said. "But that's sometime never. I want us to get married before the baby's born."

Her eyes widened.

He took the little box from his pocket, opening it, and the diamond winked in the soft light. "This has got a matching wedding ring," he said. "So I don't want you to put it on unless you agree, and I'll understand if you don't."

It was a gamble; pinning Judy down to any commitment wasn't easy, and pinning her down to a wedding date had thus far proved impossible. Even now he didn't dare actually name a day. But she wouldn't go back on a promise, a real promise. And that was what he was asking her to make.

"Well?" he said after a moment. "*Are* you going to put it on?"

She looked back at him, shaking her head. "No," she said. "I'm not going to put it on, Lloyd."

He tried hard not to let his face show what he felt; he was usually good at that, but not this time. He had thought it was a gamble he would win. He looked away, to give himself a moment to recover. And when he looked back, she was smiling.

She held out her left hand. "You are," she said.